Outfit: The "Spur" of B

Destination: Montana—b
Trail.

Chore: To deliver 2700 head of longhorns for the market.

Problem: 2000 miles of dust, drought, and death.

As foreman Adam Childress ordered the great drive to begin, he wondered how his men would hold up under the relentless pressure of guarding and guiding the huge herd over the long, treacherous trail to Montana.

Part of the trouble came from the trail itself—crisscrossed now with barbed-wire fences and dotted with homesteads whose iron plows scarred the land more deeply than the cattle hoofs ever had. And part came from the men—a strange crew of tough, hard-eyed loners with nothing in common except a grim dedication to their job.

THE LONG WAY NORTH is a dramatic novel about the last of the great cattle drives, a gripping story of the men who pitted their endurance and courage against the land, against the animals in their care, and—against each other.

THE LONG WAY NORTH

JIM
BOSWORTH

ace books

A Division of Charter Communications Inc.
A GROSSET & DUNLAP COMPANY
360 Park Avenue South
New York, New York 10010

An ACE Book

Published Simultaneously in Canada

Printed in U.S.A.

I

I ride an old paint; I'm leading old Dan,
I'm off to Montana for to throw the hoolihan.

— I'M A-LEADING OLD DAN

THE FIRST MAN fell, crying out as he hit, and
sprawled face down in the rutted road that goes to
Brownsville. For a moment, he did not move. It
was good not to move. He let the night touch him
softly with the scent of dust and mesquite and
sweet agarita, and the faint salt smells that came
with the wind from Laguna Madre. He had forgotten how it was to sleep, and he could have slept
now where he lay, but the hoarse and worried cry
of a dog tugged him from it. Charles P. Wood
raised his head and looked toward the sky. He saw
the gate dark against the stars, and beyond it a low
roof rising. He crawled painfully toward the gate,
and using it for support, pulled himself to his feet.

The gate squealed under his weight, and the
dog's barking became frenzied. In desperation, he
fought to open it, and then stumbled uncertainly
forward. But before he could take many steps,
something else moved between him and the stars.
He bumped against it and nearly fell, but a hand
reached down and held him and he knew then of

the horse, the creaking of leather, and a man's head high above his.

"Katherine!" a voice cried out.

He tried to talk, to move of his own accord, but the will was gone, and the rest came like a dream. With what strength was left, that was all it could be. The vague and yellow light of a lamp, the face of a girl. He remembered the bite of whisky and the taste of soup. There were gentle hands and a wooden tub that steamed in the center of the room. It ended there.

The second man removed his saddle from the bayo coyote, rubbed him down with the blanket, and turned him loose in the corral. He wondered about the man he had found wandering half-dead toward the house. There had been no way to really see him in the dim light of the stars, but there had been an impression of pale skin, of a man tall and thin, and of expensive clothes. This perhaps made him an easterner, and why would an easterner be wandering around in southern Texas, in the night and in that condition?

Adam Childress walked back toward the house and looked at the sky and tested the wind that had come up only in the last hour. It would bring fog from the Gulf, he knew. But what about rain?

When his boots echoed hollowly on the front porch, Katherine Nance came outside.

"What's the matter with him?" he asked.

"Tired, starved, and dirty. He'll be all right with a little sleep. Who is he?"

"I don't know. We'll find out in the morning."

"He doesn't look like a tramp," Katherine said.

"No. Maybe just a man down on his luck."

"You're still short a hand, aren't you?"

Adam nodded, and leaned in the doorway to look at the stranger.

"Well, he don't look like much, but send him out to see me in the morning," he said and turned back down the steps.

Adam Childress walked to the bunkhouse, pushing the stranger from his mind. He had too many things to think about. The Mexican Spur herd was bedded down on the holding ground. Twenty-seven hundred head of Texas longhorns. In the morning, he would start them north toward Montana Territory.

He knew he wouldn't sleep. The first light was not far away. He could almost feel it in the air. Maybe it was twenty years of driving them north, coming now like a habit, to make this bed no good for sleeping. No matter what happened on the way, it was good going north. Good to kill the restlessness, and move, as did the whispering wind outside.

In Brownsville, the third man knocked over a bottle of whisky in the saloon called Matanza. For a moment, with a grin of foolish ecstasy, he stared at it and then fell asleep with his face buried in his arms.

The bartender came over and, with the gentleness of habit, took him under the arms and pulled him outside to the watering trough. Before he could begin the business of sobering him up, a wagon lurched by in the street, and the bartender hailed it.

"Hey, Price! You heading out by Mexican Spur?"

"You bet," the man in the wagon answered and stopped. "That Charlie Baggett again?"

"Who else? I want to close up and go home."

Charlie mumbled thickly in a sodden dream as they lifted him onto the wagon bed.

"Just push him out by the gate. They'll find him."

The man named Price shook his head.

"Don't know how he stays on old Jake Nance's pay roll."

"Well, he's a good man when he's sober."

"Yeah? When's that?"

The bartender laughed, and the wagon jolted its way out of town and along the road that led under the stars.

The fourth man sat up and listened to the Mexican girl breathe deeper. Quietly, he dressed and carried his boots to the window. He climbed out and dropped to the ground. The air was colder now, and damp with the beginnings of fog coming in from the Gulf. John Preble pulled his boots on and shivered for a minute. He whistled for his horse, and when the little roan came to him, rode across the field away from her house. He looked back at the adobe and the dark square her window made. He wondered if it was the roselike scent of prickly pear he smelled, or her perfume remaining with him somehow, like the other things . . . her voice and its sweet accents which spoke softly of Sonora, her laughter, and her shy singing. She would cry in the morning when she awakened. She would reach for him and find him gone, and cry. They always did, it seemed.

He settled back and began to whistle softly as he

headed for the Mexican Spur.

The fifth man walked with a burden of wood, and because it was heavy, the fog felt good on his face. Slowly, he followed the gentle sounds of the longhorns until the place where they were held was just ahead.

He found the wagon in the darkness and eased the wood to the ground. He sat with his back against a wheel, and pulled his Saltillo blanket around against the chill of the fog. The old Mexican touched the little bag suspended from his neck and studied the two gold coins with his fingers as if they were the beads of the church. A gift of wood and gold. He did not know the men who would gather here in the first light. He hoped it would be enough.

Out with the herd, riding around the longhorns slowly, Ben Sweet and Revelation Marsh waited for dawn to come. Rev's rich Negro voice sang softly, and Ben rode lost in thought. Tomorrow, April began. Tomorrow, the long way, endlessly north, compelled and directed by the trail of a million hooves.

The rest slept in the bunkhouse. For them, the last long sleep before it all began again, while young Peewee Hand, the wrangler, who sleeplessly like the child he almost was, wandered the dew-wet grasses and watched the horses in his keeping.

II

Some boys goes up the trail for pleasure,
But that's where you get it most awfully wrong;
For you haven't any idea the trouble they give us
While we go driving them along.

    —GIT ALONG, LITTLE DOGIES

HE HAD BEEN dreaming of Boston and running down its wet streets and it seemed all right as long as he could keep on running. There were familiar faces everywhere. No strange ones. The entire population of Boston consisted of people he knew. He could not avoid them, and the sight of them was not so frightening. The horror was in that they might say something to him and the words would somehow mire him down and stop him from running. He had dreamed of this and then was aware of Katherine in the chill darkness of the room, shaking him and pulling the blankets back.

"Adam Childress wants to talk to you."

There was no explanation. He remembered vaguely her eyes and hands, her strength from the night before and the way she had tended him like some unquestioning angel. He wanted to sink back and sleep forever, but in turn, he could not question her.

So, still heavy with sleep, he found himself a few

6

minutes later sitting in a saddle that smelled of fresh neetsfoot oil, riding in the direction Katherine had indicated.

The wind had died and the fog settled close to the earth to hide the hour of dawn. The only evidence of beginning day was in the sound of cattle grazing out from their bed ground, and in the smell of mesquite smoke and the glow of the fire just ahead.

Wood found Adam squatting on his heels near the fire with a tin plate of food. He was a short and rather spare man, in his fifties, with white hair and a silvery stubble on his cheeks and chin, and pale eyes that were either blue or gray. His eyes were clear and cheerful and unfogged by the hour or lack of sleep.

Wood got down and looked for a place to tie the horse.

"Peewee!" Adam yelled, and a sallow-faced boy of thirteen or fourteen came to take the horse. "The name is Childress."

"Charles Wood," he said, taking the older man's hand.

"Better eat. You'll find some hardware in the wagon."

Wood got himself a plate and an iron knife and fork and a cup, and went over to where the cook was working at the fire.

"Well, goddamn it, you got to come closer than that unless you want me to throw it at you!"

As it was, the cook nearly did throw the big slab of beef on his plate and Wood almost lost it. Next came a pile of boiled rice and raisins, and some stewed tomatoes, and coffee from the big pot hanging over the fire.

"The way them rannies came whooping in here this morning, it'll assay about eighty per cent sand! But you look like you could use a little grit in your craw anyway!"

Wood was too tired to make any reply, and only turned and walked carefully back to where Adam Childress waited.

"Don't mind old coosie," Adam grinned. "He'd die if he thought someone had caught him smiling. His name is Red Bellah, and inside he's the biggest bleeding heart you ever saw."

Wood watched Red start cleaning up. He was the biggest man he had ever seen. Red Bellah stood at least six foot five and weighed a solid two hundred or so. His hair was the violent color of fire, although he appeared to be nearing sixty.

"I'd never have known," Wood observed.

"Well, he likes to be hard on the new faces that show up at his fire on the first day. Claims he don't like getting up in the dark to cook for a bunch of boys who don't appreciate it anyway. But I know him. Why, if he never had to cook another meal, he'd still get up before dawn and build a mesquite fire and boil coffee just so he could see what sunup was like that morning. There's the other new face over there."

Adam pointed at an old Mexican, wrapped in a blanket, eating as he stared off through the fog.

"He was sleeping by the wagon when Red came this morning. He brought a little money, and a load of wood for the coonie," Adam indicated the cowhide stretched under the wagon. "Enough to break your back or mine. The old boy wants to go north with us. Why, I don't know. He doesn't talk. He's called Cimarron."

"Cimarron," Wood said, trying it on his own tongue.

"Well, it ain't his real handle. A name like that gets tied on a man when he has to live the life of a loner . . . a *cimarrón*. It also means wild one. The man who earns the name ain't wanted by his own people or anyone else, including his enemies, I don't know why he didn't give his own name when he came here. None of us would've known the difference. But maybe it's just honesty, or habit. Maybe he carries it like a penance."

"You mean he might've committed some crime, and you'll still let him along?"

"He seems harmless enough. And Red says he could use a little help."

Wood looked at him, surprised.

"You're very broad-minded, Mister Childress."

"My business is cattle, and getting them north. I can't afford to worry about what a man's done before he came to me. I don't like talking about another man behind his back, but you're new to the country and I had a reason for asking you to come out here this morning. I might as well make it real clear. Take Charlie Baggett there. Charlie drinks too much, and there ain't no place for drunks in a cow camp. But as long as he's sober in camp it doesn't concern me. Charlie's a good man. And Floyd Rogers is wanted, we've heard. But unless Floyd tells us himself, it ain't so. As long as he don't bring us trouble, it don't matter."

Wood looked at Floyd and it was almost enough to make him flinch. The ridges of his brow were bony and prominent to the point of exaggeration. His eyes were small and piggish and his nose was misshapen with the nostrils pointing almost straight out. His mouth twisted, and his head was too large for his body, balancing precariously on a bent and scrawny neck.

The old Mexican brought his plate back, and Wood saw the wet-black hair falling from one side of his sombrero, and the beginnings of gray that made it seem like iron, and the fierce mustache that turned down around the ends of his mouth. His deep-seamed face spoke of age, and yet, at the same time, the intensity of one who could never really grow old. Wood wondered what it was he had done to earn his name and how it was he could still walk with so much dignity.

He felt stiff and uncomfortable in the presence of these two. And what kind of men were these others who found nothing wrong in it and didn't seem to care?

The smell of fried meat and boiled coffee came to him then and he remembered the plate he was holding. He was hungry now, and was surprised at how good the food turned out to be.

"You wanted to talk to me?" he said between mouthfuls.

"Yes. You look like a man who could use a job and I'm short a hand."

"I see."

"Well?"

"I don't know, Mister Childress. I'm not sure."

"If you're worried because you ain't done anything like this before, forget it. I don't like to go north short a hand, and if you can sit a horse without falling off, that's all I care about."

"I used to ride some at home in Boston."

"Well, you'd have to forget those pimples . . . those eastern saddles . . . and that business of standing up in your stirrups ever time the horse moves a leg. Some of these fuzz tails out here'd think that was awful funny."

"What makes you think I'm the right man?"

"You can learn, and like I said, it's important to me to have a full crew."

"And how long does it last?"

"Well, we're taking twenty-seven hundred head to Montana Territory. It'll be September when we get there. It's a long walk, Mister Wood."

"Montana . . ." he shook his head. He was even less sure.

"Once we only had to go to Dodge and Newton and Abilene. Then those Kansas sod-busters started hollering about Texas cattle giving their stock the fever, and trampling down crops. They threw up a quarantine and now we have to go around and farther north. It gets worse every year. Fences, more quarantines, more nesters crowding us off the grass. This is the fourth time the Mexican Spur's headed for Montana. Went up to Fort Benton six years ago . . . 1880 that was . . . the army was paying a good price for Indian beef. Went again in '84. Last year we were headed that way but sold out in Colorado to a man who wanted to stock his range in Ogallala. It was a fair price and we missed the blizzards that hit Montana."

Adam shook his head and grinned. "I didn't call you out here to talk about old times. We'll hit all kinds of weather, and the work is hard and gets harder. Those longhorns will probably get it in their heads now and then to run to hell. I've taken up only one bunch that didn't. The nights you're working you'll wish you were sleeping, and the nights you can sleep, something will happen to stop you. You'll roast and freeze, dry out to a piece of leather and then drown if the wind ain't stopped up your gullet with sand first. And the pay is thirty dollars a month, which don't go a hell of a way to making up for it. These boys you see here ain't known anything else. They don't think nothing of it. Maybe you look at things differently. But the job is yours if you want it, and I need you."

"Thirty a month?"

"You look like you're used to getting more."

"Maybe I am," he said, putting his plate down.

He thought back to Boston. Only a few months ago. More money than he needed. Fine clothes, a mansion to call home . . . never a day's labor in his life. The son of a famous judge.

That's how it was. The wealthy and lazy son of a wealthy man. A darling of society who did nothing in a society that did nothing, and who, if the spark of ambition so moved him, would have studied law and practiced in social circles.

It had been wonderful, doing what he pleased. Year in and year out until he seemed to sense a smell of decay and time went dead, and the air forgot how to move.

It had come one night in a sickening sweat. He had suddenly seen himself and the tight wall of familiar faces . . . the traditions and friendships that were not made but acquired by a system which was determined by blood, ancestry, and the weight of money. What had ever been worth while in it? Where did it go except in an increasingly tight little circle?

On December 23, 1885, he had left Boston without really knowing what it was he was looking for. A life with more purpose in it, more honesty,

and openness . . . but that was too general, and he
had no idea of where to look. He had wandered
aimlessly for weeks and eventually began moving
west with California as a possibility.

Now in April he was asked to go north with a
herd of cattle.

"Well, if you had your own string of horses, I
could pay you fifty a month. But without them,
thirty is the regular pay."

"I don't have a choice, Mister Childress. I have
no experience in any kind of work. That doesn't
make it easy to go out and find a position just like
that. I got off the train at a town called Pena with
a hundred dollars in my pocket. The train was having some kind of bearing trouble. I couldn't continue the trip to San Francisco until the next morning.
My money and tickets were stolen from me at the
hotel while I was asleep. Wherever I went from
there had to be on boot, and the best direction
seemed to be south. I had an idea that if I could get
to the Gulf and a harbor, I could find work."

"You know something about ships?"

"Not really. But there's a harbor in Boston, and
any waterfront would be more familiar to me than
this dry country. At any rate, I walked from Pena.
Sold a watch and a ring to eat on, and when that
ran out . . . well, you saw me last night. I won't
pretend I like the job, but I'll take it, and the thirty
dollars a month sounds fine."

They shook on it. Wood took a deep breath,
trying not to think of Cimarron and Rogers and
the others.

At that moment, Katherine rode into camp and
held out a bundle for him. It was the first time he
had a real chance to see her. Her hair was the color

of chestnuts, and her eyes some indeterminate shade of brown. Her face was neither softly pretty nor was it hard and weathered like so many he had seen. It was strong and clean and handsome. She rode a man's saddle, like a man, and she wore the clothes of a man. But the way they fit would never have allowed any mistake to be made about her sex.

"You're taking the job, aren't you?"

Her eyes met his with a directness that was almost a dare. She was measuring him, he was sure.

"Yes, I am."

"Then you'll need these," she said, seeming to look at him with approval. "Those clothes of yours wouldn't last two days."

He took the bundle, wondering at the weight of it.

"Thank you. I hope I can return the favor some day."

Color came to Katherine's cheeks and she wheeled her horse around and left.

"She's very beautiful," he said to Adam.

"From here, I'd say she was kinda taken with you too," Adam grinned.

"Nonsense. She's just been very kind."

Wood opened the bundle and found a linsey-woolsey shirt, a pair of Levi's, and a Colt .45. Adam nodded when the change was made.

"First town, I'll stand you to boots and a John B. for your head. There's a bedroll and slicker in the wagon you can have."

Adam climbed on the buckskin with the black stripe down its spine, the one called a bayo coyote, and they rode out to the herd.

It was getting light now, though the fog had not

yet begun to lift. Wood reined in and got his first look at the cattle.

They were grazing slowly, their numbers in the illusion of the fog seemingly reaching out to infinity. Wood was silenced at the sight of them. They were too long-legged and lean to carry much meat. They gave more of an impression of wildness and speed, as an elk would, and had the equipage of a fighting animal. The horns, black-tipped and gleaming like sabers, struck him more than anything else. They looked to be about four feet from tip to tip, extending sideways from the head, forward, and then up. On the left flank of each animal was a brand which looked both like a sunburst and a spur rowel of the type for which it was named.

Adam rolled himself a smoke and looked around.

"They ain't like they used to be. The cattle we take north these days are younger. Two-year-olds, some threes, and long threes. When this business was just beginning, right after the war, those horns were spreading out to five feet. Now and then, we'd get one of six feet. We got one old *ladino* in there somewhere now who's got a spread that big. He'd been hiding out in the brush for years. Ben Sweet and I finally caught him last fall and have been gentling him down. You watch for him."

The chuck wagon was moving up, and the hands were stationing themselves around the herd.

"What is it I'm supposed to do?"

Adam blew a cloud of smoke through his nose and pointed back.

"You ride in back of the herd and just watch for a while."

They rode briskly back to the tail end of the herd.

"You can't see all the boys with the fog like this. But Ben Sweet and Charlie Baggett ride right and left point, working with the lead steers and guiding them in the direction we want to go. Behind them are John Preble and Revelation Marsh at right and left swing. Floyd Rogers and Bob Skinner are holding right and left flank. And this man closest to us is Andy Giles. Andy was going to have to run back and forth between the two, but after you get the hang of it, you'll take left drag. The whole idea is to keep them moving and together. If one of the critters falls back or starts to take a walk on his lonesome, you get him back in. You watch Andy. You'll catch on quick."

Adam paused and took a last pull on his cigarette.

"Riding drag, except maybe wrangling where a kid like Peewee works day and night and don't get much sleep, is the worst job you can draw. Every pound of dust these coasters kick up, you'll eat back here. We'll move hard the next two or three days. Get them out of familiar ground quick so that they'll settle down. By the way, friend, if the yell goes up for Arbuckle, that's you."

Adam grinned at him and rode away.

A moment later a shout went up and the Mexican Spur crew urged the longhornns into motion. Yelling, slapping out with ropes, cursing, they prodded the great beasts into a steady, distance-consuming pace. Wood sat, not moving, transfixed by the scene.

"Well, goddamn it, you coming or ain't you?"

Wood looked around and saw Red Bellah and

Cimarron coming up in the wagon.

"I'm coming," he said, urging his horse forward. Then as an afterthought, he spoke to Bellah again. "Why would anyone call me Arbuckle?"

"Why son, you're such a sterling example of a cowhand, the boss must've saved up his Arbuckle coffee coupons to get you!"

Except for the noon meal, the pace never halted or slowed that day. The Mexican Spur rolled like a ragged tide, bawling, tossing their noble horns, reaching out with their long-legged stride until the miles vanished behind them.

Late in the day, he saw the *ladino* that Childress had mentioned. The half-wild animal broke from the herd, his great horns catching the fire of the low-angling sun. He ran swiftly as a horse would run, breaking for the heavy tangle of brush where freedom and mesquite smelled sweetly in the warmth of afternoon.

Ben Sweet let out a yell and took out after him. When he caught up, the old steer turned and stood defiantly, ready to fight. But Ben's horse had plenty of cow savvy and didn't bluff. Ben hollered and slapped the air with his hat and came around in back of the *ladino*. The try for freedom was over.

For a moment, Wood felt a chill that left him trembling. The mere shape, the stature of this animal told him that this was not mere beef on the hoof. The *ladino* was something out of heroic poetry, an image from legends not yet left to memory, and for a moment it had come alive to act out the scene of wildness.

It was still with him that night when they crossed the Arroyo Colorado and stopped on the other side, twenty miles north of the home range.

He waited for sleep to ease his aching bones and muscles, wrapped in a soogan as the others called it, watching the Dipper swing around the North Star.

It was either in remembering or in the half dreams that come just before sleep, that he saw the *ladino* again, and he wondered. Wealthy son of a famous judge, with your soft bones and muscles, coming to tremble at the sight of a fighting animal . . . what makes you think you can fit in here?

III

*I'll sell my horse, and I'll sell my saddle.
And I'll bid farewell to th' longhorn cattle.*
                    —THE OLD CHISHOLM TRAIL

ON THE EVENING of April 12, Adam threw the Mexican Spur off the trail and grazed them into their bed ground. Two miles ahead was the Nueces, but there was no need to reach it that day. Water had been no problem. They had followed a tributary of that river since dawn. Yesterday they had met the Agua Dulce at noon, and before that it had been a fork of Anacuas Creek.

It was true, he decided, that the water was lower than usual, and the blue-spiked grama grass could use rain to freshen and speed its growth. But it was not yet time to worry.

He studied the sky and the feathering of high clouds. It could turn into rain, but it did not come into his mind to try and predict. He had driven cattle up the trails for twenty years, and had learned long ago that the unpredictable was almost normal. He had seen blizzards in west Texas in the middle of July.

When the herd was settled in its bed ground, Adam headed back to the camp Red had set up. He turned his horse over to Peewee's care and went to get a cup of coffee. He saw Wood, sitting far out from the fire, and he reminded Adam of a gentle, thoroughbred mare he had seen once, pushed into a corral with a bunch of Mexican *mesteñas*. She had crowded the fence, nervously, wanting out of there.

"I reckon it's the way Arbuckle talks," Red told him. "The boys been having a little fun with him. That Boston talk of his would hooraw a coyote."

"It'll stop after a while. Doesn't Wood know that?"

"Sure, it'd stop, if Arbuckle'd let 'em. But you know, he's a hot-headed juniper. He ought to be put out to soak for a while."

"He's just got a few things to learn yet, that's all. It's all as stiff as new boots."

"There's another thing. Why did he come here? You say the boy's folks was rich and he lived in a big house, and was always spraddled out in good duds like ever' day was Sunday."

"He never told me why he left. But the boy's all right."

"I reckon he is, but the way things are going, there's going to be a little dust kicked up."

Adam wandered over to where Wood sat, and sat down beside him and watched the stars coming out.

"How'd it go today?"

Wood shrugged.

"Andy tells me you're holding left drag pretty good now."

Adam saw Wood relax a little. Perhaps he thought the subject of the others kidding him was going to be broached.

"There doesn't seem to be much to it."

"Well, maybe if you decide you like working for Mexican Spur you can get out of the drag spot next time."

"A job is a job, and I'm grateful. But I doubt I'll want to continue in it."

"There's easier ways of making a living, I'll admit."

"Oh, it isn't the work so much. I guess I'll get used to it. I'm finding fewer sore muscles each day, and when I turn in, I sleep like a child. If only . . ."

Adam knew what it was, and he wanted to make a suggestion. He'd seen how the boy acted. Every day he acted like he was meeting the boys for the first time, kind of stiff and unnatural and so damned formal. It was like he wasn't sure he approved of those rawbone, rough-cut cowhands, or like he might be a little afraid of them. But Charles Wood, whatever his reasons, was not turning into the kind of a man the rest could call Charlie.

"If the work is hard now, it'll be harder after tomorrow."

"What's going to happen?"

"A couple months ago, Jake Nance contracted to buy three hundred head from a man who's got a spread near here. Bert Summers is his name. Jake didn't say much about it, but I reckon Summers is breaking up his herd. Can't go to Kansas no more, fences popping up like weeds, those quarantines I told you about, and more grass getting turned under by plows every day. The price for cattle is dropping, and it sure as hell don't pay a man to ship by rail when he can drive for half as much. It ain't a pretty picture when you've lost a lot or went broke in Montana in last winter's blizzards. I reckon he's scared and wants out. Anyway, tomorrow morning

Summer's boys will bring them out here and we'll be slapping the Mexican Spur on them. When we get rolling again, we'll have three thousand head to play nursemaid to."

"It's all right with me, boys!" Red Bellah roared.

"Let's see what coosie dug up this time." Adam got up.

Wood walked with him slowly.

"Looks like the cattle industry is in a bad way."

Adam nodded.

"It'll straighten out. Times have been bad before —'71 and '74 were read bad. But we came through all right."

"And Jake Nance?"

"Not too bad off. Like I told you once before, we sold the herd to that Ogallala man on the last drive. We got a good price, considering the time and what it dropped to later in the year. It was lucky, seeing what the blizzards did. We didn't sink like some. We're swimming. Prices are a little better this year. If they'll hold, Jake will manage."

"But what if they keep closing off the trails with homesteads?"

"That won't happen to this one. It was set aside by law."

"I do believe," Bob Skinner cried out in a high-pitched voice and lifted his tin cup with his little finger, "that I would surely love some more of that goddamn pink tea!"

Charlie Baggett threw his hamlike hands up in the air. His round, darkly-grizzled face screwed up and he tittered like a woman who had been caught with her skirts up.

"Why yes, Robert dear, let's do!" he replied, his

wheezing, gravel voice transformed into a cracking falsetto.

Adam grinned at the horseplay until he saw Wood's color rising.

"My dear," Skinner jumped to his feet and minced obscenely around the chuck wagon, "have you seen the latest step from Boston?"

Skinner wiped the sandy hair out of his eyes, somehow managing to work a coy look into his hard-boned face, and kicked up his heels to launch himself into a hip-flapping kind of jig.

Everyone was enjoying it at Wood's expense. Rev Marsh's teeth were wide and bright against his black face. Tears were streaming down Baggett's cheeks as he laughed, and an odd little smirk had come to Floyd Rogers's ugly features. Andy Giles beat time on his knees to some imaginary music.

Adam was about to say enough was enough, and that it was almost eight o'clock and time to send out a relief for Ben and John, but before he could, Wood was on his feet.

His first blow caught Skinner off balance, and the cowhand went down hard. But he gathered himself and piled into Wood with a series of blows that would have torn the easterner to pieces if he hadn't fallen so quickly.

Wood got to his knees, shaking his head, the blood running from his nose and making dark places on the ground.

He got to his feet slowly and jumped into it again, his fists lashing out as before, but not reaching their mark. Skinner, who had the quickness of a road runner fighting a sidewinder, had only to stand his ground and throw them into Wood's face.

Adam watched Wood get knocked down several times, only to get up and try again. Several times, he thought he ought to step in and break it up, but there was something in Wood's face that told him not to interfere.

Humor had fled the situation, and the expressions of those who watched changed to regret. Even Skinner had begun to back off.

Finally, when Wood fell once more and could hardly struggle to his feet, Skinner turned his back and went for a walk. Silence fell over the camp, and for the first time in several minutes, they could hear the longhorns on the bed ground, and the crickets, and a banded owl way off. Baggett nudged Rev and said something about it being time to take over for Sweet and Preble.

Peewee brought them a change of horses ... their favorite night horses, whose night vision surpassed any of the others in their strings. But before he left, Charlie went over to Wood.

"I reckon we rode with our gut hooks in a little too deep. I know you talk different, and come from a different place. But from what we've seen, we were pretty wrong about the pink tea. I don't find it hard to apologize, and I reckon that goes for the rest of the boys. We all sort of got our britches caught on the same nail."

Charlie, having said his piece, rode out to the herd.

Adam got himself another cup of coffee and stared into the fire, wondering what had brought Wood to Texas, away from the things he knew. Only one thing was certain. He had shown courage, and with it gained the respect of the others. It was up to him now, where it went from there . . .

Before the sun had cleared the eastern hills, wood was gathered for several fires. The branding irons, brought along from the home ranch for this occasion, were thrown into the fire. Before they had a chance to glow cherry-red, Summers's boys showed with the three hundred head. As they appeared over a low rise and pointed down to the open ground by the fires, Adam took one look and dropped the cigarette he was making.

"Sweet God a'mighty!" he roared.

"What's the matter?" Bellah asked as he came up in the wagon.

"Herefords!"

"Well I'll be goddamned!" Bellah hissed between his teeth.

Adam ran for his horse and rode out to meet them. There was no mistaking them. It was Summers's Forked S brand all right. Their top hand rode out to meet him.

"I'm MacDonald. You Childress?"

"That's right. What's the idea of the short-horns?"

"That's what the contract called for. What's wrong?"

"Why they ain't worth a pee in hell, that's what wrong!"

"They look all right to me."

"Well, you look at them short, stumpy legs and tell me how in hell they're supposed to even walk with a longhorn bunch. Why those steers I got will walk 'em to death. Herefords! They ain't got the savvy of a jack rabbit! When my critters are sticking together in a stompede, these hothouse cows of yours will scatter like ants looking up and seeing a new cow chip fall. I ain't got no use for them. You'd better take 'em back."

"But they're already paid for!"

Adam took a deep breath and looked back toward the Mexican Spur longhorns. It was happening, he thought, wasn't it? First the trouble in Kansas, and then the railroads coming in, and fences closing up the land. Even in Texas now, Glidden and his barbed invention closing off what used to be free. It didn't seem so bad at first. With the buffalo gone in the northwest and people pouring in, there was a waiting market for Texas cattle.

But then Texas Fever caused trouble there too and more quarantine lines rose against them. The new trail solved that problem, but the northwest now had its own cattle, fat and beef-heavy, and no need to walk them. It was stiff competition. A lot of men shook their heads and said there was nothing for it but to switch to a better breed and head for the rail yards.

Better ... what was better about a breed that could not forage as well in a hard, bitter land? What shorthorn ever had the sense to sit in water up to its neck all day to drown screwworms? And what fancy breed ever had enough savvy to take turns going down to drink while the others stayed with the calves and stood guard against lobos and coyotes? And indeed, what of the fancy breeds that came into southern Texas and died from the fever that never touched a longhorn? The Texas steer might be short on meat and heavy on horn, but they were right for the country.

Yes, it was happening . . . it wouldn't come in his time, Adam knew. But he could see it coming.

"I said, they've already been paid for."

"I heard you." Adam nodded.

He didn't have to take them. He could go on north without them, or he could turn the whole works south again and resign when he got there. Adam looked back to where the fires were burning, their smoke rising and mingling gray in the new morning sun. He took a deep breath and calmed a little. He had to admit it. He knew the story.

Jake Nance had bought them out of generosity, not because he wanted them. These were times of trouble, and a friend had needed a hand. That was all there was to it. And because it was that way, he had no real right to do anything but accept them. Jake hadn't been in any position, money-wise, to buy them. Now he had to recoup on as many as could be gotten north.

Adam lifted his Stetson and scratched his head.

"Summers lose any to fever since he had them?"

"Some, but it's tapered off."

Maybe they had gained some immunity to the fever then, and whatever caused it. That was one saving feature anyway.

"All right, let's put the iron to them."

The three hundred were driven down to the fires and the branding began. The Herefords were roped and thrown hard, and held down, and their bawling and the smell of dust and burning hair and scorched hide filled the air. First the Forked S was burned on another part of the animal to make the *venta,* which indicated a change of ownership, and then the Mexican Spur was made. Thus marked, a steer got to his feet, wild-eyed and scared, and was run over to the waiting longhorns and kept by the men riding there.

Near midday, Adam chased one in toward a fire and, his rope singing out fast, forefooted the steer hard. A big horse of a man and his limping, dried up little partner leaped on the sprawling steer and held him down.

"Now goddamn you," the little one yelled to the man at the fire, "hit him with the arn! Lean on it this time and make some smoke!"

The man who rose, red-faced, dirty and staggering with the cherry-red iron in his hand was Wood. Adam saw him stand there, the bruises and cut places on his face from last night, shaking with fury and tears rolling from his smoke-burned eyes.

The two men fought to keep the steer down.

"Goddamn you, hit him with it! What're you waitin' for? Why . . . I'll take that arn and burn your ass with it if . . ."

"Why don't you try!" Wood yelled back.

The little man almost let go of the steer to go after Wood, but Adam stopped him.

He jumped down and took the iron from Wood and slapped it on the bawling animal. He jumped to the fire and made the final burn with the Mexican Spur and the steer was released.

The two stood there wiping their necks and faces with their bandanas, glaring at Wood. The little one spat in the dust.

"That son of a bitch there . . ."

"Take it easy, shorty. He's a new man."

"Well, you got at least a dozen critters out there that ain't much more'n hair-branded on account of him!"

"I'm sorry, Adam. I guess I'm not doing so well."

"It's my fault. I wasn't thinking when I sent you out here with the others. Maybe you better ride herd instead."

"Yeah, you make sure it's somebody who ain't afraid to burn 'em on! While I'm waitin' I'm goin' to hit that water barrel!"

Wood picked up his hat.

"I think I'd better stay here," he said.

Adam watched the little man walking away, and understood.

"Don't mind him, Wood. He's all right. It's like working in a frying pan out here. What's your problem?"

"I guess it's like he said. I'm afraid of hurting them."

"Afraid of hurting them? Forget it, boy. It don't hurt them much. These critters got thicker hide than you and me. All that bawling they do is mostly from being chased and thrown and held down. Just slap those irons on hard and fast. The hotter the iron, the better. You sure you want to stick?"

Wood nodded.

"You do all right, boy. Just keep at it," Adam turned and then stopped again, grinning. "You ought to see yourself, boy. I'll be goddamned if you look like anything that came from Boston!"

With both outfits roping and branding, it didn't take too long. Adam had lost sight of his anger in the rush to get it done. But he had little to say that night around the fire. It took a long time to find sleep, and when it finally did come, he dreamed. There was a single longhorn, a rangy dun standing alone against the wide horizons. It was dark, and the stars were bright, and he had been riding somewhere, and he found this longhorn standing close-legged and kind of hunched up, bellowing at the stars. The dun's voice carried for miles, but there was nothing to answer him and he seemed to be a creature lost and in mourning. Adam glanced up at the North Star to get his direction, and when he looked again, the dun was gone. It was as if he had never been, and barbed-wire fences stretched for as far as he could see.

IV

Sure it's one cent for coffee and two cents for bread,
Three for a steak and five for a bed,
Sea breeze from the gutter wafts a salt-water smell,
To the festive cowboy in the Southwestern hotel.

—UNKNOWN

EACH DAY CAME its round and passed, each like the slow march of the seasons. Darkness at times seemed bleak until Red built his fire and the first light of dawn came creeping. This was the winter of a day. Spring was in the swift rising of the sun and in the warmth and merriment it brought to the low, rolling hills. Summer was the afternoon, its heat and the boiling dust that came up to choke and blind, for after all, this was a thirsty land. Autumn was the gentling of evening, at sundown when the big country turned golden and red, and the scent of cooling dust rose to revive and hearten.

Wood watched the days and wondered if the others saw them that way. At first, he wondered about many things. There was such a sameness to the country. They were going north, but in an odd fashion. This side of north and then that, as if feeling their way. It seemed strange after Red saw to it nightly that the wagon tongue pointed to the North

Star. This, used with the sun the next day provided a compass almost as unerring as that which guided a ship. It was not until he watched the land more closely that he realized that the real compass was grass and water. The best grass, the nearest water. As much as the occasional fence would allow.

He had remembered talk of having to stick to the trail, a trail set aside by law, and wondered why nobody tried to stop them. But he had learned about that too, in the slow talk that drifted across the fire at night. There was grimness in the talk, and it was of something yet to come. It was farther north that this trail began, near the Colorado . . . farther north where Texas was free of the thing that caused the fever. They were strict about the trail there, and it was understandable, but it would be hard on the cattle from then on.

It would be hard for them, when everything should go according to what was best for the cattle. Time was only time, distance merely a measurement. The bad market Adam talked about might be worsening, but it would do no good to try and catch it before prices fell any lower if they had to arrive in Montana with cattle reduced to skeletons. The best way was the slow way, following grass and water and getting them there in better shape than when they left. But confined to a narrow trail, this practice would suffer.

These things he understood now, but there were others he did not.

They needed rain and needed it bad. Grass was beginning to dry up, and the water they had come to since they left the Nueces . . . the Frio, Laguna Creek, the Atascosa, and San Antonio Creek, which they had crossed that day . . . was not as high as it should have been.

So there was weather, which was hardest of all, and up ahead, a narrow, restrictive corridor through which cattle could walk slowly while time killed grass and water and prices.

He had heard the others talk of the trails which existed before this one, when cattlemen fought with nesters, and cut fences, and fought over water and ran the blockades of Kansas Jayhawkers. It had been a long time since the day when a man could take his herd north in his own fashion. It had not been easy even then, because the weather had always been there, and there had been more than one man to die from the swift, Indian arrow, and more than one herd to stampede and be lost as the red man darted among them. But there was no doubt that earlier times had been better for the cattlemen. They had only trouble now.

And yet there were railroads that eliminated these troubles. What Wood couldn't understand was why Adam didn't use them.

Adam had snorted, almost angrily, at the mention of it.

"Hell, I can take this herd up the trail for seventy-five cents or no more than a dollar a head. The railroad would cost us a dollar and a half, and riding them cars don't put weight on a critter. It takes it off. And another thing. In order to keep from needing a train a hundred miles long to ship your longhorns, you got to dehorn them so you can get more into each box car. You'll think twice before dehorning three thousand head of cattle. No, I been walking them for twenty years, and I ain't seen no better way yet!"

The explanation had meant little. So it cost

more, and the cattle lost a little weight, and maybe it was hard to dehorn them. It seemed better than the dangers of the trail. Didn't those who shipped the year before fare better by getting to Montana early and selling before prices and blizzards played havoc?

The real answer seemed to be in the man himself. He was too stubborn and too set in his ways to see the value of progress.

The other men . . . he didn't know what to think about them.

In some ways he thought he liked them. But when he tried to fix the liking in his mind, he could not. It seemed to be composed of little things, and nothing more . . . like Baggett not feeling bad about apologizing to him that time, and the obvious kindness they felt toward the animals in their care . . . like Adam taking on a man who needed a job, whether he had experience or not. And there was that girl . . . Katherine . . . who was not part of the crew but somehow necessary to the thinking . . . taking care of a complete stranger in a way that would have left other women blushing, if they were able to do it at all. It had been a kindness and a strength which the women he had known could not have understood. In her kindness there seemed to have been some kind of challenge, and imagined or not, he did not know how to accept it or where to begin, because of these other men. But he could not forget her.

They treated him with respect now. They still called him Arbuckle, but he couldn't deny it himself that he was green and new.

But still, there was distance, a remoteness in the way they talked to him and in the way he replied.

He could not get close to them.

Perhaps it was because they seemed crude and rough-cut at times, and apparently locked in a past where progress couldn't touch them in their peculiar kind of ignorance.

Perhaps, simply, it was this kind of existence . . . being dirty most of the time, with the sweet smell of cattle heavy in the clothes . . . the grueling hours and being constantly at the mercy of the weather. Maybe it was something to which he could not adjust . . . an alien world. Not bad, but merely different and the difference could not be bridged.

He had thought of quitting this job, and was thinking of it now. It seemed to be as good a time as any. It was the twenty-first of April and they had stopped a few miles out from San Antonio.

But he could not straighten the thing out in his mind.

He sat by the fire, trying to come to grips with it. There might be something in town, some sort of luck that would lead him to a life more to his liking. But he couldn't turn his back on the trail drive and not give it a second thought.

There was something here . . .

Something about the life . . . and Katherine.

"Well, you coming to town, or not?"

Wood snapped out of his thoughts and looked at Baggett.

"Guess I was thinking too hard. Yes, I'm going in."

When the guard on the cattle was established, those who could saddled a fresh horse, and rode toward town.

Adam was going, of course, to see if any mail had been forwarded, and also to write a letter to

Jake Nance to keep him informed on the progress of the drive. Bob Skinner and Rev Marsh had to ride herd until one o'clock in the morning when the graveyard boys took over. Floyd stayed behind, though he didn't have to.

It was more than an hour's ride into town, and that again coming back, leaving some with only a couple hours to play with. Others, if they didn't want to sleep, could spend the night as long as they showed up at the fire in the morning.

They all rode in together, whooping it up the first mile or so and then settling back in happy, relaxed contemplation of a time in town after three weeks on the trail.

Wood hung back and kept pretty much to himself, and after a while, Adam came back and joined him.

"Any plans in town?"

Wood shook his head, looking at the lights of it ahead.

"No. Just to get away from it for a while."

"You've only got a couple hours. Maybe you could work out a trade with one of the boys."

"No. That's all right."

"Well, I can buy you a drink, anyway."

They rode into town and tied up at a likely looking place called the Jamboree, and went inside.

Andy Giles had a quick drink and went for a hotel to enjoy sleeping in a bed. The others bought bottles and sat down at a couple of the tables and drank and let the garish paint and the tinny piano music glaze over the days on the trail. Later, maybe they'd look for women or put their pay against the perfidy of professional cardboard.

Wood and Adam stood at the bar.

"Well, here's hoping for a little rain."

Wood nodded and drank. The eternal prayer of the cattleman. Rain. Rain to come and touch the dryness of the land. The low and rolling land that had seemed to him forever dry. And yet, it had its own beauty. Morning smelled good and there was something about the way the first and last light touched the land in a day, and something too in the great, reaching and unbroken sky as they moved under it from sunrise to sundown. Sometimes at night, riding graveyard, with his companion riding over on the other side of the herd, he felt the greatness of space filled with stars and the hidden night scents, the lost places that huddled under the Dipper as it swung around the North Star. *El reloj de los Indios,* Adam called it. The clock of the Indians. They could tell time by it, Adam and the others, and be accurate within fifteen or twenty minutes. But there was no time in it for him. Time was lost out there, and sometimes he felt he only had to turn loose of the reins to be swept away forever in the timelessness. The lonely place. And yet there was little comfort now, in the lights and sounds of a town. It was still like being alone.

"Thanks for the drink," he said to Adam. "I think I'll look around."

"Any place in particular?"

"No. Just sight-seeing. Maybe the Alamo."

Wood walked out and got his horse. First he had come to town to escape the silence, and now he sought to find it again, but not in the familiarity of Bellah's fire. He had to be where he could look at the whole thing from a distance.

In a little while, after asking the way, he found the Alamo. He had seen it so many times in history books, it was almost as if he had been there before. He climbed down, tethered his horse, and sat where he could look at it.

Crickets sang softly, and there was a perfume to the night, and a quietness different from the bottomless silence he had felt beyond the cattle on the graveyard shift. It was peace, and yet it moved and stirred and whispered to him in the darkness. Perhaps it was the voices of fifty years ago still echoing. He did not know. He was not superstitious, but neither could he deny that perhaps the quality of a place could bring something like that back if one listened close enough.

"Hey, wake up, boy! Come on, it's nearly midnight."

Wood opened his eyes and found Adam bending over him. He looked around and saw the Alamo, and remembered where he was.

"I came to think. Looks like I never got around to it."

"That ain't hard to do here. It's a wonderful place."

"I always wondered about it. I used to come across it now and then in history books. The battle seemed like such a futile gesture, and yet such a glorious one. Buying time for Houston, taking such a toll of the enemy, and then dying to the last man. It makes me wonder what kind of people you raise out here."

Adam shrugged, as if embarrassed to talk of such weighty matters.

"I don't reckon they're any different than your people in the East. The circumstances is a little different, that's all."

"There's civilization here, too. But I see people

still trying to do near-impossible things."

"Like what?"

"Like trying to scratch out a living on a piece of land that doesn't look like it'd grow anything but brush when there's better land to be had. And like driving three thousand head of cattle a couple thousand miles to market."

"You do with what you got, and do the best you can. It was the same way with your eastern country once."

"I guess I'm still thinking of the things you said about trail driving and railroads. Railroads are progress, and yet you won't accept them. It's almost as if you wanted the country to never change."

"I don't figure changing it would do it any good."

"Then it's true. You'd rather have things stay half wild, rough, and crude . . . like savages."

"That what you reckon we are, Wood?"

"I didn't mean it that way . . . it's what I keep expecting, and I keep seeing hints of it, but it never materializes. I've heard about men killing one another at the slightest excuse, and of men shooting up a town and riding off with the women. I've heard how ignorant and brutal they are. But I never see it."

"Well, I reckon it kind of grows with the talking by the time you hear about in Boston. But I'll allow it has happened."

"But there's this other thing. Not wanting things to get better. Not wanting change. I've *seen* that."

They rode for a long time and said nothing until they reached the brightness of the stars outside of town.

"If I explained again, I'd only be saying what I said before. There's nothing complicated in liking things as they are. What's really bothering you, Wood?"

"What makes you think something's bothering me?"

"Our little talk back there."

Wood kept his eyes straight ahead, almost angrily.

"I was thinking about quitting."

Adam said nothing, and in a moment, Wood went on with it.

"I guess I could say I don't belong here. And it'd be true."

"I don't believe that. A man who doesn't quit while someone like Skinner tears him to pieces wouldn't quit easy on something else. You've got another reason."

Wood thought about it and shrugged.

"All right. I guess I don't care for the company. Floyd. Cimarron. And because nobody talks about it or seems to care, I wonder what kind of history the rest of you have."

"I suppose you object to Rev Marsh too, because he's black."

"I . . ." he started to deny the accusation.

"Once I said that a man's past didn't matter. That goes for his color, too. I won't make excuses for others. I know Rev had a hard time before he came to me. It took time for him to realize he didn't have no fight here and that the boys like him. He's full of pride . . . can't take anybody getting worried over him. Like him needing a good coat or working too hard to fill the gap when someone is laid up, or trying to make up for the color of his skin by trying to do his job twice as good as anybody else. But he's pretty happy now. I don't want you to spoil it!"

"You're jumping to conclusions. The color of Rev's skin makes no difference to me!"

"Then it's just what Floyd and Cimarron have done, and what the rest of us might have done that's eating on you?"

"I don't know what they've done."

"All right. I heard Floyd shot and killed a man in Abilene."

"You act as if it were nothing! My God!"

"Slow down, Wood. That was only the word I got, from other men who told me about him. You can't trust talk like that. The rest of the boys don't know about it, so don't go spreading the word. They got an idea he's done *something,* but that's all. But suppose it is true. You look at the strains that push on a man. He leads a lonely life out here, and he works hours that almost kill. Fourteen hours in the saddle, five more riding night herd, and five left to sleep if he's lucky. Put him in a cowtown somewhere after months of that and he blows off steam. There's others in that town doing the same, or maybe those who ain't got no use for a cowhand. Maybe somebody rubs him the wrong way or cheats him at cards or waters his whisky or tries to steal his woman. Anyway you look at it, an argument comes easy. Maybe it's his fault and maybe it isn't."

Wood tried to digest what Adam had told him.

"I don't know," he told him. "I don't know."

"Cimarron, I can't say. I don't know anymore about him than you do. And the rest of us? I don't know that either. I figure a man is what you make him, not what he was before you knew him."

"And what about Peewee?"

"God a'mighty! You don't suspect him of something, do you?"

"I just wonder why you let a kid his age work at a job like that. He ought to be home, going to school."

"Peewee has no folks. We found him lying in the gutter in Brownsville, sick and nearly starved. We're the only family he has and wants. He's happy. Besides, a lot of kids his age start learning the cattle business by hiring on as a wrangler."

Adam reined in at the top of the rise and Wood stopped too. They could see Red's fire flickerinng in the distance.

"You're acting like a man who ain't really sure what he wants to complain about. But let me tell you something. A man sitting on a post at noon puts a shadow on both sides of the fence."

"What's that supposed to mean?"

"The boys are probably curious about a man who's got plenty of money and all the fine things. Why should a man leave all that and go looking for something else? It might be that *you're* wanted by the law for all any of us know."

Adam spurred his horse on and Wood sat for a while.

Why all the talk, he wondered. Why all the worry? You're looking for a way of living that has purpose, and friendship that has honesty. If you don't find these things here, you will find them elsewhere. Why worry about it?

He couldn't answer any of it. Maybe for the moment a job was a job, and until he had a little more money in his pocket it was the best he could do. But he couldn't turn his back on it.

Not just yet.

Wood spurred his horse and followed Adam to the fire.

V

He ne'er would sleep within a tent,
No comforts would he know,
But like a brave old Texian,
A-ranging he would go.

—MUSTANG GRAY

THE TRAIL WIDENED at San Antonio, cut deep by many herds. So plain was it, and so wide, a man could wonder why there had ever been any need for the star that beckoned to them at night. Near Bandera, some four days to the northwest, the swath cut on the face of the earth was even deeper, for here what was left of the old Western Trail began and would be followed until it gave way to the new National Trail farther north. And here was the first real evidence of the numbers in the great bawling tide that rolled north. It was only the twenty-fourth of April, and already the herd had to be driven far to one side of the trail to find the grass they needed.

Floyd Rogers watched as the mile-long reach of the Mexican Spur bunch shortened and slowed. Red had swung his wagon in and started his fire. The noon meal was coming, but there would be little rest. The crew would alternate between right and left in coming in to eat, and then ride out to relieve the others. No rest until sundown, and even then, not for some.

It was warm for April. Rogers could see faint heat ghosts rising from the ground, and there was no breeze to cool the dark places of his shirt.

To the north, on the horizon, was a thin smear of cloud, and they all watched it, checking on it every hour or so to see if it had moved closer, looking for the faint shadow beneath that meant it was raining there. Adam watched it longer than anybody.

The thing that was on the trail boss's mind was what was on everyone's mind now. There had to be rain, and a lot of it soon, or there was going to be trouble later. In the cloud was hope.

In a few minutes the whole herd was grazing quietly, and Floyd checked the cloud again. It never seemed to come any closer. Adam was coming down off the rise, and Red was giving his yell a half mile back. His voice carried easily.

Floyd turned toward the wagon and broke into a gentle lope. The cloud . . . rain . . . he didn't care. The miles ahead, the months . . . he didn't care about that either. It was better where he was, no matter how hard things got. It was peace, a place to be.

He rode to the edge of the noon camp and unsaddled his horse and slapped him on the rump. The tired animal trotted willingly out to where Peewee held the cavvy.

Standing under the fly of his wagon, Red dished out slabs of fat beef and steaming frijoles and the tomato and bread stew called cooch. Floyd grabbed a cup of coffee and went over to where the others were gathering and squatted down to eat. His gaze wandered around from face to face.

Ben Sweet's long angular frame was folded awkwardly against a wheel of the wagon as he silently ate. Ben might look like he was watching something. But then you'd notice his eyes weren't moving. Ben was always staring off like that, into nothing. He never said much and claimed he was thinking. Baggett always swore he was asleep, like a horse he once knew who always leaned up against the corral fence and went to sleep with his eyes open.

John Preble stood up to eat, watching Cimarron gathering dry cow chips and chunks of mesquite wood to throw in the coonie. Floyd flicked his eyes on past him in near resentment. John was one of those boys who was almost pretty. His face was pink and smooth and fine-boned, with the pink running to brown now. The gals in any town they hit couldn't leave him alone. But what did it matter? He ought to have a face like mine, Floyd thought, that lets a man lie only with fat *pelados*.

Andy Giles wobbled unsteadily on his haunches, spooning in the Mexican beans and sipping noisily at his coffee.

Floyd smirked and put his entire attention to eating. Andy was no better than a dirt farmer, and that's all he wanted to be. Andy couldn't hold a job anywhere for long except on a ranch. And the only reason he worked on ranches and went on drives like this was to save money to buy a piece of farmland. His wife worked in some cafe in Brownsville toward the same idea. A man wondered how long Andy would last, pushing a plow, half stooped in the sun all day long. Already he was getting bald and wearing glasses.

Floyd felt the resentment he held for these men

and tried to forget it and push it aside. It was only envy, and it didn't matter. There was peace here. It was lonely, but there was peace. Rev was the only one who mattered.

He looked out at the herd and the small figures riding around it. There were better jobs. Once he thought he might like to be a teacher, until he found out what his looks did to people. And for a while, he had liked driving a stage until he grew tired of hearing fancy-dressed women making quiet remarks among themselves about his face while he waited for the mail sack to be thrown aboard. There were a lot of things he had wanted to do more than this. But it seemed like the world didn't like an ugly man. The way it turned out, working cattle seemed like the only place where it didn't matter.

He watched Sweet go out and Baggett come in.

"You never told me how you made out with that yellow-haired girl, John," Andy said. "The one in San Antone."

Preble shook his head dreamily.

"If I'd had just a little more time!"

"You mean you didn't?"

"Hell, no! I only saw her for about fifteen minutes. Things was shaping up real right, and then I had to come back."

"You could've traded with somebody," Baggett wheezed and brought his plate over. "Arbuckle would've done it for you."

"He had the graveyard that night," Giles said.

"Floyd then. Floyd had the whole night, and he stayed."

Preble made no reply, and Floyd tensed up.

"You just don't plan things, John. If you're

standing around now pawing the ground and bellering, it's your own fault."

"Hell, Charlie, I don't like to ask anybody to do that."

"Well, what's there to it? You go up to Floyd and he says he can't or don't want to go in town and . . ."

"What are you getting at, Baggett!" Floyd stood up.

"Why . . . like you ain't got any money, or need to mend your saddle . . . what's the matter with you?"

Floyd advanced slowly. Anger grew and his heart pounded.

"It's my business what I do with my own time!"

"That's right," Baggett said quietly, getting up.

"What did you really mean by saying I *can't* go in?"

"You're making something out of nothing, Rogers. But as long as you feel like wrinkling your hump, suppose you tell us?"

Floyd jumped for Baggett, but immediately a strong shoulder caught him in the chest and Floyd found himself looking into the pale eyes of Adam Childress.

"That'll be enough," he said quietly.

Baggett backed off and Floyd looked around at the others as they began to relax from the sudden tension. Peewee had a fresh horse out of his string singled out and ready to go. Floyd saddled him and rode out to the herd.

Maybe it was the unusual warmth of the day, and worrying about the need for rain, and being pretty tired out most of the time. It could make men edgy. Maybe it would be all right. Maybe all it had to do was settle down again and be forgotten.

But some things are never forgotten, and what would he do if this was one of them? He'd have to move on, and he didn't want to leave. Even if they didn't like him much here, it was a place of peace, a place to be.

Floyd tried to push the worry and the hurt from his mind and turned his attention to the cloud again as the Mexican Spur bunch was moved out again and they reached for the horizon.

The cloud never seemed to come any closer, nor become any darker. It was as if it were a product of the heat ghosts rising from the ground and not real after all. The rain they had hoped for never came, and by sundown, the cloud was gone.

VI

It's forgot how to rain, and the river's mighty low,
And the herd is going to suffer when the dust begins
* to blow.*

—THE OLD CHISHOLM TRAIL

ADAM HAD GONE ahead in the afternoon to scout
out the Pedernales, and then, having seen it in the
distance from a hill, had returned to direct the herd
to reach the river at the nearest point of its wandering course. They moved toward it now, slowly,
throwing their dust cloud into a low-falling sun.
Before the stars were out, they would drink and
rest in the cool of evening with another ten or
twelve miles behind them. Another day . . .

The days were beginning to reach out now. The
long sun and the long sky, endless, stretching, it
must seem, from pole to pole, held together by the
barest thread of sleep until it was hard to tell at
first thought where one day ended and the next
began.

Adam gathered it to him as a man clutches at
warmth, the desire to wander being fed now . . .
happy in the openness and change where the wind
wandered. But sometimes, as now, when he looked
at the tossing horns and the hooves that reached
out for the long walk, he had an inkling that this

50

was not enough . . . and the wish to move and the
hunger that lay beyond it unidentified became a
fierceness, an unsatisfied loving of the land.

It was at such moments that he required company, not for the talking but the sharing of the
time. He joined Ben Sweet and they rode together
for a long time without a word. The herd was doing
well. The cattle were gaining a little weight, and
they moved north each day without interruption,
peacefully and quietly. There had been no trouble,
though there was added work in keeping the Herefords from falling behind. No, it was going well
enough, but Adam noticed Ben watching the sky as
he was. The same question was there.

"How did the Pedernales look?"

"I saw the sun shining on it, Ben. It looked all
right."

"Was the shine broken or solid?"

"It was broken, but it was probably brush on the
banks."

Ben nodded and Adam knew he wasn't convinced. He wasn't so sure himself. Oh, there was
water there. The sun had shone on it, and from that
hill, he had almost been able to smell it in the dryness of the air. Was there enough? Yes, he was certain of that too. But there was a feeling in the air,
a part of this dryness, a part of this dust that rose
thickly, a part of the slowness and dull color of the
grass that came like silence and a slow pounding of
the pulse.

There were antelope, now and then, standing
from afar to watch, and the sweet trilling of meadowlarks, but memory saw these things, and heard,
and wondered, and tried to compare with all the
years before. It seemed like there had not been as

few antelope before. And didn't the meadowlark's voice seem subdued? It was a feeling that the whole world was slowly coming to a stop.

Adam rode back and intercepted the chuck wagon.

"How far, Adam?" Red stopped.

"Another hour, maybe."

He pulled the lid off the water barrel and pulled out a dipper full. It was warm and sweet.

"How's your passenger?"

Bellah glanced at Cimarron, who sat on the seat next to him with his eyes closed and his arms folded on his chest.

"Well, he's a quiet one, but I sure ain't had to go looking for chips or wood. He's a tough old bird."

"Maybe he doesn't speak English."

"He spoke it well enough that first morning. He just ain't got nothing to say, that's all. But that's all right with me. We get along, and with the time he saves me, I ought to be able to dig up something special more often. I seen some sandhill plums somewhere up this way last time."

Adam closed the barrel. Red made a good pie.

"Or I could make some bear-sign."

"Well, I wouldn't mention it out loud if I were you."

"I reckon it would go pretty good."

Adam gave him a knowing look. Those boys could stand around eating doughnuts as long as coosie turned them out.

At sundown, they spotted the Pedernales and before it was dark, Ben Sweet and Charlie Baggett were heading the lead cattle downstream while those following were moved above them, so that each group of cattle would not have to drink the

muddied water stirred up by those preceding them.
But the move was almost unnecessary. The water
was barely moving. And it had not been brush on
the banks interrupting the reflection of the sun that
Adam had seen from the hill. It was sand and rock.

There was enough to drink, and enough to fill
the water barrels, but the Pedernales was drying
up. They were in good shape for now. They had
reached the Rio Guadalupe the day before. None
of the animals had gone thirsty so far, and they
would sleep satisfied that night. But what about the
country ahead?

Red was as good as his word about the doughnuts, and the cry of bear-sign went up in the camp
among the boys, and there was little talk of anything else.

"I remember a man," Charlie Baggett chuckled
asthmatically with a full mouth, "I met up in Kansas. It was at Drover's Cottage, in Abilene. He
used to work for Charles Goodnight. Anyway, this
boy claimed he could sit down and eat three dozen
without stopping. I reckon I said something that
made him think I doubted his word, because first
thing you know, him and me was riding out to
some cow camp. It wasn't his outfit. He wasn't
heading back for Texas yet, and had drawn his pay
and stayed behind. Well, we came up to this wagon
where the coosie and another man were sitting
around drinking coffee.

"I could see they'd sold their bunch and were
going to head for home in the morning. None of
their boys was there. They was all over in Texas
Town with the rest, drinking the place dry. So this
man I'm telling you about rides up to their fire as
big as you please and pulls his Sam Colt out and

says he'd appreciate it mightily if old coosie would make up a batch of bear-sign.

"Well, there was nothing the *cocinero* could do but make up a batch, and all the while, my friend sat there with that Colt, as straight-faced and serious as a dead man."

Baggett speared another doughnut and reflectively took a bite.

"Well, with the Colt in one hand, and the other hand snagging bear-sign, and those two waiting there with their back hair standing up, he ate his three dozen. And then, like it didn't matter, got a cup of coffee off of them and then ate six or eight more. Well, coosie hadn't seen anything like that before, and forgot about being mad. We was invited to spend the night, and told that there'd be another batch in the morning. Well, there was, sure enough! When we woke up, coosie was standing over my friend with a pistol in his hand. He made him get up and start eating bear-sign. Well, he ate his three dozen and them some and when he tried to stop, coosie would stick that pistol barrel up his nostril and make him eat some more. It looked like he was going to have to eat his way clear to the bottom of that barrel. But finally it seemed like it'd be better to be shot than go on eating, and he quit. He couldn't move. Coosie and the other man pulled out of there and headed for Texas. My friend looked up at me, powerful sad, and said 'Charlie, you go back to town. No use waiting on me. I'm going to set a spell.' You know, I rode out that way a week later, heading for Texas, and that man hadn't moved an inch."

Adam laughed with the rest, and then walked away from the fire. He saddled the bayo coyote and rode out to the herd, going slowly until his eyes accustomed themselves to the darkness and found the stars sweeping across the heavens like a swarm of fireflies.

He rode slowly around the herd, until a shadow came up in the darkness.

"That you, boss?"

"Yes, Rev. How are they?"

"They're fine. How's that bear-sign? They savin' any for us?"

"Sure. You'll be relieved pretty quick."

"Hell, boss, I ain't in no hurry. Any time. Any time is all right. Don't you worry about me none."

Adam rode on around, the Negro's rich voice coming back to him over his shoulder, singing happily.

> *Two little niggers upstairs in bed,*
> *One turned over to the oder and said,*
> *"How 'boud dat short'nin' bread,*
> *How 'bout dat short'nin' bread?"*

"Bob?" a voice came softly.

"No, it's me. Adam."

"Oh," Wood came up, "I thought it was Skinner."

"I was just taking a check before turning in."

"You sound worried about something."

"Well, you saw how the river was."

"Yes. It was low."

"Too low. The creeks that normally feed it have gone dry. I've seen it like this around here before. That means there ain't any water between here and the Llano."

Wood digested this and there was concern in his voice.

"How far?"

"Well, it ain't really bad. It's thirty or thirty-five miles. We'll push the herd a little faster. We've had longer dry drives."

"Then what are you worried about?"

Adam shook his head.

"It's the rest of it, farther north. I don't like to think about how it's going to be if we don't get some rain soon."

"That bad?"

"It looks like a drought. I could be wrong. It's been late to rain before, but . . . well, we got all the signs."

VII

I look across the plains,
And wonder why it never rains,
Till Gabriel blows his trumpet sound
And says the rain's just gone around.

—DAKOTA LAND

THE DIPPER was still sharp and brilliant in the sky when Wood groaned and opened his eyes. He felt the dew, wet on his face and in his hair, and the pang of hunger in his belly. He rubbed his face with his hands, shook his head, and swung his legs out. Red was a belligerent figure, looking tall in the light of his fire.

"I got half a mind to throw it out!"

Wood pulled his boots on and stumped out to the edge of camp and relieved himself. Then he walked back, conscious of being fully awake and deliciously aware of the scent of mesquite smoke and boiled coffee and frying beef.

"Goddamn it, you act like you was getting up in the middle of the night! You ought to get up when I do!"

"Nothin' could get me to raise my nose," an irate voice piped up, "until you got your boots on you son of a bitch!"

Wood listened to the scattered, halfhearted

57

laughter that came, and got his clothes on. It was
earlier than usual at that, and he remembered
about the dry drive. They were going to get a head
start on the sun. They would take them down to
the Pedernales again to get their fill, and then start
them rolling before the sun began to beat down
hard, and keep them going fast until night fell
again and the air was cool. This was the way Adam
said it had to be done. Get the miles covered
before thirst really got bad. Thirty miles to the
Llano. Pushing hard, they'd make it by the afternoon of the next day.

Breakfast was hot and quick, with no dallying
around afterward reaching for sacks of Bull
Durham or Duke's Mixture or whatever a man's
particular favorite happened to be. They saddled
the horses they planned to start the day with, and
rode out to the herd.

When it was figured the cattle had eaten their fill
and were ready to go, they were taken down to the
river and allowed to drink. Wood rode out into the
center of the river to stop any cattle that might decide to come across and head in the wrong direction. He sat and watched, the taste of coffee bitter
in his mouth, sleepiness falling swiftly away. The
smell of the dying river was strong in the air, and
the sky was beginning to pale.

Up on the ground beyond the bank, coosie and
Cimarron provided a shadow play. Red hitched his
mules to the chuck wagon, and Cimarron killed the
fire. It was a pleasant scene, a charming painting of
black against light, of shadows moving against
what was becoming a lemon sky. One would want
to remember it, and wish to capture it somehow so
that it would not be lost . . . until the silence was

felt. The silence beyond the noise of the herd. Red Bellah was a part of it, but the silence emanated from Cimarron.

He seemed content to remain wordless, to do what he could to help Red, to eat a little, and sleep a little. There was nothing more. And all of this was done with a simple but undeniable dignity. It spoke of innocence. But these things did not show anything, anymore than did his face. The question was still there.

Where was he going? To Montana, it was said. There might be an answer when they arrived. But why would an old Mexican want to go to the Territory of Montana, and why with a trail herd at that?

He was all right, Red claimed. And Adam repeated it. And as long as he behaved himself and earned his keep, he was welcome. Wood still was not easy about it. The trust seemed childish. The old man did not carry a gun, but had a wicked knife. What did an old man need with a knife like that? It was long and balanced like a weapon; not the kind used for cutting meat or rope. Red and Adam seemed to be ignoring the obvious.

Shortly, the herd was doubled back from the water and pressed into a walk, and then pushed and slapped at with ropes and hollered at until they were walking fast.

Adam came back to talk to him and Andy before they were out of sight of the river.

"You'll have trouble with the shorthorns. Do the best you can to keep them up, but don't be surprised if you lose a few."

The heat began to get bad around ten o'clock, but the pace never slackened. As Adam had predicted, there was trouble with the Herefords. They

simply could not walk the way a longhorn could.
Wood and Giles had to chase them continually.

It seemed impossible for the day to progress and
for the miles to go by in that fashion.

By the time they halted at noon to eat and rest
briefly, he had gone through three of the horses in
his string. He sprawled on the ground too tired to
feel hungry.

"What's the matter there, Arbuckle?" Bob
Skinner asked him.

"Why hell, man, he's been workin' harder'n
you," Rev Marsh spoke up. "He been chousin' up
them shorthorns all mornin'."

"That's for damn sure," Andy eased down to the
ground and got his plate. "Those animals are the
worst mistake I ever seen."

"Well, it's better than farming, ain't it Andy?"

Andy snorted at Baggett.

"Just give me a half section, a couple of milk
cows, some good mules, and a plow and I'll show
you what's better. Plenty of milk and vegetables for
the kids, and everything coming up tall and green,
a nice house to live in, and a place for my wife to
grow flowers. After this trip, I'm going to have it."

"Kinda looks like we caught a nester for sure,"
Baggett looked at him and laughed.

Ben stared dreamily toward the herd and shook
his head.

"I don't know't that's so bad," he drawled. "It's
nice to own something and settle on it. Just give me
fifty sections of good grazing country and a few
hundred head of longhorns, and I don't care if I
ever see a trail drive again."

"What about you. Arbuckle?" Baggett wheezed

THE LONG WAY NORTH

in that asthmatic voice of his. "What are you going
to do after this trip?"

"I don't know. I haven't any plans."

Wood looked out to the herd. Maybe it would be
the sea and a thousand places before he found what
he wanted.

"Floyd looks happy," Skinner said.

"Yeah, he'll be staying with cows as long as
there are any left to walk north!" Baggett agreed.
"Just like me."

Rogers's eyes darted uneasily from face to face
and then back to the plate he held.

Wood looked at the man who hid behind a wall
of silence and gave nothing. He felt uneasiness
strengthen again.

Maybe I'm asking too much, he thought. The
most important thing is to find something to do.
Something I can believe in. But there's the people
around me, too . . . a man's smile has to go beyond
his mouth, his grip beyond the strength of his
hand.

Sometimes it seemed like there was nothing like
that in Boston . . . as if there were no sincere people
there, no honesty or professions of value for a man
to follow. This was not true. But face it, he told
himself, it was true for him or anyone who was
caught up in that tight little society and suddenly
found himself wanting out. That was the difference. Wanting out, and knowing that the well-
known son of a well-known judge could never be
left alone in his own town, no matter what he tried
to do or be. There were a lot of good people there,
but it did not take many bad ones to spoil the
whole thing.

Wood took a deep breath, thinking about Rogers and Cimarron, and was unable to eat anymore. It was no better here.

There was no stopping for the rest of the day. The herd was pushed as unmercifully as ever until well after dark, when the air cooled and made a dry camp less miserable.

Adam Childress had been right. Wood had seen the dry beds of creeks where they would normally have found water. They were nothing but traces of cracked and dry mud, or sand and rock bleaching like bones under the sun, or if there was water at all, small, stinking pools of green that were not fit for drinking.

Wood turned in early that night. He had the graveyard and needed to get all the sleep he could. But it would not come. He kept thinking of the cattle out there on the bed ground, restless with thirst. And it was as if they radiated a heart that crept through the ground. He felt stifled, devoid of any moisture in his body. There was only temporary relief in the water barrel.

"You just ain't used to it yet," Adam said, coming over.

"I feel like we came a hundred miles." Wood sat up.

"I reckon we made twenty. We'll hit the Llano early in the afternoon. Try and sleep. You've only got a couple hours."

Not used to it yet, Wood thought. Would he ever be?

They were rolling before sunup. Slowly at first, grazing while the dew was still on the grass, and then as the first sun touched them, hard and fast again. The Herefords were harder to manage than before, and while the longhorns seemed to be taking the pace with no more than the usual effort, their tongues were beginning to hang from their mouths, and they bawled ceaselessly.

At times throughout the morning, Wood spotted Adam way up ahead looking for the Llano. And he kept looking for it himself when he was not chasing shorthorns back into the bunch.

The dust was intolerable. He wore his bandana, or wipe, as the others called it, over his nose, but after a while it was of little value. The heat seemed worse than the day before.

He spent long periods of time thinking about the Llano and what it would look like, and what it would feel like to run and go sprawling in it, wallowing in its delicious, wet coolness. He thought of it as a great, wide, rolling river that he could hardly see across. And then he thought of it as a slow moving, deep stream with shade trees and cool grasses and flowers lining its banks.

But then the visions faded and fell to despair. A glance at the horizon ahead showed nothing green and soft. Nothing but the same harsh, flinty ground, an intolerable repetition of what was in back of them.

He felt sick and disheartened. What kind of a place was this, and what kind of a life? Maybe these men were like savages, as he once had thought, to endure only what savages could endure. Existing in a land forgotten by anything that could ever be described as gentle. If they were not like savages, then they were like those trees now appearing ahead. Dry and brittle-looking, stunted with deep roots looking for water that wasn't there.

Those trees . . .

Suddenly they meant something and the cattle were quickening their pace, and Adam was back from his scout ahead.

"Let 'em go, boys! No point in trying to stop them! Just let 'em go!"

The cattle broke into a run and the trail crew just went along for the ride.

Ahead, the sight of it shimmering in heat ghosts, the Llano. Adam grinned at him, and Wood cracked a smile back.

VIII

Oh ... I sashayed into town to have a little fun,
But the sheriff come around and he pulled his gun.
                                    —THE OLD CHISHOLM TRAIL

THEY HAD REMAINED at the Llano when they reached it, and for the whole of the next day as well to let the cattle recover from the hurried and dry thirty miles. There was no hurry now. On the second day of May, they reached the San Saba. Noon of the next day found them at Brady Creek, and not too many miles ahead lay the big Colorado. Water, once again, was no problem.

Sometimes it was simple like that, even when there was no rain. But they still worried about the lack of it, thinking of the long time still ahead. It made a man want to abandon the slow pace and hurry across the land and the dry days before matters became worse. But there was no hurrying, and all that was left was to watch the sky with the hope that is the same as praying.

However, spirits began to rise at Brady Creek. Once the creek was crossed, the town of Brady was not far away.

The camp was full of talk of it that evening.

Floyd Rogers listened to it. So and so was going to drink the town dry. Another was going to ruin six women . . . that is, if dance-hall women weren't already ruined. Another, even though he could spend only three or four hours there, was going to rent a hotel room and sleep in a bed, like he had done at San Antonio.

Floyd stopped listening and stared between his knees at the ground. How long had it been? A drink, a woman, and the simple act of being somewhere and standing still in it for just a little while. How long? Too long. Nearly a year now.

"Well, Floyd won't be going. Why not ask him?"

He snapped out of his reverie at the mention of his name.

"Maybe so," Skinner said and then turned to him. "How about it, Floyd? Do my graveyard for me tonight, and I'll do the next two you pull. That's good trade ain't it?"

Floyd turned away. A good trade . . . it depended on how you looked at it. When he came to saying something about it, he realized he had waited too long. Skinner was turning away.

"Well, it was worth a try," Baggett wheezed. "Too bad, Bob."

Something gave ground in Rogers. He whirled on Baggett.

"Who said I ain't going to town? Nobody stopped to ask!"

"All right, all right."

"Sure, I'm going into Brady! Why shouldn't I?"

"It ain't none of my business," Baggett shrugged.

"You bet it ain't!"

Floyd got his warbag out of the wagon and changed into a clean shirt and another pair of pants. For a moment, he thought of the consequences. But now that he had moved in that direction, there was no stopping it. Maybe it would be all right. A year was a long time for a face to be remembered. Sure, it was all right.

He saddled a horse and got ready to go, and saw Marsh leaning up against the wagon, drinking coffee.

"Hey Rev. Come with me, boy."

The big Negro shook his head.

"I don't want to go, Floyd."

"Don't be a dumb nigger. Get your horse."

Rev shook his head, and then stopped pretending.

"You know how it is with me, Floyd."

"So what! Come on. We can see the sights, get a couple of drinks, maybe even some women. How about that, Marsh?"

"You mean drinkin' out in back instead of inside with folks. That's the way it'd be. And it'd be tough findin' the right kind of gal for me."

"All right, I probably couldn't find one either. You know this face of mine. But a drink is a drink."

"Well . . ."

"If you don't go, I reckon I won't either."

Marsh grinned and took a playful slap at him. "I'll go."

Most of the others had already gone by the time Floyd and Rev rode away from camp. Neither of them said much on the short ride into town. They were too full of the need to go, too full of the hunger to give vent to excitement.

They rode silently down the street of Brady, looking at the lights and listening to the sounds. A

piano being thumped, boots on the wooden side-
walks, the slamming of a door ... how important
this door seemed to be, to have it open and close
and make its comforting sound ... a woman's
laughter coming hard and shrill, and yet infinitely
soft, through an open window.

They stopped in front of a saloon called Heaven
and tied the horses to the rail.

"What outfit you boys from? Mexican Spur?"

Rogers turned and saw the man leaning on the
post.

"Why?"

"Just wondering. Saw a few come in a little while
ago."

"You got us wrong, mister. Ours is the Boot
Heel."

"Never heard of that brand."

"Lots of brands in Texas."

They walked away and up to the doors of the
Heaven.

"What for you tell him that, Floyd?"

He had never told Rev about Abilene. He shook
his head.

"Just pulling the old man's leg. Let's get a
drink."

"I'll wait out here. You go ahead."

"Now listen ... all right, Rev. I'll go buy us a
bottle."

He stepped through the swinging doors which
were done up fancily in mother-of-pearl.

It was smoky inside. The air was heavy with it.
There was also the smell of cheap whisky, and a
trace of perfume from the girls, and the sounds of
glasses, and the soft slap of cards almost drowned
out by the man at the piano.

He drank it all in. He stared at one of the girls and the halfhearted way her clothes covered her body. She started to come over, but the automatic smile on her face faded and she changed her mind.

The face, Floyd remembered. Always this face. Angrily, he turned to the bar and decided to drink one there.

He tossed it down quick and felt the hard, hot jolt of it. He watched the girl, hating her, but wanting her too.

"Don't I know you?"

Floyd turned back to the bartender. There were two at the Heaven and this was not the man who had waited on him. He felt his pulse go heavy.

"No. I never been in Brady before."

"I mean from somewhere else, mister."

"I don't know you."

"I come from Abilene, Texas," the bartender said, searching.

"That so?"

"Yeah. Used to tend bar up there."

"All right, how about tending a little bar here and selling me a bottle of what I been drinking."

Floyd flipped the money down on the bar top.

"You ever been in Abilene?"

"How about the bottle?"

"Sure. Sure. No need to get sore."

Floyd took the bottle and headed for the door.

"Come on, Rev, let's go around in back where it's quiet."

"Sure, tha's a better place anyway."

"That's right, Rev. Those places stink," he said.

They went down a dark side street, found a water trough and sat down on the edge of it. Floyd opened the bottle. He nodded down at the water with green scum growing at the edges.

"If we get tired drinking it straight, we got water."

He took a couple of long pulls and handed it to Marsh.

"It'd blind a horse, but it's all right with me."

Marsh nodded and took another drink.

"There he is! Up by the trough!"

Floyd looked down toward the street and saw the bartender with his white apron and another man with him.

"I knew I seen him somewhere, Sheriff. Can't forget forget a face like that!"

Floyd jumped to his feet and ran farther into the darkness. He heard Rev's startled cry, and the drumming of boots on the ground in back of him. He ducked down behind a stack of barrels at the edge of an alley and pulled his pistol out.

The figures rushed by, plunging into the darkness beyond him heedlessly. Quickly, he stood up and ran back out to the street. Floyd jumped on his horse and wheeled away from the rail.

"There he goes!"

He ducked down low as the cry went up and flinched as the shots rang out, spurting flame behind him.

Floyd didn't sleep that night. He did nothing but sit and stare at the coals. It was the same old story. His face! Like the brand on those cows out there. He had shaken them easily, riding in long circles, keeping to low ground and brush and coming around behind them before striking out for the camp. There was nothing but peace beyond the fire now. But . . . his face! It would be that way in any town he went to. The thing at Abilene hadn't been forgotten. Of course it hadn't. He should've known better!

Skinner and Sweet drifted in around one. They said nothing, but saddled up their night horses and rode out to take the graveyard. The rest didn't begin to come in until just before dawn, when Red Bellah woke up and began to fix breakfast.

Marsh had a hurt expression in his face. Baggett and Preble watched him with narrowed eyes, and Wood, coming from where he had slept and still buttoning his pants seemed to sense something was wrong. He hung back as if there were a sidewinder loose.

"Tell him, Rev," Baggett ordered.

"Nothin' to tell, Charlie," Rev muttered in embarrassed tones.

"All right, if you won't then I will! Rogers, when you skittered out of town, they grabbed Marsh and held him most of the night, asking questions. They even roughed him up."

"I jus' kept tellin' them some stranger had a bottle and give me a drink," Rev lowered his eyes and went on reluctantly. "No nigger could get a drink any other way . . . that's what I said, but they don' believe me."

"There was some old timer there," Baggett continued, "who said something about the Boot Heel brand. You said that was your outfit. I reckon that's what clinched it, when we came in and said we was from the Mexican Spur and Marsh was one of our boys. They let him go then, with us to back him up."

Rogers turned away and fixed his eyes on the fire.

"Well?" Baggett pursued. "Ain't you got something to say?"

"Sure. I'm sorry."

"Being sorry ain't enough!"

"Floyd?" Rev's voice begged. "It ain't true is it? I knew you done somethin', but it ain't true about the man in Abilene, is it? You didn't go kill no man?"

Floyd stood up and faced them.

"No man in the Mexican Spur's going to get roughed up on account of another without a little explaining," Baggett told him.

Floyd took a deep brreath. He'd have to leave now, and he didn't want to leave. But it was no good like this.

"All right," he said quietly. "I did kill a man in Abilene. I got drunk. Crazy drunk ... and I wanted a woman. Hadn't been in town for months ...

Floyd sat down and suddenly felt like crying.

"You look at the face I got and tell me what woman'd have me. Nothing but fat *pelados* and gals who are as ugly as I am! Well ... when I'm sober I know better, but that night in Abilene I was making a try for one of the gals in a saloon. She kept pushing me away. The more she pushed, the more I tried to change her mind. The sheriff stepped in, after several men tried to pull me off. I didn't know it was the sheriff. I just went blind and pulled my pistol and shot the closest man. I've been on the *cuidado* ever since. Well, that's what you wanted ain't it? Are you satisfied?"

"I am," Baggett said.

"Then I reckon I'd better pull out of here."

Adam Childress stepped up to the fire.

"That'd leave us shorthanded, Floyd."

"We weren't asking him to leave," Baggett told the boss. "The air needed clearing, that's all. I figure when a man gets roughed up, he ought to know why."

Floyd looked at Adam and let his breath out.

Red yelled them to breakfast then and the subject was dropped. Floyd looked around him gratefully. It was good to have the secret gone, and find that he was still welcome here.

He went over to Rev to talk to him but found himself trembling and close to crying again. He snorted and tried to laugh.

"Look at me, acting like a kid! Well, it's all done with and it's all right."

Rev didn't look at him, but slowly turned away.

IX

Oh ... it's cloudy in the west, and it looks like rain,
And the damned old slicker is in the wagon again.

THE OLD CHISHOLM TRAIL

CHARLES WOOD WOKE up on the morning of May 5
to find Adam Childress dancing a little jig around
the fire and roaring with glee. He acted like a
drunk man, at first glance, but then there was the
realization that he was not. Wood looked around
at the others who were coming up out of their
soogans to watch. They grinned and seemed to
know what it was all about.

Wood dressed, and by that time, Adam had quieted down enough to stand quietly smiling with a
cup of coffee in his hand.

"How do you like it, boy?" Adam asked him.

"What? What's happening?"

"Why look around and see. Smell it?"

Wood looked around the camp, sniffing. He
saw nothing and smelled nothing that was not
there every morning. The cool morning air, the
smell of Red's fire and breakfast cooking.

"I don't notice anything."

Adam laughed like a man with a new plaything.

"Well, I can see you got to have another month
or two on the trail. Look up, boy, and take a deep
breath."

Wood looked toward the sky and saw nothing, and he took a deep breath. There was still nothing, but suddenly he looked up again. There were no stars, and no sign of dawn, and yet he had been awakened at the usual time. It was black as pitch up there, and there did seem to be a dampness to the wind. He turned quickly to Adam, understanding the other's pleasure.

"It's going to rain!"

"Now you got it!"

The lightheartedness was a source of new strength, and it stayed with everyone all through breakfast and through the time of grazing the herd onto the trail.

When light came, it was a gray light, and the wind strengthened and blew hard and damp across their faces.

Wood watched the clouds roll dark across the sky. He saw the others, the expressions on their faces which almost trembled. Their cheeks and chins were dark and stubbled, and there were traces of smoke and yesterday's dust, and their clothes were stiff and dirty. But they came as close to presenting a picture of absolute joy as Wood had ever seen. For the first time, he fully understood the meaning of rain to them.

Before it was time to make the noon stop, a tire came loose on one of the wheels, and Red, instead of cursing mightily as would have been usual, treated it as if it were only a joke. In good nature, he tied the tire in place with green rawhide that would shrink and hold like iron. And then, smiling in the damp wind, decided he might as well start cooking.

* * *

That afternoon, when they started again, anticipation was like drunkenness.

Perhaps the drought would end this day. The rain would come and kill the dust. Perhaps more would follow, in the days to come, to soak down to the roots of grass and bring new life. The country would turn green and the rivers would rise and the small creeks and washes would run with music.

Grazing would be better. The cattle would fatten, and if kept that way, bring a better price on the Musselshell. Water would be less of a problem along the trail.

Wood remembered home and Boston, where rain meant nothing more than a nuisance, a reason to carry an umbrella, or to stay inside.

He looked at himself and wondered why it really mattered. He was not in the cattle business, or staying with the herd any longer than the time it took to deliver the herd in Montana. His life led somewhere else. Where, he did not know. He was not the same kind of man these others were.

But still, here he was, just as excited as they were about the prospect of a simple thing like rain. It was a brief and strange feeling of kinship.

Perhaps it was only natural. Any man would find a new appreciation for rain after the dry days of that country, after eating dust for mile after mile.

"Here she comes," a yell came back to him in the wind.

It came in hard, stinging gusts for several minutes, and with it the land changed. The air was softer and sweetly scented with the dying dust, and the thirsty country softened to the eye.

Ben Sweet took off his hat and turned his face to

it. Adam laughed and cried up ahead like the sinner who had found salvation. Rev pulled his shirt off and his black body twisted into the rain, seeking it as a cold man seeks the sun. Only Giles and Preble bothered with their slickers. Wood untied his, but the fish-oil smell of it suddenly seemed wrong. He smiled and put it back.

The rain settled down to a light drizzle which lasted an hour or so. And then, it quit.

The wind picked up a little more, and patches of blue appeared between scudding clouds and it didn't rain anymore after that. Before too long the sky was clear and the sun shone down again. It was too late in the day for the sun to get hot, and it was a peaceful time, cool, refreshed, and the singing of the meadowlarks was like that of better times.

There was little time to think about it or wonder if there would be more just beyond the horizon. Wood saw Adam ride back with a short word for each man, which was yelled across to the other side. He came back to Wood and Wood could tell by his face that he had come to advise on something new in a young juniper's experience. Adam was careful about that.

"We've reached the Colorado, and she's high. Melting snow or a cloudburst up in the mountains. Longhorns don't like crossing high water, so we've got to run them in. Keep the tail cattle up close to the rest so no water shows between or they might turn and cause trouble. And watch yourself. It's bad when critters get spooked up and start milling in the water."

Wood nodded and watched Adam return to the front.

A few minutes later, he saw Ben Sweet start slap-

ping the air with his hat and a yell went up. The
longhorns broke into a run under the urging of
each man.

Wood heard a yell from Giles and knew right
away what he was yelling about. The Herefords
were falling back.

But the longhorns were not running at full tilt,
and between them, yelling, and crowding the
animals with their horses, Wood and Giles managed to close the gap.

The yelling up front took on new strength,
punctuated with short sharp whistles, and Wood
saw the river then and the lead cattle balking and
trying to edge away from it. Trouble nearly came,
but before it could start, the great *ladino* stepped
out and plunged into the river and the rest followed. He saw the tossing of their heads and the
wild fright in their eyes, and Sweet and Baggett
angling them upstream. Quickly, the others were
made to follow. Wood caught a quick look before
his own turn came, of the herd stretching across the
river like disembodied heads, a sea fraught with
horns.

He kept the Herefords running hard and saw
them slam into the water. He felt the gait of his
horse turn short and jerky, and the cold water fill
his boots and crawl up his legs, and then the sudden buoyant feeling as his horse began to swim.

It happened cleanly and without trouble, and in
a few minutes they were on the other side, driving
the herd onto their bed ground.

For a time the rain had been forgotten, but as
they settled down for the night, the thoughts slowly
came back.

Wood knew it hadn't been enough. He would

have known it even if he hadn't seen the faces of the others.

Adam Childress sat by the fire, running the heel of his boot along the ground to make a furrow of barely dampened soil, like a man with a broken heart.

X

There's a yellow rose in Texas that I am going to see.
No other darky knows her. No darky, only me.
She cried so when I left her it like to broke my heart,
And if I ever find her we never more will part.

THE YELLOW ROSE OF TEXAS

THE BEND OF a river, a wagon tongue pointing at the North Star, a lone but eternal tree, a certain mountain, the passing of time, and remembrance from years past ... these had been the things that gave them the direction. It was a free-moving course, for one still had to follow grass and water. But this was changing.

There were fences patchworking across Texas now, and while they were regrettable, the country was big and there was a lot of cattle to move, and generally a man could depend on another to help keep the way clear. Fences were a shame in what they did to the land, but up to a certain point north, it wasn't often that a man had to depart far from his trail to go around one.

At the Colorado River, it had changed. Here, prejudice and law took over. Here, the National Cattle Trail began.

The wagon tongue was no longer needed, and landmarks were out of date. A river only marked time. The Mexican Spur had reached the Colorado, and then the Clear Fork of the Brazos, and while there was no longer any meaning of direction, there was a feeling for most of the men that that much had at least been done. For Revelation Marsh, it had come to mean nothing.

A day was a day, a mile a mile, and the next, only repetition. Time was a numbness lost in the dust boiling up from the feet of those northering cattle.

Think only of the cattle. Think only of the work. Lose yourself in this, because in this there is no hurt. It was better that way. Many things are lost in the high cry of a day.

But in the here and now, with the Dipper swinging around, there was no way to stop thinking about other things. Abilene . . . Abilene was yonder, to the west a few miles. Abilene was where most of the Mexican Spur men were now. Those who had no reason to stay behind. Floyd Rogers slept in camp, not far from the fire. And his reasons were clear.

This thing with Floyd Rogers. How had it begun? And for himself, how had he begun?

A place in eastern Texas. Those years were faded and dim now. There had been a big house, with a lot of little shacks out in back, and great fields of growing cotton where his father and mother worked . . . his mother naming him Revelation because it was from the Bible, and it was a pretty word . . . and there was a grandmother he could remember only vaguely. He had been very young and she had been very old and strange, and he had always been afraid of her . . . the blacker than black skin, the fires behind her eyes casting shadows from another and wilder place, the stories she

told of this place, and the strange things she believed . . . it had turned to shame and embarrassment in him before she died, and later he found it
again in the others who lived and worked there . . .
this strangeness, this old earth thing coming just
beneath the surface when the sun set and work was
done and the fires were lighted. It came in the singing and dancing and the passions there in the fire-
light, boiling close to a single ingredient that the
brain could not remember but somehow felt . . .

He remembered the owner and his clean, shining
buggy, and it was the only thing that seemed desirable in the world. A wagon, a horse . . . it took
a man out of the mud to where the sunlight seemed
cleaner somehow.

He remembered that buggy and the owner's
horses, and they still held the same importance
when he was no longer a child and worked for a
time in the fields himself. But the war had come
along and with it things changed. The owner came
out to them one day and said they didn't have to
stay any longer. They were free to go.

Some did and some didn't. His father and mother stayed. The man they worked for was kind to his
people.

And he had stayed too, until the man died and
they had to go. He remembered the funeral and
wondering as they lowered the casket into the
ground whether his father and mother cried because they were sorry for the man who was gone,
or because it meant hard times.

There had been Lorena. Lorena was a fine girl,
and he had wanted to marry her. He had wanted to
take her West, because he had grown tired of cotton and trying to scratch out a life in the soil. There

had to be better things, but she would not come. It was home and she wouldn't leave.

And so he had reluctantly left to wander, working here and there. The mean little jobs because of his color ... cleaning out stables, sweeping of a morning in stores and saloons, splitting wood for fence posts ... never anymore than that. Never anything better. Home had been home, and Lorena would not leave, and maybe she had been right ... but then wandering by the Mexican Spur, and suddenly working for Adam Childress. Real man's work, and the strange delight of it ... learning how to use rope and branding iron, wearing the proud boots, and most of all, riding high on a horse's back ... yes, the sunlight was cleaner up there.

There, he had been happy. There, it hadn't seemed to matter that he was ... Marsh shook his head ... that he was a nigger, he had started to tell himself. Of course, it had made a difference. They'd try to tell you it didn't. The boys would joke with him and slap him on the back, and sit down with him around the fire to eat, and where they threw their bedrolls, he could throw his.

But there was a fence. No matter how hard he tried not to see it, a fence was there.

On Saturday nights, when some of the boys decided to go into Brownsville, they never asked him to go along. They knew he couldn't go to the same places or do the same things. They were right. He could not. If he went, he went alone and to his own kind, and it wasn't enough to drink homemade whisky on the sly or to sprawl with a nigger gal in the crawling filth of a shack or in the rutted shadows of an alley. He went only when he had to go. And that was the heart of it. The others *knew* this.

They *remembered*. And they constantly reminded
him of this knowledge by never asking him to go
with them, and by softening the hurt by bringing
back little gifts from town. Whisky, candy . . . it
made him feel like an ugly and pitied child who
could not stand up and exist without help. They
liked him and he liked them, but it was not enough.

But then Floyd Rogers came along during last
fall's roundup. Quiet, ugly . . . it seemed like an evil
accident, one of nature's cruelties that a man
should be so ugly.

Maybe it was his ugliness, which like black skin,
pushed him away from other men. Maybe this was
why he and Floyd seemed to hit it off so naturally.

Rogers had never looked at him as a nigger.
Sometimes it seemed like Rogers was never aware
of the fact. Like in the town of Brady. When he was
reminded of it in camp, before going, it seemed like
Floyd promptly forgot. Rogers had acted surprised
at the notion that he, Rev, couldn't go into that
saloon and drink like anyone else . . . sure, like
he'd never thought of it before.

Rev rode around slowly, letting his horse grab a
little grass now and then. He felt sick and empty.

It was the bad treatment he got from the law in
Brady, having to lie about not knowing Floyd. But
worst of all, it was having to say those things to a
stranger about being just a nigger . . . nigger ain't
good enough to drink inside with white folks . . .
only way a nigger could get a drink . . . saying these
things to a man who kept yelling "tell the truth you
black bastard!"

He was as good as any man, black or white. He
knew that deep down, and it hurt to say otherwise,
no matter the reason.

And it was no good, not being told about Abilene.

And then Floyd acting like nothing had happened after he had stayed in town, covering Floyd's tracks, lying for him, getting roughed up and dragged low for him.

What was the use?

He thought of giving the whole thing up . . . this place out here . . . go back to Lorena and the other life . . . your skin is black, so remember it and act like a nigger . . . so why not go back?

Rev rode, not watching the time told by the Dipper, not seeing the approach of day and the men who wearily drifted into camp.

They were through with breakfast, and getting ready to throw the cattle onto the trail, when a man came riding up from the direction of Abilene. Rev noticed that the man looked around considerably as he came in, examining the face of each man.

"I'd like to talk to the trail boss," he said.

"Adam Childress is the name. What's on your mind?"

"I'm C. J. Peters, U. S. Marshal. I'm looking for a Floyd Rogers. He's wanted on a charge of murder."

"I see," Adam said quietly.

"We got word from Brady that he showed up there. There was no way of knowing whether he was just drifting, of if he was coming through with some trail outfit. I'm checking all the outfits coming through, Mister Childress. Especially yours, since he was seen drinking with a Mexican Spur man."

Rev watched the men in camp. Adam, and all of

them. Nobody made a move to give Peters any information. He looked around again, by the wagon, and saw Floyd's bedroll still lying on the ground, hunched up a little like Floyd had wanted someone to think someone was sleeping there, or like he had merely neglected to put it in the wagon. But in either case, Floyd was gone. It was funny that no one had noticed. But he was gone.

"I'll have to ask it, Childress. Is Rogers one of your boys?"

Before Adam could speak, Rev stepped up.

"Yes, sir. He was."

"Let me handle this, Rev," Adam told him sharply.

"No, let him talk," the Marshal said. "Was or is?"

Rev looked around him and saw the surprise in the others.

"It kinda looks like he took off in the night. He ain't here now."

"Mister Childress, you know it's against the law to protect a wanted man, or to keep information about him to yourself."

"Yes," Adam nodded. "I reckon I do. But for that matter, we didn't know the whole story until after we left Brady. It's hard to find a good hand these days. To be frank, I don't much care what a man's done as long as he does his job with me."

Peters smiled a little.

"I understand."

He looked slowly and carefully around the horizon.

"I don't suppose you know how long ago he slipped away, or what direction he took?"

"No," Adam shook his head. "I don't."

"You?" Peters turned to Rev.

"No," he said. "No, sir. I reckon it was while I was on graveyard, but I didn't see anythin'."

Marshal Peters squatted down on his heels and poked in the sand with a stick. Adam bent down beside him.

"I'll go along with the law and what it stands for most of the time. But I can't say I'm glad you caught up with us. I'd be a liar if I did. It's too bad about Floyd. Believe it or not, he's a good man. Ugly feller. Glum. Didn't seem to collect friends. But he worked hard and minded his own business. I reckon sometimes a man's face can make it pretty hard."

"I know," Peters said, climbing into his saddle again. "It doesn't seem fair, sometimes, the way things work out. But there's no other choice. There never is."

"I reckon not."

Peters gave him a wave and rode away.

Rev turned away from the exchange just ended and set about saddling a fresh horse.

He looked around at the distant hills and had a feeling they had not seen the last of Floyd Rogers. He was out there somewhere.

XI

The road to those bright, happy regions
Is a dim, narrow trail, so they say;
But the broad one that leads to perdition
Is posted and blazed all the way.
— The Cowboy's Dream

THEY ROLLED FROM the Clear Fork of the Brazos,
heading north from Abilene. Then, slowly, the
town of Albany, and Fort Griffin and Camp Coop-
er. Elm Creek, Boggy Creek, the Salt Fork of the
Brazos. Ever slowly.

It seemed little different. A week could do that.
Floyd Rogers was gone, and he had never been
close to any of them, except Rev, and it was natural
to have to stop and think before deciding he had
only been gone a week.

But Adam wondered as they moved north. What
was Floyd doing? Moving west or east or south,
trying to find peace and a place where he was not
known or remembered? Or maybe just beyond that
line of low hills, watching, following, trying to hold
out one more day like a hungry coyote looking for
straggling dogies . . .

The wondering was there that evening when they
crossed the North Fork of the Lower Wichita, and
after they crossed the main Wichita itself the next

evening, Adam rode out to the top of a hill and
looked around.

Nothing moved out there. He swung around to
the east and west and saw only ghosts of the
dark . . . the pattern of brush and stunted tree and
low hills stretching away for uncounted miles. To
the north he saw a light. It looked like a small fire
flickering feebly against the darkness. But then he
wasn't sure. It could have been a star, hanging on
the horizon, flashing white and red in the distance.

On the twenty-second of May, Adam did not
wait for the herd to begin its daily march. As soon
as he had eaten, he rode north.

Ahead, not far away, rolled the big Red. Along
its course, they would cross the Pease and reach
Doan's Store. And from Doan's they would move
up the divide between the Salt and North Fork of
the Red. And once the North Fork was crossed,
they would edge along the eastern border of the
Panhandle with Indian Territory in sight all the
way.

Cheyenne and Arapaho land . . . he could remember the day, like the day of the buffalo, when
a man going north had to think about them too.
When they came wildly, their cries cutting the air,
it was a hard thing to try and save your skin and a
herd of longhorns too. But time had changed that.
Later they had come to the passing herds, asking
for *wohaw,* merely poor people like crippled
hunters coming to ask for beeves. A ghost of the
old wildness came sometimes, when they weren't
satisfied. They might try to stampede and steal
some cattle. But still, the old days were gone.

When they reached nearly to the northern edge

of the Panhandle, they would swing west for several days and then north again, across Public Lands into the narrow corridor of eastern Colorado's federal lands. No more fighting quarantine lines and inspectors, and no more fighting nesters and their fences on that narrow passage. But grass would be poorer, and water would be taken in the way it cut the trail, instead of aiming a herd for its nearest point like it used to be. Yes, take it as it crossed the trail and nowhere else, if it hadn't dried up . . .

There were a lot of things to worry about. These were the things spoken of quietly around the fires. There wasn't much use in it, but a man found it hard to turn loose of habit, the things to which he was accustomed, no matter how many changes were made.

For now, find the Red and see how far it was. That was a part of habit too. They had to keep to the trail. But he did want to get out and see the land in front of them, to see how bad or good it was going to be. He would not have been comfortable doing otherwise.

At midmorning, Adam stopped and looked at the ground. He dismounted and stood toeing the dead ashes of a fire with his boot. It was fresh, and he remembered what had looked like a star on the horizon two nights before. This would not be the same fire, if it had been a fire he had seen. But he was almost sure that if he rode south the distance a man could ride in a day, he'd find the ashes of another gently blowing in the wind. And another day south, perhaps another.

He climbed back into the saddle, thinking about Floyd.

The loneliest man in the world.

*   *   *

The Mexican Spur turned to the northwest when it came to the Red River. They watered the cattle and then moved on without crossing. That worry would come later. The Red was high, with the color that had given it its name. The sediment of the water had marked the timber along its coursing, and driftwood lodged in the trees along its banks gave sign of what it was like when it was really angry.

XII

The boss said, "Dammit, I ain't fired you—
Come and trail this herd with the rest of the crew."
                    —THE OLD CHISHOLM TRAIL

THE BUSINESS Judge C. F. Doan started with his
nephew Corwin, there on the bank of the Red, had
grown into a dozen shacks that held just about
anything a man needed to buy. It was situated in
Willbarger County, at an easy ford where the herds
were best crossed, just a few miles north of the
towns of Vernon and Julia. Across the river was
Indian Territory.

Cattle no longer crossed there, if a drover or trail
boss held to the trail, but old man Doan's estab-
lishment didn't suffer, since the new National
passed close.

Floyd Rogers watched and waited there, not
moving around and showing himself much, until
Red Bellah and Adam pulled up in the wagon.
Then, quietly, he eased into the same shack they
entered, and sat on a barrel in the far corner. They
hadn't seen him yet. The clerk was going over the
list of supplies Red had handed him.

" . . . Flour, sugar, rice, beans, coffee, syrup,
soda, baking powder, salt, pepper . . . onions . . .
pickles . . . bacon . . . we're short on syrup. I ain't

sure I can get you any syrup."

"Why we got to have lick! These boys I cook for got a powerful sweet tooth, and if you think fixing bear-sign for 'em ever' day is going to cure it, you're crazy!"

"I'll do what I can, mister. Now, how about air-tights?"

Floyd saw Adam turn as if he somehow had sensed there was someone watching. But there was no surprise in his face when he discovered who it was. Adam came over slowly.

"Had an idea we'd be seeing you soon. I saw the ashes of your fire a little way back."

"Sorry I had to leave you shorthanded, boss. But you saw how it was. I'm kinda hoping you'll let me come back."

"Sure, you can come back if you want."

Floyd relaxed and stood up.

"Thanks for covering for me."

"We didn't cover for you. We didn't know where you were, and we told the marshal that. You know I can't protect you, Floyd. I ain't going to turn you over to the law, but at the same time, I can't do nothing for you if the law comes looking."

"I reckon that's fair enough."

"I don't understand why you came back, Floyd. It's a big country."

Floyd went up the counter and began helping with the supplies.

"Maybe I'm just partial to Red's cooking."

It wasn't an attempt at levity. It was the kind of reply a man makes when he doesn't know what else to say or doesn't want to talk about what is really on his mind.

Maybe you've forgotten about my face, he

thought, and what it does to me. You've forgotten.
That's why I want to stay.

Adam didn't seem inclined to push the question
any farther.

"I reckon we can start loading up the wagon.
Cimarron will give us a hand outside."

Floyd watched Adam gratefully. Adam was a
fair man. He took a deep breath. It wasn't easy to
stay away from towns, and limit yourself to the
boundaries of a cow camp. A man could think of
better things. But there was an element of peace on
the trail, and a sense of belonging. He did not fight
society out there. He struggled only against the
forces of the elements, and whether they were
cataclysmic or only a gentle stirring of the afternoon dust, they were at least something to be accepted and understood.

The rest of the boys seemed to think the same
way as Adam. They hadn't asked questions until
that incident in Brady, and they had a right to then.
And when the questions were answered, that was
the end of it. Only that easterner, Wood, and
strangely, Rev Marsh seemed to feel differently
about it.

He and Marsh had been close friends. Too close
for the sudden break not to hurt. How Wood felt
didn't matter, but he hoped Marsh would have forgotten his anger by now.

These were the only worries he had. Marsh, and
the chance that he had not seen the last of the
marshal.

The Mexican Spur had not meant as much
before the marshal came looking for him. It was a

place of peace, a place to be, and he never lost sight
of the fact. But he had hungered for a real home
and a real family of his own. It would be nice to
pick out a piece of land and do something that left
a mark for a little while after he was gone. Maybe
being somewhere where his face didn't matter had
eased the pain and let hope come creeping back.

It wasn't until the time in Brady, and afterwards
outside of Abilene when that sudden warning
came, that crawling intuition pricked at his sleep
and sent him riding off into the predawn darkness,
that he began to realize how wrong he had been.
His face had come back over the space of a year, in
the mind of another man, to try and hurt and take
what little he had.

There had been several days to think about it.
Several days of hiding, living like an animal. Afraid
of the sun, and a fugitive from the stars themselves.
A trail drive was still the best thing for him. Only
his mistake at Brady had changed that, and time
and distance and waiting it out would erase that
mistake. A trail drive. It moved and never rested
for long, and in that was the lesson that killed the
little hope that had seemed to grow. If one little
mistake could ruin his place of peace with northering cattle, how would it be with the home and
family . . . that did not move at all? It couldn't be
his.

During those days, he had crawled to a high
place and looked down on the sleeping herd and
the friendly fire. At times, he had heard the gentleness of song drifting up from the night herd, and
the voice of Red Bellah resounding in the dawn
stillness like a rough-hewn benediction.

It was the only place, for as long as it would last.

When they came to the Salt Fork of the Red River, and found a place to ford, Adam took to his horse. He and Floyd tied their ropes to the wagon to hold it steady against the current and slowly eased it across. On the other side, Adam remained in the saddle, and Cimarron crawled up from the inside of the wagon to take his place on the seat by Red.

They intercepted the herd five or six miles above the point where they had been held for the night, just beyond the river now, and Red fell into his usual spot. Adam rode up the lead, and Floyd relieved Wood at right flank.

At noon, when the fire was built and the herd grazed to a standstill, the crew alternated to come and eat.

Floyd saw Rev getting his plate filled and walking off to one side with it. Floyd grabbed his and followed. Rev was pretending not to see him.

"How you been, boy?" he asked.

Rev didn't look up.

"I reckon we got a lot of talking to do."

Rev said nothing, but ate silently, staring off at nothing.

Floyd smiled nervously, unsure of how to handle it. Sometimes it was hard for a person to start talking again after he was angry about something.

"Aw, don't be a dumb nigger! You and I been friends!"

Marsh looked up like he had been struck in the face.

"Who you callin' a nigger!"

"Now you know I didn't mean it that way!"

Marsh's eyes blazed hot and he got to his feet.

"Don't be callin' me nigger! I don't like it! I'm as good as any man here!"

"Hell, I know that, boy."

"I'm better'n you! I ain't no murderer!"

"I know you ain't."

Floyd watched something churning around inside the big Negro. It was almost out of control.

"You're nothin' but an ugly murderer!"

Floyd went cold inside and stood up.

"Enough's enough, Rev."

"Maybe the boys here ain't goin' to turn you in if they gets the chance! But I will! I'll watch you jerkin' on the rope, and I'll stand there laughin' until you ain't movin' no more!"

Floyd felt anger coming fast, like it always did. He wanted to forget it and turn away and let things cool off. He and Rev had been friends. But Rev wouldn't let him. Rev was hurting and he wanted to hurt back.

"I guess I was wrong about you, Rev. You are a nigger. Nothing but a big, dumb, thick-skulled nigger!"

Rev screamed like an animal, and a cry went up from the others to stop him, but they had waited too long, listening, watching quietly. Rev threw his plate and cup to the ground and swung out with the terrible strength of his big arms.

The first blow brought a dull pain and knocked him off balance. The second brought blackness.

Floyd wasn't coming around yet when it was time to roll, so Adam had him put in the wagon. He had just swung into the saddle when Ben came riding in from the herd, angry and worried.

"It's them shorthorns, Adam. Three of them got it."

Adam looked out toward the tail cattle.

"It's all there. Weak in the legs, peeing red, yellow in the nose holes."

"Let's take a look, Ben."

They rode out to the herd and Adam had a look at the sick Herefords. There was no doubt. They had Texas fever.

"I wonder how many we're going to lose," Ben muttered.

"Hard to say, but you can bet there'll be more. Give us a mile, Ben, then shoot them."

The Mexican Spur moved on, with Ben staying behind with the stricken Herefords. Adam listened, and a few minutes later, the shots came faintly. The black carrion birds would find them soon. If it got bad enough, they might even begin to follow where the Mexican Spur's dust rose into the sky.

XIII

Take me to the green valley,
There lay the sod o'er me,
For I'm a young cowboy
And I know I've done wrong.

—THE STREETS OF LAREDO

FOR A WEEK they had moved up the divide between
the two forks of the Red, crossing Marcy and
Camp creeks and all the dry fingerlets that came
down from the hills. The longhorns walked as if
they had walked forever, slow and easily and
belonging to it and nothing else. The Herefords
were something apart, holding to the pace painfully, wearily, their misery growing with each mile until a day ended and night let them rest. Some would
somehow make it, some would scatter or fall behind, some would die as they were dying now with
their bodies shot through with fever. They were not
a part of this forever that stretched behind and the
forever that reached ahead.

It was the last day of May and the North Fork
could now be seen in the distance ahead. Rev
focused on it and tried to keep his mind empty so
that he could stay away from the hurt and anger
and the despair that had dogged him for days.
Days . . . maybe that too was forever.

Don't be a dumb nigger . . . the words kept coming back. Once words that meant nothing, but were supposedly a part of friendship. The word could be used several ways. It was the thinking behind it that made it good or bad, endearment or insult . . . *nigger* . . . it had been nothing, coming from Floyd, or so it seemed . . . it was like saying *you're crazy* in a good-humored way, or like calling a short man *shorty,* or a bowlegged man *wishbone* . . . *wedding ring* . . . *rainbow* . . . or like the way Baggett sometimes kidded Andy Giles for wanting to be a farmer, and called him *churn twister* . . . *plow chaser* . . . don't be a dumb nigger . . . nothing to it until that night in Brady . . . being left behind, not knowing why, not being taken into confidence, thinking a man was clean and honest and good and then being beaten for it and dragged low . . . yes, remember that. The single dim lamp, the almost bare room of the sheriff's office . . . the sheriff and a couple of his deputies standing over him . . . *all right, nigger, start talking* . . . *where's your friend* . . . *what do you mean you don't know who he is? We know who he is! A killer named Floyd Rogers you black bastard* . . . the fists coming down to stun and hurt and degrade . . . *we want to know where he hangs out and you're going to tell us* . . . *you know what happens to niggers who don't do as they're told? The same thing that happens to bull calves at branding time! That's right! We're going to make a big black steer out of you!*

Familiar faces then . . . familiar voices coming to argue and save . . . and the long hurting ride back to the familiar wagon and fire to face a man who acted like nothing had happened.

Don't be a dumb nigger, he had said. And then

. . . I guess I was wrong about you, Rev. You are a nigger. Nothing but a big, dumb, thick-skulled nigger!

Anger had boiled over and he had swung out and hit the man, and then hit him again and watched him double up and wilt to the ground.

And so now it sat, a twisting, hurting thing in the mind. He tried to forget it, to push it away, but those things never are forgotten.

He watched the longhorns stretched out in front of him for a half a mile, and a half mile in back of him, and heard their lusty voices in the afternoon, and smelled their sweet smell. He watched the sun lowering and the shadows lengthen, and the dust turn red with the hour.

He saw Adam Childress ride ahead like a casual general, and the ultimate grace of Ben Sweet combined with his horse in one fluid motion . . . Ben, who, walking became an apparition of flapping hands, churning elbows and knees that revolved at angles . . . he saw the *ladino* with its great spread of horns walking quietly but unsubdued at the lead in front of his tamer fellows . . . he saw light touch a wheel of the chuck wagon a certain way . . . and he kept thinking, the wonderful time, the wonderful place . . . but what was so wonderful about it now?

You get a friend, he thought. A real friend for the first time in your life. You can see times with this friend stretching way out, farther than all the herds that went up the trail put together. You count on it and then it's gone and you find out it wasn't ever there, really. And it cuts! It hurts deep . . . so what was the good, what was the use of any of this now! You might as well be back chopping cotton. . . .

Rev spurred away from the herd for a few yards to chase a cow back in, and he paused for a moment, looking back to see what had caught his eye.

He looked back toward the southern horizon, and saw the rider coming in the distance.

Marshal C. J. Peters. He hadn't given up after all.

Rev felt a sudden impulse to yell and tell the others, but he held it back and smiled grimly to himself.

Don't be a dumb nigger . . .

He didn't have to listen to things like that.

The river was close now. He didn't have to worry about Floyd looking back and seeing the marshal coming. They would be too busy now, getting the herd into the water and making them cross.

He got a good look at the river then. She was high and rolling hard. Adam Childress, in scouting it out that day had said it looked like there had been a cloudburst up in the mountains somewhere. The North Fork was swollen and angry, and it would be hard to cross. It could be done, but they would be bumping stirrups with the devil all the way.

Ben Sweet and Charlie Baggett, with the *ladino* striking right out, got the lead cattle in, and with a hard yell, the others were pushed in behind them. The leaders rolled their eyes and bawled and fought against the hard push of the current.

Just before his section of the herd reached the water, Rev looked around for the marshal and saw him no more than a quarter of a mile or so away. Then, with a yell, he kept his swing cattle running and hit the water.

It had a way of happening, sudden and quick.

One moment it looked like everything was all right. The water was moving fast and deep, but the Mexican Spur cattle seemed to be taking it in stride . . . and then, twisting, turning down from upstream, the broken limb of a tree.

Rev saw it coming and tried to avoid it. The cattle on the left side saw it coming and bawled with fright and tried to turn downstream. But they were blocked by cattle who angled against the current and could not see it for them. The panicked cattle then tried to turn against the current and head back for the shore they had just left. They began to mill and scrabble and churn in the deep water.

Rev yelled and slapped his hat at them and tried to push them back with the weight of his horse, but it was no good and no place to be now. He tried to turn them again and failed and then couldn't dodge them. As he was scraped out of the saddle, he heard Floyd yell.

The herd was breaking down the middle. Rev saw it as he grabbed his horse's tail and tried to hang on. Floyd swung around through the break.

"Hang on, boy! I'm getting there! I'll pull you out!"

Floyd reached out a hand and caught him under the shoulder just as Rev lost his grip on the horse's tail. He felt Floyd pull, but then something happened to his horse and the grip weakened and before Floyd could gather himself again, he was off his horse and somewhere in the water.

Rev went under, and it was like falling sideways . . . his ears roared and he saw dimly the bubbles rising from his own mouth, and beyond them the headless bodies bobbing massively, their legs and hooves silently thrashing the cold, murky places.

With panic coming close, he pointed himself toward the eddying surface and flailed his arms, and when his lungs seemed ready to burst, he broke the surface. With his last strength he reached out and grabbed the hard, bony tail of a steer who in confusion had struck out again for the opposite shore.

The longhorn pulled hard and sure in his fright and Rev held on until his feet touched bottom and the current began to lessen.

He sprawled in the sand, choking on the water he had swallowed. Andy helped him up to the top of the bank and retrieved his horse. By now, the others had gone over again to round up the cattle who hadn't made it across. With hard pushing and threats of mayhem, these finally made it. And with them came the marshal.

Rev saw Peters question Adam, and Adam turned around to look, rising in his stirrups as he did.

The question suddenly came to Rev then. Where was Floyd? He looked across at the western bank of the river, and then around where the herd was being held. He looked at the faces of the crew, and then looked at them again.

Quickly, he spurred his horse and followed the river downstream, his heart pounding heavily.

"Floyd!" he called out, his voice flat and echoless, lost against the rush of the river. "Floyd!"

Two Herefords were caught in the snarl of a dead and fallen tree. Their bodies, weakened from the beginnings of fever, had lost to the current and come to rest here, bobbing slowly.

The sight of them seemed to be an omen, their sightless eyes a warning, but it couldn't be true. Not Floyd . . .

But it was true, and there was not far to go or long to search. Rev found him, floating face down in a backwater.

The others, sensing the urgency of his ride, had followed and now sat there, looking down at Floyd.

"It looks like you're too late, Peters," Adam said quietly.

Rev turned and rode away from there. He rode back to the remuda and turned his horse loose.

He sat down on a rock and put his face in his hands.

Floyd had tried to apologize. He had tried to explain that he hadn't known that business in Brady would happen . . . and Rev could see how it was. A lonely man trying to have a single hour of lights and people and drinks. The short and gay time to take the deadliness out of his days. And the rest . . .

Rev shook his head and began to weep . . . he's gone now. It's too late for you to find it out now! He's gone . . . but he was just like you! You find a friend, and he's the only real friend, and he's got something that might spoil it . . . so he keeps it hidden.

Don't be a dumb nigger . . . sure, smile at it, and take it as it was intended to be taken . . . like you weren't black at all, like you weren't really a nigger, and it was some kind of a joke. Try not to talk like one, or act like one, or think like one as if there was a difference . . . because you were afraid that really being like a nigger might spoil the friendship. Both alike, both afraid.

"So what you goin' to do now," he said almost aloud. "What you goin' to do now, you big, dumb nigger! He's dead!"

He looked up at a touch on his shoulder. It was Adam.

"We're going to bury him now."

Rev shook his head.

"I ain't got no right, Mister Childress. I wasn't bein' right to him. I was hatin' him and he come to he'p. A man ain't got no right to get he'p from a man he hates! It was my fault!"

"No, it wasn't. It wasn't anybody's fault. Hell, men die in this river every year. I don't think you hated Floyd. You were sore, maybe, but you didn't have any hate down in your gut."

"How do you know!"

"Well, Rev, give me a little credit for my age. I seen a whole lot of men go up the trail. Old, young, good, and bad. Just about every kind. If there was any bad feeling, then the thing was settled right then and there. They had it out with guns or knives, or tried to kill each other with their fists and it kept on until one was dead or one left for other parts. No, you didn't hate him. I've seen the likes of you and him before."

Rev stared at the ground, not caring.

"I never did remember names. But I remember two boys who stuck together, and then fought, and then stuck together again. Nothing could pull them apart until the next fight they had. But that was to be expected. They was brothers."

Rev looked up.

"You think maybe tha's how it was with me and Floyd?"

"Like you had the same last name."

"I'd like to think tha's the way it was."

"Well, come on and let's go take care of him."

Red had wrapped the body in a sheet of canvas,

and Ben had dug a hole. Charlie Baggett and Andy Giles had lowered Floyd into it, and were scooping the earth back over him, and the Mexican was bringing rocks to mark the grave and keep the coyotes out.

When it was all done, Adam took his hat off and looked around.

"I reckon there ain't too much to say, or much that has to be said. None of us was ever much on words."

Adam cleared his throat, uncomfortable in his task.

"There's some that might say Floyd was a bad man, and others who'd say he could stand among the good. I don't know that it makes a difference out here. Floyd didn't have many friends, but he placed a high value on friendship. That was the way it happened for him and he was lonely. Well, I know a lot of men who wait on the banks of rivers now, or out on the open where the cattle ran. Floyd isn't alone here. This country we've come across is mother to all of them. I can't say that this is an unhappy place."

XIV

Lay still, little dogies, since you have laid down;
Stretch away out on the big open ground.
Snore loud little dogies, don't mind the wild sound.
It will go when the day rolls around.
Lay still, little dogies, lay still.

—Night Herding Song

At sunrise, June the first, the Mexican Spur moved northward on the new course begun the afternoon before. The North Fork of the Red behind them, they edged along the eastern border of the Panhandle. To the east, a mile or so, was Indian Territory.

Charles Wood looked back toward the river he could no longer see, at the country catching the first warm rays of the sun. He wondered why he felt no relief over the sudden end of Floyd Rogers. Sooner or later, justice caught up and society was better off, but there was no feeling of betterment here. Perhaps it was the manner of his going. It might have been more fitting if death had found him in an act of evil. But for a man to be brought full circle in the midst of doing something good . . . Wood never thought he'd feel regret over a man like Floyd, but he did now.

Adam Childress came back to speak to him then.

"You take Floyd's spot now."

Wood nodded and moved up to ride right flank. "What's the next river?"

"The Washita. That's where I'm headed now. Want to see how far away she is. I ain't come this far west before."

Adam wheeled away and rode off to the north.

Wood followed Adam with his eyes for a while, and then turned his head and looked to the east. It looked so different. But he could almost hear the pulsing of drums and the warrior cry. He could nearly sense the swift-flighted arrow and the ancient chant.

Wood smiled. It was imagination. The days when the Indian held sway over this land were gone. Just as the great, dark masses of buffalo were gone. Only the remembering earth could speak of it now, with bleaching bones and rotting wisps of hair and hide.

Twice that morning, he thought he saw smoke, and once he thought he heard the drumming of horses in the distance, and once he was so sure he saw a man sitting astride a painted pony on a low hill that he let a couple of steers leave the herd and fall to one side nearly fifty yards before Andy gave him a yell.

At noon, they stopped to eat, and Baggett joined Wood.

"What's the matter, Arbuckle?" Charlie wheezed.

"Nothing. Why?"

"You seemed kind of spooked about something. Letting those critters get away from you like that."

"I thought I saw an Indian."

"You probably did. But don't worry. You ain't going to lose your hair."

Wood smiled.

"I know that. Just call it an easterner's curiosity."

"Well, we might run into a few. They got about as much respect for the border as we have. Hey, Ben, did I ever tell you about that Arapaho chief I got drunk?"

Ben shook his head and came over with his plate.

"We was running the Fiddleback bunch up past Camp Supply, along the North Fork of the Canadian. Well, this old boy comes riding up at sundown asking for *wohaw*. The boss culls out a couple of lump-jaws for him. Hell, he didn't want 'em. He was particular, that old cuss, and wanted the fattest and best. The boss got sore and wasn't going to give him anything. I decided to have a little fun. There was a jug of forty rod in the wagon. We had it on hand for liquoring up the quarantine boys up in Colorado. Well, I got it out and went over to the fire and started drinking without a word, and the old Arapaho came over and watched. He was powerful thirsty, but you couldn't tell that by his face. You couldn't tell nothing by his face. Why he could die and his face wouldn't change expression and nobody'd know anything was wrong until the coyotes come to try and drag him off.

"I decided right then and there we should call him old Iron Head. Well, after a while, I looked up at Iron Head and asked him if he wanted a drink. I don't reckon old Iron Head spoke any English, but he could tell what I meant. So he sat down by me and took the jug and drank. Expression never changed."

Wood went to where the coffee pot hung over the fire.

"Man at the pot!" someone yelled out. Wood turned and found three cups being held up. He took them and filled them.

"Make sure you get my cup back to me, and not someone else's," Baggett said to him. "Don't want to get the epizootic from one of these stump-suckers! Well, we sat there and drank quite a while, old Iron Head and me. My idea was to get him drunk enough to pass out, and then we was going to tie him on one of those lump-jaws and turn him loose near his own camp. One of those lump-jaws was almost like a pet, and would walk up to any fire looking for a handout of dried apples or salt. I figgered it would make a noble sight, old Iron Head riding into his camp on a cow.

"The boss was tickled by the idea. He'd get rid of a lump-jaw, the Indian and have a little fun as well. But you know, that idea went off in my face like a bad pistol. Old Iron Head never showed a sign of passing out. That face of his never changed, and he kept pouring that forty rod down like it was well water. I should've seen it coming, but I was in a bad way by that time. Old Iron Head suddenly opens his mouth and goes yahoo! Not real loud. But them Fiddlebacks weren't far away, and they had done some running a couple days before. Ever time he did that, they lifted their heads and began to roll their eyes. Well, I wasn't too worried, because it was a sure sign he was pretty drunk. I figgered one more drink would lay him out. Boys, I didn't know how wrong I was! He kept yelling, and I kept giving him one more drink."

Wood saw everybody staring at Baggett with

their coffee growing cold. Peewee Hand had come up to listen and his eyes were wide.

"What happened then, Charlie?" Peewee asked.

"Well, like I say, ever time Iron Head did that, the cows acted like they smelled a grass fire. It might as well been something like that, because Iron Head finally let out with a yell that would've wrinkled water, and them Fiddlebacks was off and running, to hell. The boss says, 'Goddamn it, Charlie you're fired,' and everybody grabbed leather and we ran all night, and never saw Iron Head again. We lost fifteen head, and I don't mean they was lost in the stompede. That old boy knew what he was doing when he was yelling like that. He was out grabbing strays before we could even see which way they was going."

The sun began to ease down in the west and the country reddened in its glow, and there seemed to be a sameness no matter how far they went, for mile after mile.

Perhaps it was because of this that Wood did not see them at first. There was some kind of hypnosis in the warmth and in the sameness. But one moment, the land might have been vacant of anything but the cattle and the Mexican Spur riders, and the brush and stunted trees and the grass and the meadowlarks singing somewhere in it . . . and the next, *they* were there, sitting on painted ponies, feathers blowing in the wind, the sun catching the sternness of their faces.

The herd was stopped and held, and Ben Sweet went out to meet them. Wood edged up behind Preble.

"What are they?"

"Cheyenne."

"Arbuckle!" Sweet called out, and Wood raised his head and cupped his hand behind his ear. "Cut out four of them lame shorthorns, if you still got 'em."

Andy helped him cut out four that didn't look too good and he drove them up to where the Cheyenne waited.

The three Indians looked at them and Wood saw the fluid language of the hands begin again.

"Well, goddamn it!" Sweet muttered angrily, and indicated the four shorthorns again.

The Cheyenne who was doing all the arguing pointed up front at the best longhorn steers, arrogantly, and held up eight fingers.

"Doesn't he want these Herefords?" Wood asked.

"He's suspicious of them. It ain't what he's used to. But I ain't going to give away good Texas cows when we got shorthorns. That's the boss's orders. Besides, these boys are in Texas. We don't have to give them anything if we don't want to. And they know it. So you just stick here with them four."

Ben made motions with his hands.

"Take it or leave it!" he muttered. "We ain't got all day!"

The Cheyenne leader downed his demands to six and waited.

Ben shook his head and pointed at the four. The Cheyenne held out for six and Sweet turned his back on them.

"Take 'em back."

Wood got in front of the shorthorns and turned them back to the herd. He saw the Indians whirl with an angry little cry and ride away, bright de-

mons in the dust that kicked up and blew across
the herd.

It was a full hour later when Adam joined them
again. He told them there would be a dry camp
that night. The Washita could not be reached until
the following afternoon. The herd was kept rolling
until dark.

It wasn't until they gathered around the fire for
supper that the subject of the Cheyenne came up
again.

"When I headed out this morning, I spotted
some Cheyenne coming our way. Run across
them?"

Ben nodded.

"Three of them. They wanted eight of our best."

"What did you give them?"

"I didn't give them any."

"What!"

"Well, damn it, boss, eight was too many. And
they wouldn't touch the shorthorns. I offered them
four. That was enough."

"Four is all right, unless the dickering gets hung
up there. Didn't they come down?"

"Yeah. To six."

"Then you should've gone up to five."

"But boss, they wouldn't even look at them
Herefords!"

"Goddamn it Ben, if you'd have offered them
more, they might have showed some interest!
They'd get over their suspicions about shorthorns
soon enough. Any damn fool, Indian or not, can
see there's more meat on a Hereford."

"Well, I might've gone up except they was so
damn almighty about it. We aren't in the Territory.
We're in Texas."

"They've got as much use for borders as we got. Damn it! We always got some lame critters that ain't no good to us. There ain't no reason to turn them down." Wood saw Adam stand up and stare into the darkness. "Well, you can expect trouble now. If you want the rest of your grub, you better eat fast. Then get back out and make a circle around them cows. Nobody sleeps tonight."

Wood was one of the first to finish, and rode out with Adam.

"What will happen?"

"Maybe nothing. But they might try to stompede the herd."

"Giles told me he was afraid Ben had done the wrong thing."

"Well, I can't get too sore at Ben. Sometimes those Indians do get pretty mighty about it. But if you can reach the middle and agree, it's worth it. The lum-jaws and cripples ain't no use to us. If an Indian and his folks can eat for a little while on them, it's all right with me. But if they go away ringy and unsatisfied, they might decide to get the beef anyway. It ain't hard to stompede a herd in the dark, and while everything's going to hell, grab a few head."

"How do we stop them, if this is what they plan?"

"Make a circle around the herd and try to keep them from cutting through. We'll have eight men riding around slow like, and two cutting a bigger and quicker circle around that."

Wood thought about it for a moment. It didn't seem necessary.

"Why not take a few head out where the Indians will find them?"

"No. Once you make a decision around Indians, you got to stick to it. If we gave them what they asked now, we'd lose dignity. They'd figure we was scared, and we'd be an easy target for every beef-hungry Indian from here to the Lands."

Adam stopped where they could wait and saw the others gradually coming to make a circle.

"You and I will be the outer circle, Wood. We'll turn in opposite directions. Be on the lookout for anything."

Darkness deepened, and Wood rode in silence, feeling more alone than he had ever before. The night seemed alive with sound and movement, and at first that seemed all right. To hear the owl was normal, to hear coyotes call each other under the moon, pleasant. Crickets singing, the brief shadow of a bullbat against the stars. There was friendliness in all of this. Friendliness, until something crept into the sounds that was not quite real.

He stopped as Adam came around again on his circle.

"See anything, boy?"

"No. But I'm worried about those owls."

"Sound like Cheyenne? No, they're all right. It's the quiet places when the crickets stop you got to worry about."

"That's a relief."

"Well don't get too relieved. They're here, some-where."

"What do we do?" Wood looked around, un-easily.

"Keep riding around, that's all. And watch the way your horse acts. He's got a better nose and better ears than you have."

They separated again and rode the darkness. Wood stared at blackness, trying to see until his eyes smarted and watered. He lost track of time completely, and any sense of direction he might have had became little more than a stumbling in the dark. On one round, he missed Adam completely. The only way he knew night was growing older was the changing position of the Dipper.

The night seemed long. Longer than any he had ever spent on the graveyard shift, and he began to despair of ever seeing daylight come again. He was tired and longed for sleep, but the constant awareness of something moving or waiting just beyond his range of vision kept him sharply awake.

It grew cold after a while, and there was that certain damp smell to the air, and it seemed darker than before. He knew dawn was close now and it wouldn't last much longer. He dreamed of hot coffee and food and sitting down by the fire.

His horse stopped suddenly and snuffed at something in the darkness. He went stiff-legged and began to back off. Then, squealing suddenly, the horse reared up and Wood grabbed for the saddle horn, but it was too late. He fell and slammed against the ground. He lay there, listening, close to the earth. They were here, somewhere close, but where? Only his horse had seen them in the blackness or smelled them just a few feet away.

Wood rose to his knees, hearing a faint clicking sound like rock against rock, or stone against steel. He got to his feet and tried to determine the direction of the sound, and quickly a figure darted up against the stars and ran.

Wood ran after the fleeing shape. He realized the incongruity of it . . . the son of a Boston judge chasing a Cheyenne Indian . . . what will you do if you catch him, he wondered. What happens if he stops and turns around?

They ran for what seemed a long time, the grass making a whispering around his ankles. The Indian's running seemed without effort, his own harder with each stride. Those high-heeled boots he wore were not made for walking, much less a pre-dawn sprint over ground he could barely see.

Wood stopped and pulled them off, but even as he did it he knew it was no use. The Cheyenne was gone. Angry, and relieved, he put the boots back on and stood up. He whistled for his horse, and in a moment, the animal came trotting to him in the dark.

He rode back to pick up his circle again, back to where he had heard the clicking noise. It was gone now, and he would have dismissed it from his mind, but his horse shied a little at the spot and wouldn't hold still. Then he saw the glow of a light close to the ground and almost hidden. It grew brighter, sputtering and revealing the grass around it and the crouching figure of an Indian. Wood yelled and spurred his horse forward, but it was too late and flame leaped across the sky in a wide, curving arc.

The effect was instantaneous. Before the fire arrow had completed its flight and landed to create a growing circle of smoldering grass and flame, the Mexican Spur broke into a run, their thundering shattering the silence.

Wood watched, awestruck at the sight for a moment, and then angled out to try and meet them. The Herefords were scattering and the longhorns ran with the devil. But all he could reach was their dust and the tail end of their thunder. In back of him, where smoke and the low, flickering fire of burning grass blended hazily with settling dust, he saw bare-skinned figures on painted ponies move ghostlike into where the herd had been.

"How many did we lose?" Adam asked.

"Six or eight, maybe," Baggett estimated. "Mostly shorthorns."

"Well, it could've been worse."

They had run for no more than a half an hour, if that much. Dawn was growing in the sky. It would be all right now.

Adam looked around at the herd for a moment, and then hooked one leg around the saddle horn to relax.

"I'm sorry, Adam," Wood said, joining him.

"About what? Was that you who let out that yell?"

Wood nodded.

"I guess I'm not very smart. I heard a clicking noise . . ."

"Flint and steel," Adam explained.

"I know that now. But when I first heard it, my horse had shied and thrown me. I tried to find out what it was, and an Indian jumped up and started running."

"And while you followed the decoy, the other one had time to get that fire arrow to going."

"Yes. I got back there just as he shot it."

Adam smiled.

"It takes more than one trip up the trail to learn all their tricks. Don't worry about it."

The night was over now, and sleep had been lost. In a short while they would be moving north again, as if nothing had happened.

He looked around the scene, and remembered the things he had seen and learned. There were worse places to be, he decided. He watched the others. There was something about the whole thing that was good . . . and yet . . . he still couldn't come close to it. His actions that night proved what he felt. He was a spectator. A passenger. Nothing more.

XV

I looked up and seen the city of Dodge,
But the whole damn thing was another mirage.
—THE OLD CHISHOLM TRAIL

SLOWLY NORTH, across the Washita Canadian they moved. Then to Wolf Creek and across, and swinging gradually west the next day, cutting across the Panhandle, close to Public Lands. Here, Paladora Creek, and the North Fork of the Canadian wandered and would come to them again before they reached for the north once more. It was the thirteenth of June.

The land was changing subtly. It seemed flatter to Wood, and yet, more than that. More than sunburned grass and unbroken sky. He might have seen a thousand miles in any direction, in the early morning before the air was touched by the sun.

For all the days since they turned west, they had been blessed with a hot and dry wind. It had sucked the moisture from their bodies and burned across their faces like fire.

This morning the smoke rose from the cook fire undisturbed. While he watched it, the others talked about the fever.

"I think we've seen the last of it," Baggett said. "Them Herefords look to be in good shape."

"Maybe so. But I sure thought we'd lose more than that," Adam said, putting his John B. on and standing up. "Twenty-five head . . . well, that ain't so bad. If we can get the rest up to Montana, Jake'll get most of his money back."

Wood had climbed on his horse then and rode out to the herd. He didn't think about the fever. The only thing he could think about with the sun climbing fast was how bad the heat would be and how slow the herd would move . . . as if everything were lost somewhere in time that somehow had been suspended.

An hour later, when the heat was really getting bad, he looked out to his right and saw an antelope standing a few feet away. He watched the animal, wondering how it was that it showed no sign of fear and allowed man and his cattle to approach so close.

Wood turned to see if Andy had seen the animal, and found him ignoring it. When he looked back, the antelope was gone, as if it had never been anything more than smoke . . . a sorcery belonging to this flat place. It deviled him, and somewhere in his memory was an answer, but he couldn't find it. He thought of the dust then, and pushed the whole thing away. Yes, trim and cloven feet on slender legs, springing lightly to cover in that cloud of dust that came so thickly at flank and drag.

When they stopped at noon, he thought of the antelope and told Red about it.

"You mean Old Lonesome? He's always there. Why, when you see Old Lonesome, you know damn well you're headed right. He meets all the herds coming through here."

Wood went over and sat down, knowing that his leg was being pulled. Skinner began to laugh, and Baggett almost choked on a piece of meat.

"That was just a mirage, Mister Wood," Peewee Hand explained.

"A mirage . . ." Wood suddenly understood. "I never thought they'd be so realistic."

"Now why did you have to go and tell him!" Baggett spluttered.

"Well, I reckoned he wanted to know," Peewee's face fell.

"It sure is getting hard for a man to have some fun around here!"

"Mister Wood?"

"Yes, Peewee?"

"Just what is a mirage? What makes 'em?"

"It's a trick of the heat," Baggett wheezed. "I remember the first time I seen one. I seen an old river boat, just like the one that goes up and down the Red. That boat come moving across the prairie, throwing up black smoke, with the river a hundred miles away or more. It's just a trick of the heat."

"It's got something to do with layers of hot air," Wood said. "It acts like a mirror. There were enough layers of hot air, or a big enough layer of air anyway, so that an image of the boat was reflected over a long distance. You could see it steaming over the prairie at the same time it was steaming up the river a hundred miles away."

"Is that a fact . . ." Peewee said slowly. "Like a mirror?"

Charlie Baggett sat there looking suspicious.

"For one who didn't know what that antelope was, you sure know a lot about mirages!"

"I used to read a lot. Besides, reading about them and seeing one for the first time are two different things."

There were more mirages during the day. At times, Wood could look up toward the lead steers and Baggett and Sweet, and they would look like giants towering above everything else.

There were innumerable lakes and rivers and whole forests that shimmered green for an instant before vanishing. Some lasted long and defied the imagination.

Once there was a high hill, and on the hill, three mounted Indians like a giant memorial to the land that was taken from them. It lasted a long time, their features and costume as sharp and clear as if the whole image had been painted there.

A place of ghosts, Wood thought. A place of limbo and purgatory . . . a big country without beginning or end that somehow could capture the spirit and image of everything that had ever been and turn it loose upon the air for an instant to shimmer and live again.

Late that afternoon, Wood circled back to the wagon to get a drink, and a change in horses.

Wood opened the barrel and got a dipper full of the warm, sweet water. He drank it quickly, feeling sweat suddenly flood his pores.

"Well now, there's a good one!" Red exclaimed.

Wood looked up and saw two horsemen. In reality, they could have been almost any distance away, but in illusion they were no more than a few yards distant. One was a white man and the other a young Mexican. His wide sombrero, and his tight-fitting pants and the big Chihuahua spurs could clearly be seen.

Cimarron, who had been dozing on the seat suddenly looked up and saw the mirage. His lips began to move silently, his eyes widening. He smiled and jumped down to the ground.

"Hey!" Red yelled. "Where are you going?"

Cimarron grabbed a piece of rope and ran to where Peewee was bringing the horses along. Before anyone could think about it, he made a loop at one end, slipped it over the jaw of the first horse he came to, and was riding fast toward the mirage.

"Now what the hell is the matter with him! You better go and fetch him back here, Wood."

Wood dropped the dipper back in the barrel, turned his horse, and spurred him into a run.

The Mexican, without saddle, rode fast and hard like an Indian and it wasn't easy to close the gap between them. Wood kept spurring his horse, crouching low in his saddle, heading straight for the apparition.

Cimarron began to slow down, and Wood cut in front of him. The Mexican's eyes were ablaze with a strange light.

"Go on back. You're holding up the wagon. You hear me?"

Cimarron seemed to be deaf and tried to push past.

The great image in the sky shimmered like the northern lights and grew dim, and a strange, strangled cry escaped from Cimarron's throat. His hand darted to his belt and jerked the long knife free. The blade flashed as it sliced through the air.

Wood pulled back just in time. The blade caught at the cloth of his shirt and nothing more. Angrily, he pulled the Colt out of his holster, ready to defend himself, but Cimarron seemed to collapse and go limp. The mirage had vanished, and there was nothing out there but the empty and wide sweeping horizon.

The fire flickered and sent short-lived sparks rising toward the stars.

"Something's bothering him pretty hard," Adam said. "But I wouldn't worry about him."

"He's crazy!" Wood protested. "He tried to kill me with that knife of his!"

"He isn't loco," Red entered in the conversation.

Wood kicked at an ember with his boot.

"I don't see how you can say that, Red."

"Oh, I ain't tying it down hard. He's an old man and he might be a little loco. I knew an old man who was perfectly all right as long as the front door was left unlocked. Lock it, and he'd have a walleyed fit. Once when he was young, he and his best friend were being chased by an Indian war party, down near old Fort Lancaster. He made it to the gate of the fort, but his friend's horse stumbled. Before he could climb on again and make it the rest of the way, they had to close the gate and lock it. His friend was carried away by the Comanches and never seen again. I guess this old man keeps on waiting for his friend to turn up. All right, so maybe it's something like that with Cimarron. A mirage bothers him someway. You ride out to bring him back. You startled him and he tried to defend himself with a knife."

Wood shook his head, unable to accept it.

"I never could understand why you let him come along in the first place!"

"Keep your voice down. Everyone is trying to sleep. Now listen. It was just that mirage. It got him all spooked up," Red almost whispered. "I keep feeling the old boy is looking for something. I don't see any danger for us in that."

"One was a Mexican, wasn't it? In the mirage?" Adam asked.

Red nodded. "That might have something to do with it."

"Whatever it was," Wood said angrily, "he was ready to kill anybody who tried to stop him from reaching those riders. The only thing that saved me from getting hurt or him getting shot was the fact that the mirage vanished."

"Shut up! Here he comes," Red warned.

Cimarron walked slowly into the light of the fire. He walked tall and straight, and his face was without emotion. He stood before them, and took the knife from his belt.

Wood flinched and reached for the pistol at his side, but Red stopped him. The Mexican held the knife out, offering it to him.

"Su hijito mio . . ." the old man whispered.

Wood only stared at it and then met the Mexican's eyes. They studied him for a moment. There was an almost imperceptible nod.

Cimarron put the knife on two rocks, and looked at it for a short time. Then with a sudden, swift motion of his boot, he came down on the knife and snapped it in half. Quietly, without facing them again, he went back to the front of the wagon. They heard him moving around, and then there was no sound at all, save the crackling of the fire before them.

"How much more will it take to convince you?" Wood snapped.

"I don't think so," Adam picked up the remains of the knife and studied them. "But we can keep an eye on him."

"Offhand, Wood, I'd say you got just about the strongest apology a man can make." Red stood up and began making fresh coffee for the men who would later go on graveyard.

Wood looked at Adam and the trail boss nodded.

"It might be he'll tell us what his trouble is one of these days, and we can help him, and he'll turn out to be one of the most talkative and friendly old cusses you ever saw."

"Well," Red chuckled, "you at least got him to talk."

"What was it he said?" Wood asked, remembering the whispered words.

"My young one," Red translated. "Don't ask me what he meant by it, unless he has a high regard for young junipers like you."

Wood lay awake for a long time after the others had gone to sleep. That feeling was strong in him again. That feeling of distrust. The feeling would come and go and sometimes it was like it had never been ... until something like the mirage came along to remind him.

And what was it? Something lost in silence and darkness, brought to the surface by the sight of a Mexican who, in a sense, was no more than a phantom. This frightening, evil thing, and then the unexpected gentleness that came in snapping the blade and in a short, whispered phrase. *My young one* ... what did it all mean?

XVI

Ride around the little dogies, O ride around 'em slow,
For the fieries and the snuffies are a-raring to go.
        —I'M A-LEADING OLD DAN

WHEN THE WANDERING North Fork of the Canadian found them again, they followed its curve north and left Texas behind. For three days they edged across Public Lands, and by noon of the fourth, crossed into Colorado, following the impermanent buffalo skulls that feebly marked the trail. That same evening found the Mexican Spur at rest on the north side of the Cimarron River.

Wood marked the place and time in his mind. June 18, 1886. Colorado and the Cimarron. How many more miles and days and rivers? Sometimes it was pleasant. Moments like now, with the warmth of a fire and a night's sleep ahead, a full stomach and the sound of the river quietly rolling a few yards away.

But the country he had seen . . . what kind of country was it for a man? How could he exist there? A pure expanse of dying grass and blowing dust and heat for mile after mile. It was a bitter land, and he had longed for the cool green places of gentle air and image.

The clouds that had begun to gather just before sundown were heavy and dark above them now, blotting out the stars and holding the air still. The air was warm and close and held the promise of rain. They had all watched it hopefully.

Wood went to the barrel, and while he was there, saw Cimarron remove his sombrero and examine a little ball suspended from inside the crown. His face seemed darker and more wooden than ever, and his lips moved for a moment, silently. Cimarron wiped the damp strands of hair away from his eyes and glanced at the clouds, looking almost like an aged Christ staring at the heavens in agony. His lips moved again and he put the hat on his head again and once more became an unmoving part of the wagon's shadow. Wood felt a shudder along his spine.

He turned his back on the old Mexican and went back to the fire. The pleasant time? Not now. Cimarron had somehow been a part of the clouds gathered up there, and it was as if the age-old fear of darkness had come to touch him. The whole tenor of the evening was changing rapidly.

The cattle were restless, and gave voice to it out on the bed ground. The men kept watching the sky. Adam stood with agitation growing slowly in his face. Ben was rubbing his arms as if he were cold. Skinner could not stand still. Rev's eyes shone nervously in his black face, darting back and forth from clouds to fire.

Waiting. . . .

For what? Something other than rain. Something more than the clear, wet drops they prayed for constantly.

It came time to turn in, and nobody did, and it

was strange because the very nature of the day and the work they did made sleep come easy. They merely talked in hushed voices, as if in the presence of the dead. Waiting . . .

Wood was too tired to go over to the fire and ask what was on their minds or pay much attention to the uneasiness it gave him. He turned his back on it and got his bedroll out of the wagon.

"Ain't no use in that, Wood."

He looked around at Adam, and beyond him where the others were now getting up and getting their saddles, and Peewee was bringing the horses in. There was an exaggerated silence in every movement the men made.

"What's going on, anyway?"

"I think those cows are going to run."

"I don't understand. Why should they run?"

"Electrical storm building up. You can feel it in the air."

"They seem restless, all right."

"Well, maybe it will pass and everything will quiet down. But we've got to be out there just the same. And whatever you do, keep it quiet. Anything can start them. The striking of a match, a sneeze, metal hitting against metal . . . anything. You understand?"

"What do I do if they do start running?"

"Not much you can do, boy. Hang with them until they begin to tire out, and then try to make them turn and mill."

Wood threw the bedroll back in the wagon.

"Cimarron was acting strangely again."

"How?"

"He was sort of talking to himself and looking at a little ball inside his hat."

Adam nodded and smiled at him.

"You're liable to see any Mexican do that. It's beeswax. He believes it will keep him from getting hit by lightning."

They walked back to the fire and mounted up.

"Okay, boys, let's go."

They rode out to the herd, quietly and wordlessly, and stationed themselves where they could watch and wait.

Waiting . . . how would it begin?

Nothing happened, and nothing seemed different about the night and the herd except their restlessness. Time moved slowly and though the clouds were still gathered in awesome council, it seemed like the situation might pass. But shortly after midnight, they saw a pale, almost hidden flash of light and heard the distant muttering of thunder.

The cattle tested the air and watched with their eyes rolling skyward. Some stood up nervously.

Someone began to sing to them softly, and Rev joined him.

> *Little black bull came down the hillside,*
> *Down the hillside, down the hillside,*
> *Little black bull came down the hillside,*
> *Long time ago.*

The voices carried eerily above the bawling of the herd, half lost as a voice becomes small in a wind, but there was no wind here. In spite of the bawling of the herd and the singing that fought against it, there was an immense silence and stillness touching everything.

The air was almost hot now, thick and heavy from hidden fires, and the rumbling continued.

Wood sucked his breath in at the thing that began to happen then.

It had been dark, and now it was not. Balls of fire were forming on the tips of every horn in the herd . . . like a million pale globes of light, bobbing as would exaggerated fireflies when the cattle moved their heads.

Flashing snakes rippled up and down their spines, and they pawed the ground and bawled and snuffed at the trembling air.

Wood felt a chill rattle up his own spine and sat trembling, watching the scene, feeling the power of this spectacle building, growing by degrees.

They were waiting for a giant to move.

When would it happen . . . the end of this waiting?

What was it that would finally touch off the explosion?

The answer came so quickly, the question was forgotten.

The sky cracked in a hundred places with a blinding flash of light, and a tremendous barrage of thunder rolled from horizon to horizon. But before the thunder could run its full course, the longhorn cattle hit the ground with one, concerted roar and were running, drowning the heavens with a thunder of their own.

Wood dug his heels in his horse's ribs and went with them. He did not know what to do. Adam had talked of staying with them until they tired and then trying to turn them.

But when would that moment come? How could you tell in this darkness? And how did you make a herd, three thousand terrified animals, see anything but the frightening heavens or hear anything but the numbing thunder?

Stay with them. That was all he knew. Stay with them while they ran their terror out.

When he came up close and matched his speed with that of the racing cattle, there was no longer any time to think about it.

It was a nightmarish thing. He was carried along with it, caught on a fantastic tide. He could not see, except when lightning flashed and revealed a sea of horns and wild-eyed cattle plunging head on for hell, and the desperate image of men struggling to keep horse and self free of the fatal currents. And then, darkness again . . . fraught with thunder and pounding hooves and bawling, terrorized, phantom shapes.

He wondered how his horse could see, and thought of prairie dog holes and washes, and anything else that might trip a horse. It could happen so quickly, and so easily . . .

He thought of pulling aside and slowing down and letting them go on. What good was he for this? The others, those tough-skinned, lean, hard-boned . . . those rawhide men he could hear yelling now and then against the thunder. They belonged here. This was their life, and it seemed they'd just as soon be doing this as tossing their hats on dust-devils to see how far they would fly.

But he did not dare try to guide the horse now. He wasn't sure of the cattle in back of him and what would happen if he tried to slow down. He could only give his horse his head and let him choose his own way. Hang on and hope . . .

"If a man falls in a stompede and gets killed," Adam had said once, "it ain't usually the critters that kill him, but the fall itself. Them cows try to go around anything in their way."

Wood wished he could see. Maybe those cattle would go around if he fell. Maybe, if it were light. As dark as it was, he found no comfort in Adam's words, and waited, sure that the end would come at any moment.

They ran forever, until it seemed they must reach the sea. They ran forever and then slowed and began to mill, and stopped, blowing, standing head down. Forever, and then stopping beyond that time, because that was what it was like . . .

It began to rain then, with thunder rumbling more distantly, and the cool drops were a joy to feel. Wood took his hat off and turned his face up to it.

"We lose anybody?" Adam spoke in a low voice.

"I reckon we're all here," someone answered.

"Well, we'll hold 'em like this until daylight."

"Boy howdy, I sure wish coosie'd come up with some hot coffee 'bout now!"

Wood listened to the whispering voices in the darkness. Coffee, sleep, the cheer of a fire and the comforts of routine. That was nice to think about, but for the moment he was grateful just to sit, to hold still and breathe for a while.

"He'll be rattling up soon enough."

"Yeah, providing he got them mules to move."

"Well, he ain't had no trouble with them mules ever since they seen what he done to the horse."

"What was that, Charlie?"

"He was showing how he could lift a horse."

"That's a long one!"

"Well, he didn't get the horse off the ground, but he made that horse groan powerful sad in the trying!"

A low laugh, almost silent, went up, but it was suddenly blotted out.

"There they go again!"

There had been no warning for it. They had been standing there blowing with the peace of exhaustion, and now they were off again, running, thundering, bawling in the darkness and rain.

Where the footing had been dry before, it was now wet. How many times had a horse lost its footing and slammed its rider against the unseen ground to die of a broken neck when the ground was like this, churned by rain and three thousand head of cattle into soupy mud . . . Wood hung on more desperately and with less hope for the outcome than before.

It went that way for the rest of the night. The Mexican Spur bunch ran intermittently until dawn found the men, redeyed and worn, riding around a herd beginning to graze in the growing light.

XVII

Popped my foot in the sitrrup and gave a little yell,
The tail cattle broke and the leaders went to hell.
                              —THE OLD CHISHOLM TRAIL

AFTER THE RUNNING was over, on the morning of
June 19, Red caught up with his wagon and fixed
breakfast. Those who did not have to say with the
herd while it grazed and rested, tried to catch up on
the sleep they had missed during the night. Later,
that afternoon, they would take the herd over the
remaining distance to the North Fork of the
Cimarron. There, they would cross and make camp
for the night.

Wood stretched out near Adam, yawning in the
warming sun.

"How far off the trail are we?"

"I reckon fifteen or twenty miles. Why?"

Wood came up on one elbow and blew his nose.

"I was wondering how much time we'll lose
going back to it."

"We aren't going back. We'll angle to the north-
east and pick it up again. There won't be any time
lost."

"We can't do that, can we?" Wood sat up.

"Why not?"

"On account of the fever. We had a stampede and there's not much we can do about that, but I thought we'd be obligated to retrace our steps."

"You seen any stock yet that wasn't behind a fence?"

"No, not since we left Texas."

"All right, you tell me how we can bother them."

Wood sank back down.

"You worry a hell of a lot about these people," Adam added, "when you should be worrying about us. We were here first."

"I'm sorry, Adam. There's a lot of things I don't know. You've been doing it for twenty years, and this is my first time. I'm not even sure I've got a right to talk to the boss this way."

"You know me better than that, boy."

"Well . . . you want me to tell you how we can bother anything that's fenced off. I don't know. But it seems to me if it were as simple as that, there wouldn't be any need for that National Trail. There must be cattle out in the open around here."

"I imagine there is."

"And you've told me quite a few trail drivers leave the trail to take a shortcut, and still knock down fences."

"That's right. Including me, if necessary."

"That's what I mean! A trail has been set aside, so that you won't have to fight quarantines and nesters or fences. Now you're trying to kill it off by not using it."

Adam slapped at his knee impatiently and shook his head.

"This National Trail is no solution. It's added too many miles and takes us away from places where we could count on water. There ain't enough

grass for all the herds that come across it. I guess
we're kind of lucky, especially in a dry time like
this. Maybe we got going early enough to come
across it before the grass was all grazed off. But
you think about it. What happens when there ain't
enough grass and the rivers start drying up? A man
still has to get his cattle north. He has to do it any
way he can. All right, I'll stick to the trail as long
as I can. But if things get bad, I'll swear to you
right now, we'll take our own way."

Wood closed his eyes.

"It's an odd situation. Both sides seem to have a
right to be here, but you can't exist together. And
you can't keep moving the trail west. There must
be an easier way."

"Railroads, I suppose!" Adam smoothed it over
with a grin.

"No. But there has to be a way."

"There is. Only one. Decide where you want to
take them, and walk them there."

"But . . ."

"I know what you mean. Well, this National
Trail is better than nothing. For a while it didn't
look like we were even going to have anything."

Adam told him about the convention that met in
St. Louis two years before. Jake Nance was there.
A lot of them were there. Ranchers, breeders,
packers, feeders, bankers, senators, and con-
gressmen. Adam settled back, and in the telling,
the memory of the struggle came fresh and hard.

They were scared on both sides, Northwest and
Southwest. Times were bad and they came to the
meeting in desperation. The Northwest . . . a wilderness not long before, now roared with a population boom. Time was beginning to crowd, the

breadth of the land narrowing. The Northwest
wanted Congress to allow long-term leasing of
public domain lands for grazing.

Texas cattlemen had fought one battle too many
going north. Quarantines, fences, jayhawkers, water rights . . . the great, rolling and free thing they
had known was grinding to a halt. The solution
seemed to be a trail set aside by law. A trail three
to six miles wide, from the Red River to Canada. It
wasn't like the old way. But if it could be had and
set aside from sale or settlement for at least ten
years . . . well, a man could keep going north.

"It didn't get far," Adam said. "Montana and
Wyoming said their ranges was in danger of getting
overstocked, and they didn't like trail herds coming in from Texas. So they wouldn't back the trail
idea. Well, the boys down here got sore and spat on
the grazing lease idea. We all went home empty
handed.

"There was another get-together last year. It got
just about as far. The Panhandle sided with the
north, and the north went haw-haw because we
were yawping for a trail up there without even having one in Texas for a starter. We figured there was
nothing left to do but strap on our guns and go
north the best we could. Even Governor Ireland
was hinting around about making a trail through
the Panhandle, with Texas Rangers to back us up,
so we could reach Public Lands and cross over to
the federal lands in Colorado. From there we'd be
on our own.

"Well, last May, in Dallas, north and south Texas got together and mapped out a trail and it was
agreed on. Texas was ready to move, and was
going to move. So rather than have cattle roaming

where they pleased after they left Texas, the north set up the rest of the National Trail. It don't go all the way to Canada. Just gets us around Kansas, through Colorado, and that's the end of it.

"Getting around Kansas is the important thing, but it still isn't enough. And also like I said, there is another way. Find the cause of Texas fever and get rid of it."

"What do you suppose it is?"

"I don't know. Some say it's the ticks. Some say it's something in the southern grass. Some even think a longhorn's breath is poisonous. There's several ideas. I think it's the ticks myself. It's the only thing that makes sense. You take cattle from the southern part of Texas, where you got lots of ticks, into the northern part of the state, where there ain't any . . . and bang! Them north Texas cattle got the fever. But no matter what it is, get rid of it, and we'd be a lot more welcome. I ain't saying it'd knock down all the fences or keep those god-damn sodbusters from turning the grass upside down. But we could move the trail West, away from all that."

"I guess that would be the best way," Wood agreed, sleepily.

"In the meantime, we'll go north the best way we know how."

That afternoon, they moved the herd onto the North Fork of the Cimarron and crossed over. On the other side, watered, the herd was bedded down and camp made for the night.

Adam sat with his back against a wheel of the wagon, away from the heat of the fire. He watched the stars which shone redly in the sky. The air was smoky and hard, and bitter to the taste as if there were a big fire somewhere. But it was not a fire, he knew. It was just the land and the air smouldering under the lack of rain, and there was no sign or hope that any would come.

"Katherine is quite a girl," Wood said.

Adam nodded, amused.

"She was so different than most I had seen."

"Different?"

"Well, coming down from Pena that time, I saw women in the towns or standing on the porches of houses, riding by in wagons. Most of them looked all dried up, turned to leather, gaunt looking. And they weren't old."

"A lot of the women have led a hard life. They age quick and dry out until you'd have a hard time saying which was prettiest if you stood one alongside a fence post to compare. My mother was like that. She and Paw raised a few head of cattle and farmed a little down in Lavaca County. When he went off to fight Santa Anna, she had to do all the work. And it was the same when he came back crippled up with a ball in his leg. It almost killed her and she wasn't pretty anymore. But in some ways she was one of the most beautiful women I have ever seen. They're good women. If you want to take a piece of land and put cattle on it and raise a family that'll stick and be as durable and hardy as the longhorns you own, these women are the ones for it."

"How come you left? Seems to me you had the makings for a ranch of your own, instead of working for other people."

Adam thought of it and shrugged.

"Couldn't sit still that long, I guess."

Couldn't sit still . . . a good enough answer, and

perhaps the right one, he supposed. But there was an uneasiness in thinking about it, a feeling that came to haunt. It held the same unrest the wind holds as it blows the grass and talks around the edges of a house. A feeling of almost being lost and not understanding.

The camp went suddenly quiet, and there was the sound of boots scuffing in the dust as men stood up. Adam immediately sensed something wrong, He got up and came around the end of the wagon. They were in a half circle around the fire, a dozen men with the flames reflecting angrily in their eyes. They had come like ghosts, without warning. Each sat quietly on a horse and held a gun on the crew of the Mexican Spur.

"Don't try anything, mister," one said to Adam.

Adam stopped.

"What's this all about? Who are you?"

"It doesn't matter who we are. You're more than twenty miles from your trail, mister."

"Our herd stompeded in that storm. We ain't here by choice."

"We crossed your trail just below the river. There ain't no sign of cattle doing anything but walking."

Adam walked closer until the man stopped him again.

"You should've checked a little farther south of the river. They ran all night."

The intruders snorted their disgust, knowingly.

"Convenient to have a storm come along as an excuse! We seen your kind before. That trail of yours you done so much begging for is getting to be a joke!"

"Go ahead and laugh then. I said we had a

stompede, and it ain't no concern of mine what you think!"

"You talk pretty big, considering the fix you're in now. Now let's forget how you got here and talk about how you're going to saddle up right now and turn that herd back the way you came."

"Your pistols don't mean a thing to me, anymore than talking about going back does. I plan to reach the trail north of here without losing any time, and I reckon I'll stick to that plan."

"I don't agree with that, mister. We can shoot you on the spot and drive them back to the border ourselves."

"Go ahead," Adam invited them.

"You seem anxious to commit suicide."

"Not at all. I'm just thinking what those cattle will do when you fire that first shot, mister. They're still a little jumpy from that storm. They'll run, and they'll scatter, and there'd be some you'd never find ... wandering around spreading the fever wherever they went. Think about it. And then either shoot or clear out and let us reach the trail in our own way."

"It's a bluff!" one of the others growled.

"That's what I'm thinking," the first one said.

One of the pistols lowered a fraction and spurted flame, and dirt kicked up near Adam's feet.

Almost immediately, there was the bawling of cattle and the sudden shaking of the earth as they began to run.

Adam ignored the nesters as he and the rest gathered leather and rode after the herd. The men who had sought to make them retrace their steps now sat their horses in astonishment.

Adam spurred his horse to the utmost, angling

out to the sound of thunder, plummeting headlong until the thunder was close and he could taste the dust that rose into the air behind them.

There was no stopping them. Not until the fear that started them lessened and faded. They might turn and stop in half an hour, or they might run right into sunrise.

They were headed north. Try to keep them together.

It was all they could do.

It was nearly two hours before the herd stopped. They were held there to wait until daylight, which was still a good time off.

"You reckon they'll come back?" asked Ben.

"I don't think it likely. They know now that all they got to do is fire one shot and they'd be off again," Adam muttered.

Ben chuckled.

"You know, if it wasn't for the weight them steers were running off, it'd be funny. I can't forget the look on their faces when them cows laid their navels in the sand!"

Adam thought about it for a moment and then began to grin. It was funny, the way it had turned out. They were farther north than before.

"The grass seems pretty good through here, too."

XVIII

*Now, they string bobwire till it's four strands high,
And as sure as hell there'll be fences in the sky.*
                                                        —THE OLD CHISHOLM TRAIL

THERE WAS NOT going to be any quarter from the weather. A man can keep looking at the sky, saying there was time yet for it to change, and change it could. But the time comes when he feels it in his bones that there is not going to be any rain. Adam felt it, and saw it in the dying grass and in the dust clouds that rose on the wind. Most of all, he saw it in the beginning of gauntness in his cattle. It was no longer just a dry spell, a time when a man wiped his face and sought the shade to wait patiently. This was a drought year and a bad one.

It was June 21, and a long way lay before them still. They would cross Bear Creek that evening, and beyond that, how many creeks and rivers, and how many miles?

There was a chance that weather would be normal farther north in Wyoming and Montana. It could be raining there now, the gray-bellied clouds keeping the grass deep and green. But what could not be seen could not be known. It could only be guessed at or hoped for and held impatiently in the mind.

Grass was fairly good here, good in the sense that other trail herds had not passed over it. But they could not stay long enough for it to do any good. They'd be back on the trail in a day or two. They could not hurry, for hurrying takes the flesh off an animal. But at the same time, they could not waste time. A single day saved was now as valuable as a day on good grass and a day of rain. The way they went, the time they spent . . . it came down to one thing. Weather. It was all a part of the weather.

It was in this desperation that they came to the fence.

Adam reined in and looked at it, stretching two or three miles in either direction. This was as much as he could see. How far beyond sight the fence cut the land, he could not guess. This was not the land of one nester but the combined holdings of several.

Angry and saddened, he noted the fence continuing down again across the range what must have been nearly a mile away. That wide and how long? It seemed to have no purpose as yet. There was no stock in evidence. Part of it had been plowed, but there was nothing growing there. It was no more than a barrier. No more than a line saying this land was theirs. . . .

Adam rode back to Ben and Charlie Baggett.

"Hold them here and get ready to squeeze them through a hole."

He rode on down the length of the herd, telling everybody what was to be done, until he came to Wood.

"Grab a couple of wire cutters out of the wagon and come with me. Preble can handle your spot. I need Baggett and Sweet to lead them through."

"But those farmers . . ."

"Hurry it up, boy! It's got to be quick!"

Wood rode out to the wagon and came back with the cutters.

"I had an idea we might need these," Adam told him, grimly.

"Now look here . . . this is a rotten thing to do."

"We'd lose too much time going around."

"That may be. But they own that land."

"There ain't time to talk about it now."

"You're still wrong. You can't go knocking down something that belongs to other people!"

"And I told you if things got bad enough, I wouldn't let a fence stop me!"

They came to the fence then and Adam dismounted.

"We'll start here and I'll cut to the right. You take the left. And make it quick!"

Adam worked furiously, denuding the posts of the wire. He could hear Wood doing the same. Their work sang down the uncut wire like some sort of telegraph. Wood didn't understand, but maybe he would someday. Maybe he would see how it was to have free, open land, to know its joys and its value, not to just one man but hundreds of men. If he would understand that much, then he would see what it did to the land when nesters threw up shelter and fence at random. . . .

He had cleared about twenty feet of fence, when he saw the men walking across the field from the houses. There were six or seven. There was going to be a fight, he knew. But he worked even faster. Let them argue with three thousand head of cattle moving through that hole.

He looked back to see how much Wood had done and swore softly. Wood was awkward with the cutters and slow, and his heart wasn't in it. He should have gotten someone else. Someone who had done it before and didn't mind.

A half dozen shots rang out and the bullets whistled close. He heard a sharp cry and turned to see Wood fall to the ground.

Adam dropped the cutters and ran to Wood and tried to get him to his feet. He had been hit in the chest, and it was bad.

"All right, boys, they want a fight! Let's oblige them!"

"No!" Wood coughed.

"Hold still and keep quiet! We'll take care of these goddamned nesters and then get you to the wagon."

"It isn't worth it!"

Adam pulled his pistol from its holster. He waited for the nesters to walk into range. The others in the crew were ready.

Wood struggled to get up on one arm, but lacked the strength. He talked unevenly against the shock and pain, and it was like a voice close to laughter and breathlessness.

"They have a right . . . only you're too damn stubborn . . . you don't own the land . . . just . . ." Wood squeezed it out and almost fainted. ". . . old man . . . had his way too long!"

The bullets came singing again, and the Mexican Spur boys looked around for cover, and there wasn't any.

"Them's .45—.70's!" Baggett spat. "I'd know 'em anywhere. Long-barreled Springfields. This distance ain't nothing for them!"

It was true, and Adam swore against the stone splatter of more lead. They had only three

Winchester carbines, and the pistols that made up the rest useless. The nesters, crouching down at a safe distance, could pick them off like sleeping birds. Not only could he lose some of the boys in a fight like this, he could lose some of the cattle. They had to back off and go around . . .

Nearly crying with frustrated rage, he hauled Wood up onto his saddle and climbed on himself and headed for the wagon.

"All right, head them around. We'll go west."

West, instead of passing through their fire to get to the trail . . . delay . . . and no time to delay . . .

Wood was unconscious all the way to the wagon. Adam stretched him out inside, and he came to for a moment.

"You're wrong . . . real . . . wrong . . ."

"Listen to me, Wood! I'm going to try and pull you out of this. And if I do, you can goddamn well go back and join the sodbusters you seem to love so much!"

Wood started to say something, but then was gone again.

"That's a bad place to catch one," Red said.

"Yeah, and I've got to do something about it quick. We can't hang around here. I don't think they'll bother us anymore as long as we're moving. Try to smooth out the bumps."

"That's a tall order."

"I know, but I've seen you do it before."

Adam ripped Wood's shirt away and pulled out his knife and began looking for the bullet.

A moment later the wagon stopped again and Red climbed down. Adam paid no attention, but kept on until the point of his knife found the bullet. He worked at it, slowly and carefully, until finally, it came and fell to the floor of the wagon. Only then did he wonder why they had stopped and where Red had gone. He was fixing a bandage when Red came back.

"How's he doing?"

"I got it out. A rib kept it from going too deep. If they had been fifty yards closer . . . What's holding us up?"

"It's Baggett. He was hit, too."

"Well, get him over here! Why didn't he tell somebody!"

"I reckon he's got it figured out the way I have. He knows nothing can be done for him."

"Where'd he catch it?"

"In the belly."

They made room for him in the wagon alongside Wood by lashing some of the bedrools on the back end. Red whipped up his mules and they moved once more. Adam bent over Charlie and had a look.

"That's a good one, ain't it?"

Adam managed to nod his head.

Old Charlie seemed his usual self, cheerful and ready to talk. But that hole in his belly was another matter.

"Y'know, Adam, it's too damn bad. If this wasn't going to kill me, it could've made me famous. Hitting me right on the knot like that. Stitch it up just so and I'd have been the only man in the whole state of Texas who didn't have a navel!"

"Well, don't give up your fame yet, Charlie."

"Now what the hell, boss. Quit pulling my tail hair."

They moved slowly through the afternoon, and

Adam, with the rough surgery on Wood finished and Charlie made as comfortable as circumstances allowed, rode up in front of the herd.

He had a bad feeling inside. Charlie was an old friend . . . why, he and Charlie had trailed herds together off and on almost ever since the first Texas herd moved north and crossed the Red. Old Charlie, with his stories and his way of talking. It was wrong that he should go this way. And Wood . . . he had come to like Wood. Wood, soft and pale, taking on the task of forgetting another way of living and trying to learn a new one . . . growing brown and hard, learning slowly, but learning. And now . . . he could be dying as surely as Charlie was dying.

Adam regretted his anger and yelling at the boy like that. Wood didn't understand. Of course he didn't understand! The way the land was and the thing it was coming to now. A man had to see how it was before to understand . . . but in a way, he was right, too. Saving the fence wasn't worth it. The miles and time lost in going around . . . it wasn't worth risking lives.

He saw Charlie's face, sharp and clear in his mind, back there in the wagon, grinning and making jokes, and owning up to the grim fact like it didn't really matter.

Of course it wasn't worth it!

But goddamn it! What was a man supposed to do?

They were at Bear Creek and camped for the night when Charlie requested to be taken from the wagon so that he could look around and get some air.

"How do you feel?" Adam asked.

"All right, I reckon. Thirsty."

"Well, you know you can't have any water with a wound like that. Best wait a while."

"I wasn't thinking about water."

"There ain't no saloons around here, Charlie."

"No, there ain't. And I know whisky ain't allowed in camp, but . . . well, it ain't like you could exactly fire me now, is it?"

"All right," Adam said. "Where is it?"

"In my warbag, and just so's you'll know I ain't been busting the rules, you'll notice I ain't even had the cork out yet."

"Get it, Red."

"You going to let him drink?"

"Sure, it's all right. It ain't the same as water."

It was strange standing there pretending he didn't know what Charlie knew.

"That's right," Charlie said, licking his lips. "It ain't the same as water. Why, there ain't anything like a little forty rod to take care of a man. It'll hold off the epizootic, it's good for worms and a bad tooth, and a little of it in a cut will keep it from getting infected if you can stand the burn. Hell, I knew an old buffalo hunter who lost his hair to a Comanche. Well, he played dead until the Injun was gone, and then plastered his head with mud to keep from bleeding to death. That was all right for a while, but a man with an infected head ain't going to get nowhere. And that mud would infect it if anything would, seeing as he got it out of a buffalo waller. So he got the mud off when the bleeding stopped and wrapped it with a piece of his shirt. The only trouble was, his head was already beginning to rot up there, and flies bothered him something terrible. Now, he just happened to have a jug of forty rod the Comanche overlooked. He soused his head and the cloth in it, and the burn damn near killed him. Well, I don't suppose I'd be stretching it to tell you he came out about a half incher shorter than he was before, but by God it saved his life! Here, let me have that bottle, Red."

The camp was quieter than usual that night. The men just sat around, staring into the fire. Charlie drank almost half the bottle, and began to sing a little, and after a while, he went to sleep. That was how he went.

Adam went over and took the bottle from his hand.

"Here's how, Charlie," he said quietly, and raised the bottle to his own lips.

Adam stared at the empty bottle and gave it a fling into the darkness beyond the fire. He stood up and wobbled dangerously close to the flames until Ben made him sit down again.

"Poor old Charlie . . . poor old Charlie. That's one hell of a way to go. He was a good man . . ." he said thickly.

"Come on, boss," Ben told him, "you ought to turn in."

"Me? I ain't drunk, Ben. It's Charlie who's drunk. Why he's up there now, facing the Lord with whisky on his breath. But I reckon it's all right, and you know Charlie and how he could talk . . . why, I can just about hear him now. 'Sir,' he's saying, 'Sir, I'd offer you one, too, except'n I done left it back down there.' And the Lord is saying, 'It's all right, Charlie, it's all right. I don't mind.' Ben, do you reckon he'll be able to drink where he is? I always had an idea heaven was different for every man . . . heaven having all the good things a man liked while he was alive. Whisky for Charlie . . . and for me when my time comes, cow country like it ought to be. . . ."

"Come on," Ben took his arm and helped him to his feet.

Adam didn't object this time. Ben helped him turn in and went away, and Adam watched the stars for a long time, wondering about heaven and where it was. Suddenly he turned over, and burying his face in his arms, wept bitterly.

XIX

Weep, all ye little rains; wail, winds, wail,
All along and all along the Colorado Trail.
—The Colorado Trail

SLEEP HAD JUST begun and it was troubled, too full
of the darkness and depression and despair that
sleep somehow can never entirely kill. The dreams
were not real, but they were true. They were only
images that came for a moment, in the same
manner as a bird wing touching and disturbing the
calm of water for an instant and then going on.
They were a remembering, and what they remembered was true. They were a sum of the past, com-
paring what was good with what was now bad,
what was once almost easy with what was now
hard . . . the thing called progress, the event called
change . . . the sadness called fences and the
brutality called weather and distance. The dreams
were a shout into the past and the echo came from
the future to say there was no stopping it. And in
the middle of it, seeing Charlie Baggett and his
grave . . . and Wood, no longer arguing, no longer
shouting, his face in repose and life slowly trickling
away. It was a relief to be shoved from it, rattled
awake and shouted at until the night and the fire
were real and the wind blew sweet and cold across
the National Trail.

"Adam!" Wake up! Damn it. . . ."

"All right, Ben . . . quit stompin on me. I'm awake. What's the matter? Is it Wood?"

"No, it ain't Wood. Giles and Preble are gone! So's Peewee and all the horses!"

"What do you mean they're gone!"

"I woke up on my own. I don't know how. I guess expecting it and then not . . ."

"Never mind that!" Adam pulled his pants on.

"Well, I got Skinner up and we got to looking at the Dipper, and the Dipper don't lie. We went down to where Peewee had the horses and found them and Peewee gone. Well, we went out to the herd to see what was going on, and . . . like I said, Preble and Andy weren't there either."

"The herd?"

"Quiet. But what do you suppose has happened?"

"I don't know. And we ain't going to know until we find something to ride. Have Red wake the others."

They walked out to where the horses had been. Soon, the rest were out there too, looking and listening, talking and whistling softly so that if the horses were still nearby they wouldn't bolt and run from the shadowy figures looking for them. It was bad, and each man was tight with worry. A trailhand is awkward on foot, and they felt it now, stumbling around and cursing the dark. And the herd . . . without men on horseback to push them, to hold the cattle together, they would soon scatter and be lost.

An hour or so later, Adam bumped into Rev Marsh.

"Any sign?"

"No, boss. Nothin'. They wouldn't stray this far."

"No. Somebody drove them off."

The night grew older and Adam walked, wondering who it was and why, and what of Andy and John and Peewee? They hadn't just walked off. They were in trouble and whoever had forced them away had also driven off the horses to avoid being followed. Adam looked up at the sky and wondered how much time was left. There was an empty feeling that told him time was important. And the importance was not only in how long the cattle were left unguarded, but in how long it took to find his missing men.

For a long time, he heard the others call out now and then and the replies that floated back and forth were always negative. They might have to wait until daylight to find the horses, if even then they could be found, and maybe that was too long to . . .

Adam stopped and listened and heard something moving ahead. He saw a tall shape looming against the sky and heard a familiar nicker. The horse came to him and pushed against his chest with his nose. It was the bayo coyote, heading back toward camp.

"Good boy. Nothing's going to drive you off for long, is it? Good boy." He stroked the sleek neck and slipped the bit between the horse's teeth and climbed on.

At that moment, he heard a cry go up from one of the others.

"Here they are!"

"Keep talking, so we can find you!"

Adam rode in the direction of the voices and

found Skinner and Marsh on top of a low rise, looking down into a little pocket before them. Sweet hadn't reached them yet.

"You wait here and keep them in sight," Adam told them. "I'll double back to camp and saddle up. I'll bring one back with me and bridles for the rest."

"You got a plan?" Sinner asked.

"I'll take one man with me. The rest can drive the horses back in, and keep an eye on the herd until we get back."

Skinner nodded.

"You know, we're south of camp. Southwest to be sure."

Adam knew what the other was thinking. The fence they had cut was southwest.

It did not take long to ride back to camp and saddle the bayo coyote and suspend another saddle from the horn. With extra bridles and a saddle blanket under his arm, Adam turned around and retraced his steps. He rode hard, unmindful of the dark, trusting the bayo coyote to pick his ground. It only took a few minutes to return to the others. It might have been encouraging to be mounted again, but so much time had been lost already.

"All right. Skinner, you come with me."

Skinner saddled up after he caught his horse, and the others got ready to push the remuda back to camp. The horses were quieter now, with familiar voices making the darkness around them commonplace. Adam and Skinner turned away and rode southwest.

"See anything?" he asked after a little while.

"Yes," Bob was leaning down from his saddle.

"There's tracks all right. Looks like six or seven horses."

It was slow, following the markings cut faintly into the earth. In some places, they lost the trail entirely and had to circle around until it could be picked up again. They kept it up, pushing, trying to press time back and cover ground. But it was not until they had gone back almost to Bear Creek, crossed by the herd two and a half days before, and the first glimmer of dawn came that they were able to pick up speed and really move.

The wind freshened and a gentle rain fell for a few minutes. It washed cold on their faces and smelled sweet and clean, but it blew on across the paling sky before it could do any good. Even if it had been enough, there would have been little joy in it. Neither of them could stop remembering Charlie's death, and Wood, who skirted close to it even now back in the wagon. The possibilities of this night just ending were just as grim.

"How far do you reckon they took 'em?" Bob asked.

"I don't think they had more'n an hour or two start on us, judging by what time it was before all of us turned in. We've come pretty far already. Bear Creek's only eight or ten miles ahead."

"Maybe them nesters got a notion about snaking them into the law for cutting the fence," Skinner said.

Adam grunted.

"If that's what they wanted, they would've tried to bring the law to us. I'm pretty sure that ain't what they had on their mind . . . in fact, I'm certain it ain't! Look yonder, in the trees!"

The trail swung over to a wooded area. A fire flickered there. Coming closer, they could see horses, and men sitting around the fire, and suspended from the limb of a tree, three ropes.

XX

I'm a poor lonesome cowboy.
I'm a poor lonesome cowboy.
I'm a poor lonesome cowboy,
And a long way from home.
I ain't got no father.
I ain't got no mother.
No father and no mother,
To take good care of me.

—POOR LONESOME COWBOY

JOHN PREBLE STARED at the sky and watched it grow pale. The time for talking was done with. The time to be angry, and the time to argue . . . the time to be frightened . . . no, it was still time to be frightened, and to think . . . that was all that was left.

Thirty-two years on earth. Not a long time. As brief as the little rain that had fallen. It was time to wonder how much he had done with it. How much of value. He had followed the longhorn cow ever since he left grade school. Longhorns to the day he died. What would he have done with a longer time?

No fancy ideas, he thought. *It would never have changed. Cattle and the drives, and women, and once a girl who sweetened her bed with the petals of roses. Your life is as complete now as it would have been if you had lived for a long time to come.*

162

But no resignation was that simple. He could come to terms with death, but now there was a lonely feeling, an emptiness.

It would have been better at home. In some place he knew. Not here under these unaccustomed trees, but back in the gentler air and the remembered scent of agarita.

He glanced at Peewee, seeing him taut with the fear and the agony of it coming too soon. Not understanding . . . not much more than a child. What had he known in his short years? A brief happiness, a brief belonging, and before that, nothing . . .

And Giles, close to tears . . . older, with more behind him, and yet who could say he wasn't losing most of all? The time of children, the small faces in his life, the wonder of watching them grow. The woman of his final and lasting choice . . . the dream to plant the earth with seed and change its face to green.

The sky was growing lighter rapidly, and one of the sodbusters grinned and pointed at it.

"Won't be long now, you Texas boys!"

Giles closed his eyes, and Peewee stiffened, running away from it in his mind. Preble kept his eyes on the sky. Plenty of time for the final misery when the rope took hold. He wanted to look at the sky and the trees and the grass out beyond in the first light. It was a pleasant world, in spite of everything . . .

"You ever seen a hangin' before, boy?" The leader walked around the fire to the ropes.

"No, I ain't, Dutch," one of the others replied.

"Well, you goin' to see one now! Let's get horses under 'em."

They came and jerked them to their feet. The

bindings around wrist and leg bit hard when the numbness began to creep away.

Dutch grinned.

"You Texas boys got any last requests?"

"Yeah," Preble hissed, "just untie me and meet me in the middle by the fire, one at a time!"

"I allow that might be a pleasure. But I don't guess there'd be enough of you to go around. And we ain't got that much time, Texas boy! In fact, time has just about run . . ."

The clatter of hooves came suddenly, and the dust came kicking up, and before it could settle, the same thing happened from behind. Preble looked up into the angry faces of Adam and Skinner.

"Stand where you are!" Adam ordered. "Bob, untie our boys."

Skinner climbed down and untied Preble. Preble rubbed his legs and wrists.

"Get your horse, John," Adam told him.

Giles was next, and then Peewee.

"You boys all right?"

Giles nodded, unable to speak. He watched the first rim of the sun poke fire into the sky and touch the treetops with red.

"They was going to string us up just about now," Preble told him. "Look out!"

Adam had seen the gun coming up at the same instant Preble had seen it, and fired in that direction. The nester dropped the pistol and stared at them dumbly, and then fell.

"I've got a notion to hold a little rope dance of our own! I don't like sodbusters shooting my men, and then coming around in the middle of the night to ride more of them off at gunpoint. I don't like having three thousand head of cattle jeopardized and my horses run off."

Preble saw the thought sink in. He saw faces turn white and the shine of sweat.

"Scares you, don't it! The idea kind of cuts you in half," Adam grated the words between his teeth.

He motioned the others to start moving out of there.

"You're lucky. I ain't got time to do all that digging afterwards," he said, beginning to back out himself. "But let me tell you something. Don't let us see you again! Take a good look at your friend on the ground there and remember my advice!"

Preble spurred his horse, and they went away from there.

The herd was grazing peacefully when they returned. Skinner and Preble and the rest ate breakfast. In spite of their rescue, there was sadness in the camp. Baggett was dead, and Wood showed no change. The last few miles had been expensive. Peewee sat looking at the ground, unable to eat.

"I don't know . . . how they done it, Mister Childress . . . I just don't know . . . the horses started running, and somebody grabbed me . . . and they had Preble and Andy, and . . . they were going to hang us . . . I thought I was going to die . . . and I kept wondering how it was going to feel and . . ."

Peewee burst into tears, and Adam tried to comfort him, but the boy tore loose and ran behind the wagon.

Adam poured himself a cup of coffee.

Peewee Hand . . . almost a man, almost a child.

Caught in that uncertain place between. He had already seen two men die. Floyd and Charlie . . . and Wood slipping down the frightening edge of it . . . and then those ropes, and feeling the end coming. How close it would seem in the cool of morning. Fear, of the final sort, and time slipping past . . . and then, incredibly, safety as the last minute came. It had taken time for full awareness to come, to look back and think. The horses in his care . . . seeing them driven off and feeling like he ought to be big enough to do something about it and then failing . . . fear, humiliation . . . yes, and shame because of the tears he could not hold back.

It was hard.

XXI

Oh, Lord, I've never lived where churches grow
I love creation better as it stood
That day You finished it so long ago.
— THE COWBOY'S PRAYER

THERE HAD BEEN a great darkness, and dreams, and faraway voices coming from some unspeakable void. There had been a chilled Presence, and then a battle with heat. There had been half-remembered places where time and light existed briefly and then slowed and vanished to become a gentler sleep. The fight in the dark was over.

He woke to the rattling of the wagon and the smell of coal oil jolted out of the lantern. The light he saw was real and earthly and soft, coming from the front of the wagon where Red and Cimarron sat. From outside, the sound of cattle and horses . . .

There was no need to move, to look around, to drink or eat. He adopted this little world and drifted in it, listening to wood groan against bolt, the slap of canvas and the turning axles beneath. Water sloshed wetly in the barrels lashed on the outside not far from his head. He could watch the reflected light of a day move slowly across the canvas inside from left to right, down one side and across the front of his shirt and up the other. And when it faded, there was darkness and a smaller, flickering light and the smell of smoke, the rattling of pans from the other end of the wagon. There were voices then, and if he listened and sleep did not come too soon, he could find out how far they had come, where they were, and where they expected to be next evening.

And then the wheels didn't turn anymore, and the wagon was quiet, and the smell of coal oil faded. For four days now, they had not moved. They were just north of the Arkansas, and it was the thirtieth of June. They were stopping for a while to try and put flesh on the cattle. Red had told him this when he came in the first day of the halt to feed him the strong, hot beef broth. Four days now. Now was when hunger, thirst, and restlessness, and awareness of being alive came to disturb.

Wood had been asleep during the times when Adam had been able to shake his duties and check on the boy's progress. Red had been able to keep an eye on him during the day as he drove his wagon. But now, Wood was not sleeping as much. They could talk.

Adam stood thinking about it, out from the cook fire a short distance. It wasn't easy. It was pride, he supposed, and stubbornness, and the lack of patience with the young. Wood had lost his temper and said some pretty hard things. And he, in turn, had done the same. No matter about the bullet wound or anything else, it would not be easy to speak the first stiff words. It wouldn't be easy for either one of them.

He went over slowly, and climbed into the wagon. He could barely make Wood out in the dancing, reflected light of the fire.

"How do you feel?"

There was silence and Adam felt more awkward than before.

"Not so bad."

"We were worried about you."

"You're a good doctor, Adam."

Adam relaxed and laughed softly in the darkness.

"I've set a few bones, and it seems like they always come out stiff or shorter than before. Never took a bullet out before. The only time I ever saw it done was when my mother took that ball out of Papa's leg . . . too far back to remember anything excepting getting sick from looking."

The silence fell again, all the worse it seemed for what felt like a sudden and long speech. But something had to be said, and he couldn't make it come. He thought of backing out into the open air. He had paid his respects. Perhaps it was enough.

"Get me out of this wagon, won't you?" Wood broke the silence.

"I don't think you ought to."

"It won't hurt anything. I'm all right. I want to get out where I can breathe and see the stars. I feel like I remember waking up a thousand times to see the inside of this wagon."

"Well, maybe it won't hurt. Red? Give me a hand."

Adam and Red carefully lifted Wood out over the seat. They wrapped him in blankets and carried him to the fire.

"Not so close!" Wood protested. "I don't want to bake!"

"The nights are getting cool. You got to keep warm."

Red left to resume cleaning up his gear. Wood stared into the fire for a while and then watched the stars. He seemed to wander among them, half asleep.

". . . Listen, boy . . ." Adam began awkwardly. "About the other day when you got shot . . ."

"Don't worry about it. That's all done with."

"No. I shouldn't have taken off on you like that."

"Let's forget about it."

"We can't."

Wood looked at him and nodded.

"I guess not," he said. "And I suppose the first thing to do is be honest about it. I can apologize for losing my temper and saying some of the things I did . . . but I can't apologize for saying you were wrong in tearing down that fence."

Adam tossed a pebble into the fire.

"A cowman's first interest is grass and water and the critters he puts on it. I guess he loves his cows more than anything else. Hell, let him find a dogie who's gone potbellied and will be runty and never amount to much, and he'll give the little feller his first taste of milk, and fuss and worry over him until he can do for himself. He'll half kill his crew taking his cows out of a bad place to where there's grass and water, and it's the cows who eat and drink first, and then the horses, before that miserable sack of rattling bones called a cowhand gets his turn."

Adam went and got two cups of coffee and brought them back.

"It's natural then, that anything that cuts down on his supply of grass and water is going to be his enemy. Bad weather, plows turning the grass under, bobwire . . ."

"I know," Wood said. "I understand that. But look at those people. Maybe all they can ever remember is being crowded up against somebody else, with no chance of bettering themselves. Out here the country is open. Here he can bring his family and make a new start. He has the weather to fight, and the soil to fight. Maybe some of them don't make it. But some do. Their crops come in, and they get to where they can build a decent house. Soon you've got a little farming community. This is how the country grows. You're wrong in trying to fight them. And even if you were right, you can't stop them. That's the way it's going to be."

Adam said nothing for a long time. He felt anger coming again, and he didn't want it to come. He looked up at the Dipper . . . *el reloj de los Indios* . . . turning slowly.

"Remember that fence? Charlie caught one there, too. He's dead."

"Baggett?"

Wood set his coffee down and stared into the fire.

Adam thought of the slower, deadlier things other than weather and stampedes and the deep currents of rivers. He remembered the slender, shining strands of wire.

"Charlie was one of my best friends," he said, the words tasting bitter.

"I guess," Wood murmured, "I'm supposed to say I told you so. Maybe I'm supposed to be angry. It's not a part of my nature to understand men who kill over a piece of wire. At home, these things are settled on paper and in court rooms."

"Charlie's cashing in don't mean anything to you?"

"Of course it does. But . . . well, his shooting at someone is as strange to me as going up to another man's property and destroying it. We wanted to save a few miles, and they wanted to save their fence. What was accomplished? A man lost his life, and another will remember pulling the trigger for the rest of his life. And we had to go around, finally, after all. It's all so damn irrational! And the worst of it is, I've got an idea you'd do the same thing all over again tomorrow."

"The stubborn old man who's had his own way too long," Adam repeated Wood's words of the other day and wanted to laugh.

"As long as you're bringing it up . . . yes."

"And maybe you're right about the next fence, if we come up against one. Probably because there's nothing for me and the rest of the boys if this thing closes us out."

"I don't see why. Methods will change, but there'll always be men raising cattle and a demand for beef."

Adam shook his head and stood up. Angrily, he took the cups back to the wagon, wishing he could find a way to explain the thing inside. He was as sorry as hell about what happened at the fence, but a man couldn't give up his own kind of life and the thing he believed in because of the death of a friend . . . especially when the friend had believed in it too. If men had stopped crossing rivers because a man drowned in one . . . if men stopped trailing cattle because a friend had died in a stampede . . .

if a man lowered his weapon at the first sting of a Comanche arrow . . . where could it all have gone . . . where would they be?

But beyond that, how could he explain this wonderful thing that was held and kept by not stopping . . . where death was a moment for regret but no more significant than a stirring of dust. This wonderful thing was grinding to a halt, dying at the edges. The numbers of the enemy were many and growing too fast. He cried inside now, and sickened against it. He was tired, but he couldn't stop and wouldn't, and how could Wood be made to understand?

Adam took a deep breath. What did it matter? What difference did it make whether the boy understood or not . . .

"You better get some sleep."

Wood nodded.

"I think I'll sleep out here. I'll be warm enough."

Adam got an extra blanket and stretched it over Wood and he seemed close to sleep. Adam started to walk away.

"Adam . . ."

"Yes?"

"I've seen and learned a lot of things. Some of it I like, and some I don't, and I guess I still deserve to be called Arbuckle."

"You're doing all right."

"Well, I wanted you to know one thing."

"What's that?"

"Getting away from what's right and wrong and what has to be and all that . . . I don't like to see it happen either."

Wood went to sleep and Adam went to spread his roll.

He wondered what bright dream the future held for Wood and others of his age. It would hold many things, no doubt, and Wood was the kind who could go far in it, once he found what he wanted.

But what of himself? What was there for him? He was getting old, and perhaps he need not worry about it too much. But it was a sad and lonely feeling.

Bitterness welled up in him, and it couldn't be shaken off. Being squeezed onto a narrow trail, away from the free places and the better way . . . forced on to it by plow and wire, by guns and fence posts and time . . . by so many things . . . and Charlie was dead. Charlie would have understood and gone ahead at the fence, even if he had known what was coming . . . but nevertheless, Charlie was dead!

Adam sat up, knowing there would be no sleep that night. He rolled a smoke and sat watching Wood sleep. Anger returned to bolster bitterness in spite of the boy's comment. He had liked Wood and liked him now, but he felt resentful about it. Wood seemed so far away. Wood and his eastern notions . . . he didn't have to like or dislike a man according to that man's ideas. That wouldn't be fair. Each man had to have his own beliefs. But as far as he felt about Wood, it seemed different. He wished Wood would somehow wake up some morning and see everything as he saw it. Wake up and understand . . . but he wouldn't.

If only time could be changed and the boy could have come into this wonderful country sooner, back when things were new and its life was young . . . the way it was when he himself had left home

and, looking for something, struck out on his own
... home, how long ago it was. What was it he had
looked for ... the final place, and dreamed-of
place. He had looked for it, like Wood. Perhaps no
man ever found it, or could really identify it ahead
of time. But the country as it once was would have
been enough.

XXII

We've reached the land of hills and stones
Where all is strewn with buffalo bones.
O buffalo bones, bleached buffalo bones,
I seem to hear your sighs and moans.

—DAKOTA LAND

THEY LEFT THE grazing ground near the Arkansas on July third, and the long way and the familiar names met on the older trails reached out and touched them on the new, the National. White Woman Creek and Ladder Creek, Smoky Hill River and the Little Beaver, and the ever-remembered Republican and Arikaree. Each a marker, a reminder of the distance behind, and of the time ahead. It had been a long way, and it remained a long way. Not until the seventeenth of July, when they reached the South Platte and crossed into Nebraska with the National behind them, did any of them feel that the northwest was close at hand. By the nineteenth, they were at the North Platte.

Rev Marsh stirred against the shaking and woke with Skinner looking down at him.

"It's time, boy. You awake?"

Rev nodded and sat up, and shivered in the cold

air. It was almost one o'clock. Skinner aroused Preble and rode back out.

They dressed quickly, cursing the cold, and then went to the fire and gulped scalding black coffee.

"You better get yourself a new coat, Rev."

Rev shrugged and wished they'd leave him alone and quit acting like he was a kid who didn't know how to take care of himself. Maybe he did need a new one, but he wanted to do his own deciding. Maybe it was prideful, but he wouldn't get one as long as they kept pushing. Adam didn't go around telling Preble he needed new boots, and Andy didn't go telling Peewee his pants were wearing out. Nobody told anybody that, except him.

"Let's go. Skinner and Arbuckle are waitin'."

They rode out and took over, and the endless circling continued for the night.

Rev wrapped the reins around the saddle horn and folded his arms against the cold. His night horse knew where to go and what to do. There was nothing to do but watch and wait while the Dipper turned and brought the dawn.

Coyotes sang somewhere in the darkness, and the mellow owls spoke too, and the moon cast a pale, milky glaze.

It was an odd time. A time for sleeping . . . even the earth slept . . . when a man simultaneously thought of sleep and yet adventured in the dark like a child on a summer night. A rock, a tree, a patching of grass . . . each was one thing in sunlight. But night transformed them, and man never grew tired of playing there or stopped feeling the mystery brought by the moon.

Along about three in the morning, the cattle gave a sudden start, and some stood up, sniffing at the air. Rev came to, and realized he had been dozing.

He bit off a little chewing tobacco and worked up a little juice. He got his finger wet with it and rubbed it under his eyelids. The burning and stinging was ferocious for a little while, but it kept his eyes open.

The cattle stood on the alert for a long time.

"What was it?" he asked when he came around to Preble.

"I don't know. I saw something move over there, but I was too far away to make out what it was."

"I thought they's goin' to run."

"They was close to it. It went by just like a ghost, and them critters snorted and rolled their eyes."

Rev glanced around warily, feeling more chill than the night provided. He didn't like the idea of ghosts.

Lots of folks went around saying there was no such thing.

He wasn't so sure.

He hadn't ever seen one. But he had seen some mighty peculiar things happen. Like with cows. Lots of ordinary things could make them run. A loco steer suddenly jumping up and crashing his head to the ground with a bellow. Or a man riding too close to a sleeping steer without whistling or singing to let him know he was there. But how many times had he been with a herd that ran for no apparent reason?

It was times like this that he wished he could see the owls that made the owl sounds, and the coyotes who made the mournful crying. Sometimes the sound of them seemed connected with death and dying, and the dark places of night where a man

should not wander . . . connected with the bones of
buffalo, where some skinner had done his work
years before. White in the moonlight, mouldering
with the seasons. This whole area was strewn with
them.

He shuddered and sang a little to drown out the
things he heard and felt. After a while, the feeling
passed.

The deeper darkness and the sharper cold that
came just before dawn touched him, and he looked
at the Dipper and saw thankfully that the night
would soon be over.

It was in the complacency of this moment that it
happened again, and happened where Rev could
see it.

The dew in the air was causing a thin, trans-
parent fogging close to the ground, and the apparition came slowly and silently toward the herd. It
looked like it was not touching the ground, but
gliding gently over it.

Rev felt the air catching in his throat, and the
sudden shock paralyze his whole body.

The cattle snorted and stood up, bawling nervously.

Rev wanted to scream, to call out, but his open
mouth could make no sound. He wanted to pull his
horse around and run, but he couldn't unwind the
reins from the saddle horn. He wished he had a
pistol, feeling that the vicious report of a .45 and its
screaming slug would somehow make things all
right.

Night had a way of disguising an image, of dab-
bling in illusion. The apparition slowly changed
shape with shadow and light and lessening distance. The gliding ceased and took on a slight up

and down motion. Shapelessness resolved itself.

Rev watched it happen and felt himself go limp, perspiration dampening his shirt.

It was the old Mex.

The cattle quieted again. They still stood and watched, but it was the eternal curiosity of the longhorn and no longer nervousness.

The old man walked toward camp, and finally out of sight.

"You see it?" Preble came around.

"Yeah. It was Cimarron."

"You know, it don't seem like he ever sleeps. I'd like to know what he's up to."

"This ain't the first time, you know," he told Preble.

"You mean he's gone out wandering before?"

"Well, I ain't seen him out by the herd before. But the last two mornin's, he ain't been in camp when coosie was fixin' breakfast. He was two, three miles ahead, sittin' and waitin' for us. You didn't see him?"

"What was he doing?"

"Nothin'. Just sittin' there wrapped up in that blanket."

"Well, we'd better tell the boss or he's going to have them cows running at everything that moves!"

They rode on around, making their separate circles.

When they came in for breakfast, Rev took his plate over to where Adam was and squatted down. He nodded to Wood, who was almost back to normal now.

"How y'feelin', boy?"

"Except for a little soreness, fine."

Rev turned to the boss. Adam wasn't eating. He looked tired and haggard, older. He only drank coffee, and sat staring red-eyed at nothing. Preble joined them.

"Then cows almost run last night. Twice," Rev told him.

"How come?"

"Cimarron was wanderin' around out there."

Red Bellah came over.

"The old man again?"

Adam nodded, his face grim and almost white.

"What's he walking around at night for, Red?"

"I don't know. But we're getting pretty far north now, and he knows it. If I ever saw an impatient man, it's him."

"Goddamn it, what's he up to?"

"I think he's all right, Adam."

"Yeah, that's what you keep saying," Adam's voice grew loud. "First he doesn't talk, and then he chases a mirage and pulls a knife on Wood! Then he starts wandering ahead of the outfit! Now this! *Sure, he's all right!* Tomorrow, it'll be something worse and you'll still say he's all right!"

Rev saw Red watch Adam with concern in his eyes and shake his head.

"I know he's acted strange," Red admitted quietly. "But I can't help feeling sorry for the old man. Don't ask me why. I don't know. Let me have a talk with him."

"How's that going to stop him from doing something else!"

The others around the fire nodded in agreement.

"I think he ought to leave now," Preble spoke up.

"My sentiments, exactly," Adam said flatly and stood up.

"Wait, Adam," Red planted himself in front of the boss. "Just what's chewing on you anyway?"

"Nothing's chewing on me!"

"But this ain't like you! You ain't been one to turn a man out to starve. But that's exactly what'd happen. You'd be condemning the old horse to his death. Look, boss, there's not a man here who doesn't wonder about him or who isn't suspicious. Lord knows he's acted crazy enough. I'm the only one who works close with him, and I still say he's all right. Whatever is bothering him has nothing to do with us. I'm sure of that. And all he needs is a little talking to. I can straighten it out."

Adam took a deep breath and sat down again.

"All right, Red. You have your little talk with him. I've got a herd to deliver on the Musselshell, and I'll do it with or without him. Make sure he gets that straight."

The discussion ended, Rev finished his breakfast and stretched out for a few minutes to rest until it was time to move on.

Cimarron still sat out beyond the fire, facing north, as if there were something to see there.

XXIII

The river's way back, and it's dry ahead.
One more mile, and these cows will be dead.
                              —THE OLD CHISHOLM TRAIL

AS TIME PASSED and the miles fell behind, it became more and more necessary to stop and try to fatten the herd whenever the opportunity presented itself. From the North Platte, they moved northwest to Snake Creek, and northwest again to Box Butte Creek, where they remained from the twenty-third of July until the sixth of August. Then, on to the Niobrara, and north to the White, and they exchanged Nebraska for Dakota Territory by the ninth. They met the approaches of the Black Hills, shimmering in the haze of heat, and stopped at the Cheyenne with spirits low.

It was here, too. The dryness. It was no longer mentioned. The cattle waded into the Cheyenne and drank long and deep. Their bones were showing again, and their motions were that of long-suffered weariness. Hope was gone. It would not change now. The men watered their horses and filled the water barrels and looked ahead into gathering night and wondered how it was ahead, and knowing at the same time it was no different.

Of the three hundred Herefords, two hundred and fifty and perhaps less remained. Some had fallen behind, unable to hold the pace. Some had succumbed to Texas fever, and some wandered alone, somewhere back where they had stampeded and scattered in the darkness. With the longhorns they had been fortunate in losing eight or ten and no more, and those few had been the ones who had gone lame and could travel no more. Some were left in hopes they would recover and wander home again, as they sometimes did. The hopeless ones were put out of their misery, and if there was no room in the wagon for the meat they provided, the carcasses were left on the trail and clouds of buzzards rose behind them.

The dryness . . . For now, there was nothing to do but eat and settle back to relax for a while. The sound of the Cheyenne was in their ears. Here, there was water, and for the night they could be numb and not think about it.

At a little after nine, Adam looked up to see two men riding into camp. They were a ragged, gaunt looking pair astride equally sorry-looking mules.

"Evening," Adam said.

The two nodded and climbed down, glancing at the pot hanging over the fire.

"I'm Pink Edwards," the first one said. "This is my partner Sol Witson. We ran out of coffee and salt and sugar last week. Your pot smells mighty good."

"You gold hunters?" Adam asked, absently.

Pink Edwards nodded, worrying about the coffee.

"Yeah, but what we found you could lose sneezing on it."

They were quiet for a while, almost in an embarrassed way, until Red suddenly stood up.

"Help yourself to the coffee. I'll rustle up some grub."

"Thank'ye," Edwards grinned. "Much obliged."

Red dished up a couple plates and brought them over to the two visitors.

Adam ignored them and remained silent. He didn't want to think about anything or talk to anyone. He only wanted to sit and watch the fire for a while and hope that he could sleep later. Really sleep. It seemed like ages since he had really slept.

When they were finished, Pink Edwards drew his sleeve across his mouth.

"You headed for the Musselshell?"

"That's right," Red told him.

"I never seen the like of it. Why, I never saw so many goddamned cows in my life! A month ago, I clumb to the top of a hill, chunking around to see if I could find any color. I looked out and saw 'em coming and going for miles!"

"You been to the Musselshell?" Red asked, glancing over at Adam.

"Yessir. I seen it. And if you boys will take my advice, you'll turn those critters around and go back. The range is overstocked up there. They got more cows waiting around up there than the grass can feed. I heard the price was dropping fast. I ain't had nothing to do with cows myself, but I talked with them as did. The price was low to begin with, but it's dropping anyhow. You'd do better to just turn around and go back."

Adam kicked at the fire and watched the sparks rise. It was no surprise. Everything else had happened to make trailing them tough. Why not this?

With bad grazing, cattle became poor, and because
of the resulting low price, not as many would be
sold and moving out. Bring in more herds from
Texas on top of this, and the circle became only
tighter.

"Too late for us to turn around," Red muttered.
"Even if we do get a bad price or do no more than
break even, it's better than we'd do heading back
through all that dry country."

Sol Witson, looking out toward the river, gave a
little grunt.

"Wait until you leave the Little Missouri!"

Edwards spat into the fire.

"Dry as bone dust. Next water after the Little
Missouri is the Powder. Sixty-five or seventy
miles!"

Adam stood up and wandered away from the
fire. He didn't want to listen to it any longer. He
pulled his bedroll out of the wagon and walked out
a ways with it. He took his boots off and in a sudden fit of anger slammed them to the ground and
sat with his face on his knees.

In a little while, Red came out to where he was
and hunkered down beside him.

"They leave?" Adam asked.

"No. I told them to throw their rolls and spend
the night. You heard what they said?"

"Yes."

"Maybe it's time to leave this goddamn trail."

Adam shook his head.

"I know this country. It don't make no difference which direction we take. It'd be dry."

"Then I guess it's hold them on the Little Missouri for a spell, and then go across. It'll be hard,
though."

"Did you think any of it would be easy?" Adam snapped.

"No. I don't reckon I did," Red eyed him quietly. "You all right?"

"I'd even be better if I was left alone!"

Red nodded and stood up and left without saying another word.

The camp quieted and sleep came easy for those near the fire. But Adam lay in his roll, staring at the haze-reddened stars, thinking.

The long miles, insufficient grass, low water, stampedes, fences, nesters, a bad market, and a low price, Herefords lost to the fever . . . and two men dead. Two men suddenly gone . . . and now *a seventy-mile dry drive!* He groaned and rolled over and rammed his fist into the sandy, dried up earth.

Seventy miles, and after it was done with, the trip still wouldn't be over. What more could be added to their troubles?

He loved those longhorns. It seemed like the good Lord had looked down on Texas and said this was the kind of cow they needed down there . . . just like the wiry little mustangs turned out to be indispensable for the country where the going was hard. What other kind of cow could walk and walk, for two thousand miles and more?

They could hold them on the Little Missouri for eight or ten days. They could hold them there for a month, but it would do only so much good. Seventy miles was seventy miles no matter how it was crossed and no matter how much water they drank first.

There had to be a limit somewhere . . .

XXIV

I'm in my saddle before daylight
And before I sleep the moon shines bright.
                                    —THE OLD CHISHOLM TRAIL

THE LITTLE MISSOURI was the last water. It was not
easy to contemplate the seventy miles that lay
beyond, stretching burned and dead to the Powder
River. They stayed there for ten days in preparation, and for each of the ten, they hoped for a
change in the weather that might alter the situation. A little rain, or even unproductive clouds to
shield them from the sun and make their trip across
it more bearable.

But it didn't come in that time, nor did any
clouds. They remembered bitterly that there had
been no reason to expect any change, and the hope
died for what it was.

The first day of September was one that should
not have been. No man could rise with its beginning and think with complete conviction that the
day, inevitable as it was, was to be accepted and
taken with a shrug. They arose at a time long
before dawn when the deceptive dew was still on
the grass, and wished this day and the next, and the
one following could somehow be skipped and for-

gotten as if the time and place had never existed.

It was not so much of themselves they thought as they gathered around the fire and ate and drank their coffee. The days would be hot, but no hotter than before. And it was hard, staying in the saddle from dawn until midnight, but it was nothing they were not accustomed to doing and certainly not as hard as some of the things they had done in their lives.

It was the cattle that were ever present in their minds. The cattle would be without water for the better part of three days. Seventy miles. Cattle were a business, and even in the best of weather they were walking to their death. But this made no difference.

The longhorn was a creature of breath and blood and intelligence, and a nobility the like of which had never before been seen. But it was more than that. These men led a lonely life. The fact that a cowhand had the other men in the outfit to talk to, to see, to work with, had little to do with it. It did not take into account the long hours of the graveyard when all was darkness and the man he worked with was way over on the other side of the herd. It did not take into account the long months on the trail when a man grew tired of the same faces and longed to see new ones. It was natural that he be lonely, and in this loneliness, find some communion with the animals in his care, to find affection for them.

Adam Childress was tight-lipped and grim as they moved them out that morning before light even began to show ghostly pale in the east. It was the same for all the others. Even Charles Wood of Boston, still fairly new to this, was aware of the brutality of the thing they had to do.

The morning was deceptive. The grass was wet and the air cool, and the cattle accepted the fast pace with ease. They were well on their way by daylight, and by noon, ten or twelve miles were already behind them.

Wood watched Adam through the morning, wondering at the sudden spark, the energy and interest that was in such sharp contrast to the way he had seemed the night before and so long before that. He seemed glad about this dry drive . . . or was it unreasoning defiance? All natural reactions to this ordeal seemed cast aside, the final straw accepted with abandon. He even seemed reluctant to make the midday halt.

They ate, and sat around for a while.

"It must be almost one o'clock," Wood guessed. "Aren't we ready to go again?"

"They have to rest a while," Adam told him.

"They seem to be doing all right. Maybe it won't be as bad as we thought."

"It'll be bad enough," Skinner grunted. "This is just the first half of the first day, and no different than any other day so far. You just think it's different because there ain't no water ahead. Wait and see how restless they are tonight when we make a dry camp, and watch how they slow down tomorrow. The third day will be the one, Arbuckle. You'll see how bad it is."

Ben Sweet looked at Wood with worry in his eyes.

"I remember a dry drive like this one. On the second evening they began to drift. And a drift is just about as bad as a stampede. You can't turn them or stop them. I don't know what it is. They get it in their heads to move off in another direction and they keep going. Maybe they think they smell water. I don't know. But this bunch I'm talking about began to drift and all we could do was go along for the ride, knowing they'd stop sooner or later. Well, in the middle of the night, a lightning storm blew the lid off and they ran. They came to a bluff. The leaders saw it and tried to stop, but those behind didn't and kept piling up against the ones in front and pushing them over. If I remember right, we had eight hundred head, and we counted three hundred or so at the bottom of the bluff in the morning."

Nearly an hour later, they got a change of horses and began again. The hard pace, the fast walk which seemed almost a trot. Pushing them across the distance, with the heat coming bad now, the ghosts of it shimmering and rising before their eyes.

The longhorns seemed to take it without much effort or visible strain, but the shorthorns began to cause trouble.

Wood fell back often to give Andy a hand in keeping them up with the rest of the herd, and Adam filled in now and then where Baggett used to ride. As the day wore on, the heat worsened.

Dust boiled up and caked in the folds of his shirt. It gummed the lids of his eyes, and the glare tortured them. He couldn't breathe without drawing dust into his lungs and aggravating an already constant thirst. His bandana had long since ceased to be of any value. It was the same for everyone else, and what touched them, touched the cattle even more, and the Herefords worst of all.

It was obvious they were going to lose more of the shorthorns. They simply were not made to walk. They were not lean and tough as were the longhorns. They were the first to suffer and the suffering came quickly.

By nightfall, some were falling too far behind and no amount of coaxing could bring them up again. Adam waved them off.

"Let them go. Maybe they'll catch up during the night. If not, it can't be helped. No point in killing off your horses trying to save something that can't be saved."

Evening brought a little relief. The air gentled and cooled and washed their eyes with darkness, but it was not the relief water could bring. Not the kind cattle could find, feet planted in cool mud, with water belly-high and cool in their mouths and the sweet scent of it on the air. But at least they could stop for a while and rest while Red practiced his art. They got up only to eat, and then stretched out on the ground again.

Adam waited for the aching in his bones to subside and wondered why it had to be. This weather . . .

It was bad enough to take shorthorn cattle along in the best of times, and now it was as bad as it could be. He didn't like shorthorns. He had no use for them. But they were animals, and maybe all right in soft pastures. He did not like to see them left behind or suffering. The fact that they did not belong on the trail did not matter now. They were on the trail and in his care, and too many would be lost before the seventy miles were done.

And those longhorns . . . standing out there

hollering for water. He wished he could go out and talk to them, make them understand. But there was no way. He had to listen to them until the rest was over and they were moving again, and he would be too busy finding their way in the dark to think of anything else.

Wood shivered in the cold air, his tired body offering no resistance to it, but it was better than the heat. The dry beds of creeks they crossed in the darkness were a reminder of tomorrow, but at least the dew would be heavy on the grass before morning.

Andy Giles untied the brown ducking jumper he kept lashed behind his saddle and put it on. Maybe it was just as well, for himself, that the drought was on now, he thought. When the winter and spring rains came again, he would be buying his section of land and putting it to the plow, and planting. He'd watch the land transform into something green and living . . . a beautiful thing all of his own, producing the things he had planted with his own hands.

It was a dream that made the dryness almost not matter. Yes, it was just as well the drought was this year and not next. Winter and spring would end this. The rains had to come.

Ben Sweet rode up in front, behind Adam, watching the North Star, wishing they could follow it and not the trail marked out with buffalo skulls. He hoped that the two gold hunters had somehow been wrong.

Red Bellah followed at the rear, with Cimarron jumping down now and then to grab a piece of wood and throw it in the coonie. They needed wood. That was certain, but they needed water more. Water to drink, water to cook with, and water for the coffee. He listened to the water sloshing around in the barrels. It was getting low, and he wondered how long it would last.

And that portion of darkness which precedes midnight went on forever, the hour when they would stop for the night perpetually receding in the distance. Stiffness and fatigue became a pain and then progressed beyond all feeling, and time hardly mattered any more.

They were used to long hours and long miles, but there was a limit. A man would open his mouth to complain, but he would remember the cattle and hear the silence of the others, and the complaint went unvoiced.

When the Dipper finally indicated the hour, the herd was halted and a dry camp made. A double guard was posted around the restless cattle. The rest turned in quickly to get what little sleep could be enjoyed. They had covered more than twenty miles.

Rev Marsh stifled a groan when Red's bull voice drove everyone from sleep. He sat up quickly and pulled on his pants and boots and rolled up his bedding to toss in the wagon. He was the first to grab a plate and begin eating, and he found pride in that. Pride in his body, and pride in his ability to shrug off and ignore the fatigue he felt.

John Preble dressed slowly and painfully. He had dreamed of the girl he had once known and always thought about. The Mexican girl who sprinkled her bed with rose petals. He wondered why she had vanished and what had happened to

her. Where was she? She had been like no other . . .
tall and dark-eyed. The day would come when he
had his own spread, and a wife and children, and
the wife would not be a Mexican girl. She was
gone. But the brand he would use would be a rose;
and the wife and the children would never know
why.

"Come on, John," Skinner grinned at him.
"You're too tired to be thinking about women, and
Red ain't going to wait forever!"

The second day was no different than the first.
Not in itself, but the cattle now showed signs of
suffering. It was harder to make them hold the
pace. They bawled constantly, and their tongues
lolled out, strung with thick ropes of slobber.

The wind died that morning and let the dust
hang in choking clouds and made a bad condition
worse. More of the shorthorns and a couple of
lame longhorns fell back and were lost. Those that
had been left behind the day before had not caught
up.

Time seemed not to move, suspended in dust and
heat that would go on forever, and the animals
they led looked like dying animals, and moved as if
heading by instinct to some vast and hidden bone
yard. It was a bad dream that encompassed not
only darkness but bright daylight as well.

Once during the day, everyone saw what looked
like a cloud, and the word was passed back and
there was hope. But it had been only the dust of
another herd ahead . . . stampeding perhaps, their
violence sending the dust high into the air. It was
gone in a while and the day returned to its slowness
and torture. It lasted until the sun slanted low and

was lost and the sky changed from blue to orange and to mauve and the stars came out. And even then, it did not stop because night too was unending.

The third day came as if they had never known anything else, normal times forgotten, the easier miles a thing of an unremembered past.

The cattle hung their heads low, their tongues lolling, swollen and dry, and the pace they held was an automatic thing beyond awareness and feeling. They could not take much more.

The thought couldn't help but come to each man. Maybe the gold hunters were wrong. Maybe it wasn't sixty-five or seventy miles. Maybe it was eighty miles or almost ninety, maybe more . . .

Maybe they would arrive at the Powder with only a pitiful, staggering and near-dead remnant of the Mexican Spur herd. And worst of all, maybe by now the Powder had gone dry too.

In the afternoon, Charles Wood chased after a longhorn that had wandered from the bunch. It showed no sign of knowing he was there until his horse grazed its side and then it reacted violently and in sudden fright. He began to notice it in the rest of the cattle. They staggered and stumbled against one another, stepping in holes and on rocks that jutted up out of the ground, as if they didn't know they were there.

Wood edged up to John Preble.

"What's wrong with them? I've never seen them act this way."

"The dust, heat and glare, lack of water. They're just going blind."

"What do we do about that?"

"Get them to water and it'll go away in a couple of days."

They halted at sundown, and there was still no sign of the Powder. They talked of going on that night. The Powder could be only four or five miles away. But on the other hand, it might not, and both cattle and men had reached too great a stage of exhaustion. It was agreed that it might be better to wait and start again in the morning. The dew would be on the grass, and the cattle would have regained some strength. They could be on the Powder before the heat came, more than likely . . .

Sleep was drugged and dream-filled. They slept on rocks, distributed at uncomfortable places beneath their bedrolls, doing it deliberately so as not to sleep too deeply with the cattle as restless and jumpy as they were that night. Dreams and the thought . . . five miles to go, maybe eight or ten . . . not so far. Not at all far on another day. But with all they had endured in three days, no man could feel with certainty that it could ever end.

Only Adam, who had ridden on briefly while the others slept, to try and locate the Powder, had seemed relaxed . . . free of the bitter thing that had held him since Baggett died. Perhaps it had been purged in those hellish miles. Or maybe it had been only put aside. But everyone had noticed it. And it was the first time anyone could ever remember hearing Red Bellah hum a little bit under his breath as he worked over his fire.

XXV

Powder River, let'r buck ... she's a mile wide ...
an inch deep ... full o' dust and flatfish ... swim-
min' holes for grasshoppers ... cross 'r anywhere ...
yeou ... uhh ... yippee ... she rolls uphill from
Texas.

—UNKNOWN

WHILE THOSE IN camp slept the troubled sleep of
the near dead, there were those unfortunate souls
who rode the kill-pecker on the night of September
3. There had been no sleep for them since the night
before, and indeed, little chance to even get out of
the saddle. Twenty-two or -three miles, stop,
change to the night horse, and then continue on
like this in the endless circle around a restless and
tortured herd. Andy Giles, Wood, Marsh, Skinner.
The guard doubled, although Wood could not see
how four men could do anymore than two, if the
cattle ran.

The night was still, there was no wind, and it
seemed like there might be a frost. The only sound
to break the silence and the deathliness was the
bawling of the cattle and occasionally from far
away, the grieving of a coyote.

Charles Wood, immensely tired, slumped in the

saddle and once again resorted to the distasteful task of rubbing tobacco juice under his eyelids.

It was perhaps the singing of Rev Marsh, and the endless circling as much as the efforts of the dry drive that made the desire for sleep so powerful.

It was a long way from Boston. The trail from Brownsville. Even the last few miles, since they left the last water, had added an immeasurable distance. But the distance was not in miles or the span of a country. It was in himself, and the thing he was doing, and the way he felt.

He thought about home, and for a moment thought longingly of the soft bed in that upstairs room. He remembered the hot baths and rich food and the fine liquors, and it seemed like a precious dream . . . but no . . . with it came his father and his ever-ready pocketbook, the never less than kind word, and his mother wrapped in her self-appointed grandeur . . . no, even this was better, and the hardest ground would be all right. He couldn't ask for more. He didn't want to. Just to sleep.

Wood remembered the girls he had known. Alicia Pomeroy, and the Benton girl, the young women in his little circle, and the ones who were not so young. He had never felt a real need for them, because they were always there.

It had been a long time, but strangely he felt no great need now, and hadn't at any time since he left Boston. There was a need, yes, but it was new and clean and fresh.

Away from them, and given a chance to breathe and think, he felt that he could see them more completely. He had known that those he had spent his time with in Boston left much to be desired. But looking back on them now, it was almost a shock to realize how false and avaricious and stunted some of them had been, compared with women like . . . like Katherine Nance.

He shook his head and thought of himself as being ridiculous. He had seen her for only a few moments.

One did not come to know a woman in this manner. There had been no chance to talk and argue and laugh together, to come to know each other's face, so that it was etched sharply in the mind and not left to hazy patterns of retrospect.

And yet . . . these things were not quite true.

He did remember her face, clearly and easily. It followed him like a warm and scented cloud.

He remembered her soft voice. And he did know her. A woman who would, without question, bathe a strange man because he needed to be bathed . . . who would spoon soup into him and care for him as if she had known him all her life . . . a woman who seemed to care whether he got a job or not . . . a woman who spoke directly and honestly and stood straightbacked and solid on her feet. . . .

Was this not easy to know?

He'd like to see her again. He had thought of her a lot lately. But when the trail ended in Montana Territory, who knew where he would go from there? A memory was all she could ever be.

Wood looked up at the North Star. Where from there?

The old discontent, the wretched feeling of unwholeness and wasted days . . . the frenzy of not belonging, and of looking . . .

It boiled up again and then vanished. He was too tired to think about anything but blessed sleep.

He nodded and slumped more, and the tobacco juice lost its power.

The horse moved on in its accustomed circling, patiently around the bawling herd, and the night grew older.

In the chill and deep darkness, the cattle began to agitate and move around more than they had before. It seemed at first that they were merely going after the dew on the grass, but then it was obviously more than that. Wood came around to Rev.

"What's doing it?"

"It's that ol' *ladino,* boy. He's acting up. Keeps tryin' to wander off west, jus' like he don't want the sun to find him here."

Skinner came over in a hurry.

"That brush popper is going to talk the whole bunch into running. I'm going to drop a rope on him and lead him out a mile or so. Arbuckle, you better go in and ask the boss what he wants done with him. I reckon he'll want him shot."

Wood nodded and headed for camp, glad to depart from the monotony of the circling, if only for a little while.

He roused Adam from his sleep and told him what was happening.

"All right, tell Skinner to shoot him. Only tell him to make sure he's far enough away so that the shot don't make the rest run."

Wood mounted up again, and rode out to the herd and took the direction Skinner had taken with the old steer. In a few minutes, he caught sight of them a short distance ahead.

"Adam says do it, but far enough out to not stampede the rest."

"That's what I figured. Well, over by that rise ought to be far enough."

"It's a shame."

"Shooting this old boy? Yeah. He's something ain't he? But sometimes it's better to shoot one than to have the whole shebang stirred up and run and maybe lose five or six. Here, take the rope and wrap it around your horn, and hold him steady. I'll go around in front of him and. . . ."

"Hold it!" the yell and the sound of a running horse came from in back of them.

"What's the matter, boss?"

Adam reined in and the relief in his face was obvious.

"Bring him back, Bob. I've changed my mind. I got an idea we almost lost a good bet. He's smart, and he's been trying to go somewhere. All right, take him back to the herd and then let him go."

"He'll take the whole herd with him," Skinner grumbled.

"Exactly what I was thinking about. You seen how he steps right out into the lead like he owned the herd? And when we come to high water, he don't hesitate but jumps right in like he was showing the rest how easy it was. He's a valuable old cuss. Too good for shooting. I'm not so sure I'll even include him with the herd when we sell out on the Musselshell. Come on, bring him back. I think he's going to lead us to water."

They returned to the herd, with the *ladino* following reluctantly at the end of the rope.

"Turn him loose. I'll get the rest of the boys shook out."

The *ladino* did what they thought he would do. As soon as the rope was taken off, he struck a straight line to the west. He bellowed, but he did not run, nor did he pause to graze the wet grass. He walked in a steady, deliberate way, head up and proud as if this were any day of the year.

The herd stirred again at his insistent calling and began to string out behind him.

"Makes you feel sort of useless, don't it?" Adam said to Wood, and Wood grinned and nodded.

"You know, Wood, my sense of direction tells me to keep to the north. It seems like we ought to cut the river there. But sometimes it's better to leave it to a cow."

"There's isn't any wind. How could the *ladino* know?"

"He's been hiding out in the *brasada* too long not to have a better sense of smell than the others. And if it ain't that, then it must be instinct, and don't ask me how that works. All I know is that now and then a longhorn will know there's water around. Something tells him where it is and he goes to it. That's all."

"It's a good thing the National is behind us. I wonder how far off course he'll take us?"

Adam tightened visibly, and rode on ahead without answering, and Wood was sorry. It looked like Adam had not forgotten the argument at the fence, or the one by the fire when he first left the wagon, in spite of seeming more like himself these last few hours.

They rode for nearly two hours, placing their faith in the *ladino*. If the wild one was wrong, they'd have even farther to go by daylight, to get to water.

Then with dawn almost upon them, the cattle began to quicken in their walking and a yell went up in front.

"Let 'em go! Let 'em go! It's the Powder!"

The cattle plunged in and gloried in it after the dry miles. Ben Sweet, who had not taken time to dress, climbed down off his horse and ran out into the shallow water in his long underwear and sat down to laugh and play like a child.

The Powder River. The dry drive was over.

XXVI

. . . and the cattle on a thousand hills.

—PSALMS 50:10

IT BEGAN TO come to an end. The rivers that, into
the depth of a continent, had signaled the incredi-
ble distances behind and the despairing miles
ahead, now signaled the end of the journey. Montana Territory was gained on the sixth day of September, and then, almost magically, the Tongue
River, the Rosebud and the Yellowstone. It seemed
to have come suddenly, as if they had not been
aware; as if the time when they were still far away
had been merely yesterday. But still, there it was
. . . those last rivers and creeks, the mountains, and
then the valley of the Musselshell opening up
before them. The eighteenth of September.

It was as the two gold hunters said it would be.
The range was overstocked, the grass was bad, and
the watering places low. Adam Childress shook his
head grimly and dismounted. It was the drought of
course, that made things bad. Weather always
made the big differences. But there were many
things in evidence here, and a sense of desperation
that could not come from weather alone. He could

not put his finger on any one part of it and say this
was the cause.

It seemed related to the small streams that
festered in stagnant little pools when they should
have been deeper and running and fresh. The
beaver had been trapped too heavily. His dams had
collapsed and vanished, and the water they would
have held and conserved through the dry season
had run off too quickly. Part of it was the number
of herds visible in the area, and the number that
must have been there just beyond sight in the hills
for miles around. There would always be a market
for beef, but there was too much here, and it
couldn't all be attributed to the fact that the
drought and low prices were causing cattlemen to
hold and wait for better times. There was a feeling
that the cattle companies, with their English and
Scottish and German and American bosses had
greedily contracted for too much.

Part of it was the same sense of time running out.
The same specter of the fence, too many boots, too
many walls rising. The tide sweeping over the land,
building, trompling down the earth, shoving aside
what used to be.

He remembered leaving, as a boy, the one piece
of land, the one house with its four crowding walls
. . . the small, fading adobe, with the smell of
leather and frijoles . . . with its iron, Spanish gate
that opened on nothing and was supported on two
posts but not a fence, and yet somehow belonged
because it was his mother's one real treasure . . .
leaving, and uprooting all that was familiar in him
and looking for the new and open grass. The feeling had come a thousand times since, but it was

strongest now. Get out. Leave this place while you can! Time has gone here . . .

"Looks bad, don't it?" Red muttered. "No place to hold them."

"After we've had some grub, I'll go over to the company and talk to Barnaby Hall and see what's to be done."

The Mexican Spur bunch was thin. They had recovered from the dry drive somewhat, but the way the grass had been, they could improve only so much. The fact that the drive from Texas was over would help considerably, but first they had to find range land not too far away where they could graze and grow lazy again and cover some of the gauntness.

Red built his fire and supper was fixed and the boys came in from the herd. They ate and sat around the fire, but none of the exuberance of trail's end enlivened the hour.

"We ain't going to stay here are we? Looks like sheep country," Ben Sweet said.

"Well probably moved out a few miles," Adam told him.

Adam finished and stood up. He climbed on the bayo coyote and sat there for a moment.

He could see cook fires scattered through the valley, and the glow of them here and there in the hills, and he wondered how many there were he could not see.

There would be those trying to fatten their herds for a few weeks, and those standing by to sell, and those already on their way home. There would be those, too, who failing here would go on up to Fort Benton, or to Canada to try and sell their beef.

Adam quietly spurred his animal around and headed in the direction of the Musselshell Cattle Company buildings.

The buildings, hasty structures that stood bleak and cheerless in the dark, were closed for the night. Adam dismounted and looked around. He saw the glow of a cigarette and a shadowy figure sitting on the front steps of the main building.

"Know where I can find Barnaby Hall?"

"He'd be in his cabin. That one over yonder," the man pointed.

"Much obliged."

Adam walked over and knocked on the door.

"Come in. It isn't locked."

Adam stepped into a sumptuously furnished little room. He walked on deep carpet, amid expensive furniture that didn't fit the rough timbers of the walls and ceiling. Hall sat at the far end, at a table. Hall was a short, bandy-legged little man with a growing paunch that directed his belt buckle toward the ceiling. He had circles under his eyes, heavy eyebrows, and a large red nose and a brush-type mustache that seemed to emphasize the mouth which slanted down to one side. Hall was eating, and the food was rich, and a near-empty bottle of brandy sat at his elbow.

"I'm Adam Childress, Mister Hall. We met in '84."

"Of course. Now I remember."

Hall shoved the bottle toward him, and Adam shook his head.

"I've got nearly three thousand head waiting south of here."

"Yes. I remember our contract."

"I need to fatten my herd. Where can I find some

decent grazing for a couple of weeks?"

Hall smiled and shook his head.

"I wouldn't say there was any decent grazing. You can move out thirty or forty miles west of here and do fair."

"I expected that, but it's my only choice. We won't even talk money yet. I'll come back in two or three weeks."

Hall shoved his chair back and pulled out a cigar.

"Frankly, Childress, I'd advise selling now. Save you time and trouble. The situation isn't going to improve."

"Maybe not, but at least I stand to gain a little on what weight I can put on them in that time. What are you paying?"

"About eight dollars. Depends on the condition of the animal."

"Eight dollars!"

"Well, they're only worth two seventy-five a hundred weight on the market, Childress. That means they're worth about twenty-seven a head. Out of that we have to pay expenses. Nobody's making much profit these days. I tell you what. Get some weight on them and maybe I can go to nine or ten."

"Ain't much profit for Jake Nance in that. We'll be lucky to break even! He's in a bad way now."

"Well, it's better than last year," Hall reminded him. "And you can't expect the old high prices this soon. Remember, market price dropped down to a dollar eighty a hundred weight last year."

"Hell," Adam muttered.

"The only thing I can say is that it can't get worse."

"You're certain of that?"

"As certain as anybody can be in this business."

"In that case, I'll hold to my original idea of waiting."

"I wish you luck, Childress. And if things don't pan out this year, maybe next year will be like it used to be."

"Good night, Mister Hall."

Adam left and got his horse.

He tried not to count the number of fires he saw, nor listen to the crackle of short and dry grass under his horse's feet, nor smell the dust that rose too quickly and too easily. It seemed prophetic of something.

Times were bad. How could it be worse, when all the things that had happened were remembered. Thinking about how much of a fight it had been, he could only realize how constant a companion bitterness and anger had become. So constant that awareness of it had dropped away until a fresh reminder like this scene around him brought it to the surface again. But how could it get worse? The fight was over. They were on the Musselshell.

The changes he had seen? It might be that the things Wood talked about were right. Of course they were true. Time would come when the trails were gone, and every cow that went to market rode the shining steel of the railroad. That was certain.

But not yet. He wouldn't have to worry about it in his time. Once the cause and cure of Texas fever was found, the trail could move west again, west of creeping progress.

Plenty of time. . . .

So what was the prophecy he could feel but not read?

It whispered darkly around him and the wind that rose was not a friendly wind.

His horse snuffed at it, as if he too found something wrong in it, and they went on in the darkness, not watching the fires.

He found Red Bellah sitting on a rock, some piece out of camp. Bellah was watching the sky.

"If you're looking for rain, it's useless."

"No, I ain't looking for rain. It's something else, and I can't figure it out. Watch them coming across the moon."

Adam looked up at the moon and the dim light of its final quarter. They were flying across it, their sound coming to him now. Birds, great flights of them winging south. The cry of geese came faintly, and the formations were orderly and as one remembered. But there was a sense of warning here, a feeling of wildness and panic where wings touched the moon too early.

"Just about every bird you ever saw. And right after you left, an arctic owl flew through the light of our fire. I've seen them in Canada, but never down here. And deer, too. Moving south. The boys out with the herd saw them by the dozens."

"Migrating," Adam said.

"It's too damn early for that!"

"Maybe a big fire somewhere. It's certainly dry enough."

"If there was a fire that big, we'd see signs of it in the air."

"Well, I suppose it could be the drought, but . . ."

Adam rolled a smoke. None of it made sense.

Adam rode on into camp and turned his horse over to Peewee. He went to the fire to pour a cup of coffee, and had settled down in its comforting glow when he heard a strange noise. Adam turned to look.

Cimarron was sitting on the wagon seat, wrapped in his blanket. He was rocking slowly from side to side, moaning or chanting something ... Adam couldn't tell. Sometimes it was meaningless, and at others it was like Latin, and the sing-song thing a priest did. But whatever, it was misery overflowing in the old man, and the misery came from the sky.

XXVII

They answered well their purpose,
But their glory must fade and go,
Because men say there's better things
In the modern cattle show.

—N. HOWARD THORP
SONGS OF THE COWBOYS

THEY MOVED WEST as if the trail had not yet ended, moving them out of the cattle-company ranges. One day, and then two, and still they had not found open ground. There were cattle everywhere, and brands they had never before seen. The men were the same. They all had that tightness around the eyes, the haunted angle to their shoulders. The time was bad, the place was bad, and they all had cattle that needed a month on good grass. A man could only wait and do the best he could, and hope the next year would be better. All it took was rain. Water to soak into the parched earth and cause the eternal miracle of grass to rise and reach for the sun. Only rain . . .

They received friendly nods from the Texas outfits, and cold, hard glances from those who waited with native cattle.

"I reckon we weren't the first to think of moving

out from company ground," Ben drawled.

"No telling how far we'll have to go," Adam said. "Maybe another day or two. Well, maybe we'll be lucky. Might be that in three weeks or a month we can all broomtail it home."

"It's going to be a cold trip."

"Yes, but we'll be heading home, and it ain't never as cold riding in that direction."

"It'll be good to see the home range and Brownsville again."

"We're all due for a bust. The boys are pretty tired. I don't reckon any of us counted on it being like this. I thought we'd get them up here fat and heavy and sell them right off and be back crossing the Red or even get home by the end of November."

"We're doing all right," Ben smiled. "We've chewed tougher leather than this."

In the middle of the afternoon, the evidences of other herds began to thin out and grass began to improve. Adam spotted one camp and rode over to get word about what it was like beyond.

The old man was from Texas, as was obvious from the rawhide coonie stretched under the wagon.

"Coffee's hot."

"Thanks."

Adam got a cup and poured the thick, black liquid and then hunkered down near the old man.

His face was wrinkled and leathery, deep with the color of weather and the years of sitting in the smoke of a fire. The old man kept his eyes fixed on some point in the distance.

"I reckon you're lookin' for a place to hold your herd. Well, there's some cattle out yonder, but

you'll find yourself some ground. Don't know
what good hit'll do, or what difference'd come of
hit. Sell now and go broke or graze 'em a month
and go broke. This grass wouldn't put taller on a
grasshopper!''

"It sure is bad. I've seen plenty of dry years in
my time, but never anything to beat this one.''

The old man nodded and spat bitterly.

"You ain't likely to see any more of hit, good or
bad.''

"I wouldn't say that. All we need is some good
rain and she'll straighten out. There's always a
market for beef.''

"Why shore," the old man agreed. "But you
watch. Prices are so low we're all gettin' busted.
We'll all go home with nothin' but the duds we're
wearin'. We'll be sellin' off our holdin's so that our
women and kids can eat. I don't stand to make
anythin' I can call my own. Had to borrow money
last year after we lost ever'thin' in the blizzards,
and I had to borrow to trail this bunch. There'll
always be cattle, but hit's goin' to be Herefords like
them you got mixed in with yours. And they'll be
goin' by rail, shipped by the boys who still got
somethin' to stand on while the likes of you and me
watch our land shrink. You own that brand or are
you just trail boss?''

"I'm trailing for Jake Nance. The Mexican
Spur.''

"I know that 'un. Down near Brownsville . . .
well, you're a little better off if'n you didn't own
nothin' to begin with. I own the Three Sevens.
West Texas, on the Pecos about a hundred miles
from where she hits the Grande. I'm gettin' too old
to trail 'em, but I had to save on wages. Got three

sons, and they're ridin' this 'un for nothin'!''

Adam listened, nodding in sympathy.

"Well, I think you're wrong. We'll all be up here next fall, and up to our knees in grass with fat cattle. The rain will come."

The old man snorted impatiently.

"You forget all the railroad tracks you seen, and the fences and sodbusters? And how about them foreigners runnin' the companies and contractin' for more than they can rightly handle?"

"The National Trail won't be so bad, when there's enough rain to keep the grass coming. As long as that's there, fences and nesters and the railroads don't need to bother us."

"I guess you ain't heard the news."

"What news? We just got here."

"Well, a big chunk of land down near Lamar, in Colorado, got opened up for settlement. Seventy mile wide and a hundred and forty-five mile long, and hit sits right across the trail."

"But they couldn't!"

"Well, you know politickin', son. Hit don't seem to matter how many pieces of paper get signed, or how something gets turned into a law, there's allus a hole somewhere. The Bent Land District they called hit. Happened last month."

Adam took a deep breath and punched his knee.

"All right, then the trail can move west again!"

"Not as long as Texas cows got the fever hit won't!"

"Someone will find a cure for it. Soon now. Then we can move west, and I don't give a damn what anybody says about railroading. It'll never work. I don't care if they knock shipping costs down to two bits a carload, it'll still be cheaper and

better to walk them! You ever see a well-fed steer
climb down out of a box car?"

"That'll get worked out too, and hit'll happen
soon, and if you don't see hit comin', you ain't got
no more sense than a little nigger with a big navel!"

"You're an old fool!" Adam snapped, losing his
temper.

The old man chuckled instead of taking offense.
"We're all old fools," he told Adam. "That's
what's kept the trails goin' as long as they have."

Adam rejoined the outfit in a deep gloom. The
trail was gone. The one way that had been left . . .
gone, like the others, like the better times . . . angrily, he repeated his arguments in his mind and tried
to shut out the words of the old man and those of
Charles Wood, and the signs that were there to see
even when no one pointed them out. They were
wrong. They had to be wrong. A thing like that
didn't happen overnight.

They found their range late that afternoon when
the *ladino,* sniffing at the air and taking over as he
had done at the Powder, led them into a small valley cut off from their sight by low hills.

It was more than likely the small creek, fed by
year-round springs, that he had smelled. But by vir-
tue of the water, the grass was better there, too. At
one end of the valley was a deserted shack and a
barn. It was better than they had hoped for.

They swung the herd in, and after watering
them, bedded them down at sunset. Red set up
camp near the shack.

"It looks good," Adam told the boys. "I think
we can count on selling in a month and then head
for home. In the meantime, we've got a shack we

can fix up as a bunkhouse, and a barn for the horses when the weather gets cold. I reckon once all this is taken care of and we got time on hand, we can split in two and go raise the lid in Judith Gap for a few days. That agreeable to everyone?"

Shouts of approval went up.

"All right then. First thing in the morning we'll see what can be done about the shack and barn. When it's done, we'll cut cards to see who gets first throw at Judith Gap."

Preble closed his eyes and the expression on his face was obvious.

"Don't you think we ought to draw straws on who's going to cut them cards?" he said.

"I'll do the cutting, John," Adam grinned at him.

"The trouble with that," Preble muttered, "is that it'd be too honest."

XXVIII

I'll drive my herd to the top of the hill
And I'll kiss my gal, by crab I will!
                    —THE OLD CHISHOLM TRAIL

THERE WASN'T MUCH to Judith Gap. It was a raw
town in a raw country. It had its gambling houses
and dance halls . . . hurdy-gurdy houses made of
canvas or board or whatever material came to
hand. It was not pretty. Its face had not mellowed,
and its voice had not yet softened. As with the
country that grew too fast, maturity could only
come to it with time.

Wood glanced at his three companions who had
drawn the high cards for the first trip. Skinner and
Preble were obviously eager and hungry from the
trail. Giles found comfort in seeing buildings and
other aspects of civilization, rough as it was, but
Wood suspected he had little else than his family
and home on his mind.

For himself, it was a change, a brief respite from
the trail and nothing more.

"I'll tell you what," Preble said. "You stick with
me and I'll show you how to squeeze the most out
of this town."

"I don't know. I'd just as soon find a good hotel

and sleep in a bed for a change."

"Is that all you're going to do?" Preble acted as if he couldn't believe what he had heard.

"Oh, I'll have a drink and walk around after supper."

Skinner snorted.

"How about that, Giles? I don't think ol' Arbuckle here knows about women!"

"You think that's the way it is, Bob?" Giles chuckled, half-embarrassed. Preble drew up alongside Wood and took it from there.

"Well, he's damn well going to find out. This place has got 'em. Real women! And I don't mean squaws or Mex's or Chinee. Real women, Wood. Better change your mind and come with me."

Wood looked around him and saw ladies walking by with their fancy dresses and carefully powdered faces. It had been a long time . . . a long while of nothing but cattle and horses and men; hard things and hard smells and nothing to soften any of it but memory.

What little remained of that day went quickly. The sun went down and lamps were lit, and the thing they drank in from the time they arrived continued around them. The slamming music, the hoarse cries of men turning loose, the rattle of wheels in the street and the sounds of boots along the walks, the brittle, high-pitched clatter of glassware. After the silences of the trail, it was one unending explosion.

Andy went somewhere to write and mail a letter, and Skinner found a card game and a little luck and decided to stay with it for a while. Preble and Wood went to one of the dance halls and stood at the bar having a few drinks.

"This the place?" Wood asked.

Preble grinned.

"Any of these places."

Wood leaned with his back against the bar and watched the dancehall girls moving around from table to table. He presumed they were the women Preble had talked about.

One of them detached herself from a bearded old-timer and came over to Preble. Wood watched, her scent coming to him soft and fast.

"Hello, Texas boy."

Preble put his arm around her and kissed her.

"How about a drink?" she asked.

"Call one of your friends over here for my partner and I'll tell you what we do want."

"All right, honey," she looked him up and down. "I think that will be agreeable."

The woman walked away and Preble winked at Wood.

"That's all there is to it. Guess you never seen anything like that in Boston. In your saloons anyway."

"I guess not," Wood murmured and finished his drink as the woman came back with one of the others.

"Come on," Preble said, and they followed the women up the stairs to the second floor and down a dark hallway.

Preble slowed down and Wood bumped into him.

"See you downstairs, boy."

A door opened and closed, and Wood stood there for a moment until a soft hand found his and led him farther down the hall.

"In here," she said.

He might have slept for a moment or two, or let time slip by in the hazy dreaming of half-opened eyes, but then he rolled over on his side and looked at her. He saw then the bad teeth, and smelled the liquor and stale smoke on her breath. He saw the lines under her eyes, and the gauntness beginning in her cheeks.

He sat up and involuntarily looked around, as if what had happened a little while ago had only been a dream and this was reality and being awake . . . as if this was another girl, and the beautiful and desirable girl of a moment ago was gone, and this one . . .

He pushed away from her. How could all those things change in the distance of a room, in the shortness of minutes? From a soft and lovely thing to something so . . . It didn't seem possible. . . .

Wood stood up, feeling dirty and disgusted. He threw open the door and ran downstairs. A half mile out of town, he was sick in the cool night air.

"Back a little early, ain't you?" Adam greeted him by the fire.

"I had enough."

Wood felt the stiffness between them. The differences between two men seemed to come closer to the surface when they were alone together. It was almost an embarrassed thing.

"It's been a long ride, Wood."

"Yes, I know. I'd just as soon not talk about it."

"What's wrong? You run into trouble?"

"No. I just made a mistake, that's all. It's nothing."

Adam poured some coffee.

"You went the rounds with Preble, didn't you?"

Wood looked up at him in irritation.

"You haven't been inclined to be very friendly of late. Why do you concern yourself with my affairs now?"

Adam shrugged.

"Maybe I been kind of hard. But if I have or haven't, I reckon I ought to try and get along with a man working for me."

Wood turned away. He suddenly wanted to apologize. Adam had either shaken off the bitterness that had eaten away at him, or had buried it deep and was trying to make amends. But Wood was too full of the thing that happened at the dance hall.

"So I made the rounds with Preble. What does it matter?"

"It wasn't a bad idea. A man gets tied up and brittle out here."

Wood let his breath out.

"Call it a good idea if you want, but leave me out of it. . . ." He shuddered and put his cup down.

Adam remained silent for a moment.

"Seems to me they look pretty good after a long drive."

"Maybe to the others."

"What do you mean by that?"

"Remember what I said in San Antonio? I came out here expecting you people to be something like savages. What I saw when I was stranded in Texas . . . the kindness I received at the ranch . . . well, I was convinced otherwise. But now I'm not so sure. It takes a pretty low type of person to find pleasure in women like those in town!"

"You went to one."

"I must have been out of my mind!"

"Is it because they aren't as pink and new as your women at home? Is it because they forgot how to blush a little or how to pretend they don't know what you want? Wood, if I didn't know you, I'd say you were a fuzz-cheeked mama's boy who believed a man never thought about more than a kiss on the cheek!"

"Now just a minute . . ."

"Let me say what I'm going to say. Then if you want to start swinging, I'll oblige you! If you don't like those gals, that's your affair. But don't come riding in here thinking you're better than the rest of the boys!"

Adam turned away, knotting his fists and then letting them relax and fall loose.

"I shouldn't get sore. I reckon they are hard, and rough, and maybe they can't keep their skin nice and their teeth fixed. I'll allow the first time a feller sees one up close, it's . . ."

"I thought she was soft and pretty," Wood interrupted, a little ashamed of his own outburst. "It wasn't until afterwards that I really saw her."

Adam sat down and smiled.

"I know. That's the way it always is."

He kicked an ember back into the fire.

"They're about all there is, Wood. There's not many women in these towns. Too few, with too many men to go around. So don't be hard on them."

Wood looked down at the toes of his boots and tried to find anger and a reply. But he found nothing, and when he looked up again, Adam was gone.

Adam trying to help him understand. Trying so hard, beyond his own bitterness, as if it were important to Adam that he accept this life and like it. Why?

XXIX

Well, first it rained, and then it blowed,
And then, by God, it up and snowed.
—THE OLD CHISHOLM TRAIL

TIME WAS SLOW now. There was little to do. The
cattle, grazing in the small valley, showed no desire
to range far from water as had been natural for
them on the Mexican Spur range. While the grass
was burned and browned, and put weight on a
steer only slowly, it was at least abundant and
more than they had seen for perhaps five hundred
miles. Even the *ladino* chose not to follow his sense
of independence and strike out from there.

No more than two men at a time rode herd now.
It was not far to Judith Gap, and every one of them
had gone, some even two or three times. But the
short pay of the cowhand tempered it after a while.
So there was little to do but sit around the fire or
make up for all the sleep lost coming up the trail. It
was pleasant and welcome at first, but it too became hard, this waiting.

Wood pushed his bedroll against the wall and
used it for a back rest. He studied the pale afternoon light coming through the window. It was the
first week of October.

"I'd settle for a good book," he said to Ben. "Going into town is all right, but it's the times in between that get me."

"Them cattle are fattening up a little," Ben said. "Another two weeks ought to see us pushing them down to the company and then heading for home."

Wood shook his head.

"It isn't a long time, really, until I start thinking about it. Damn, I wish I had something to read."

"I got a book. Ain't had time to drag it out, and no need to. I don't read unless I'm by myself and ain't got someone to talk to. Want me to get it?"

Wood wondered what kind of book a cowhand would carry around. If any of these boys had gone to school they hadn't stayed long.

"May I see it?"

Ben rummaged around in his warbag and pulled out a thick little volume with terribly small print.

"Shakespeare!"

"That feller writes funny, but I guess I read it a dozen times. You know, I can still get all spooked up reading that one called Macbeth. Damn! Try that one or Hamlet when you're sitting out all by yourself on a dark, windy night in a line camp. Why, goddamn!"

"Where did you get this?"

"Arbuckle coffee coupons. I didn't know what it was I was sending for. Just picked a name on the list and sent her in. But shucks, it's the only way a man can kill time and keep hisself company. You sit out there, riding some during the day, making sure your cows ain't straying off to the next feller's range. Sometimes it can keep you busy and it ain't so bad. But mostly you're just doing nothing. A book's the best thing."

Wood looked at him in a new light.

"The others do this too?"

"Sure, when they get the chance."

Wood sat back without opening the book. He was going to devour every page when he got started, but right now he watched Ben and the others.

It seemed like they had to be ignorant and backward. Looking at the way they lived, he had never thought they could be any other way. A minimum of schooling, if any at all, and running off to be trailhands at an early age and then never knowing anything else. The way they acted and talked . . . he stopped short . . . no, not in the way they talked. Their English wasn't so bad. It was slow and drawling, and colored from the country in which they lived and by the things they did. There was a richness in it, rather than a lack. And the way they acted? How did they act?

Wild and reckless sometimes, but quiet and mature almost beyond their ages, too. And which was easiest to remember?

They would kill rather than be walked on, fight uselessly rather than be thought cowardly. But just as quickly, they would take up another man's fight, even a stranger's, if the fight was too one-sided and their sense of fair play was disturbed. It wouldn't matter how hopeless they found the odds. But here again, which would be remembered? The quick-tempered violence, or the almost knightly valor? Society was never kind. . . .

But put a man . . . a man of the highest education and finest background, born and raised in the civilization east of this frontier . . . put him with these men and let him work with them. Would he

not become like them in time? He would still be the
same educated man. But would not his thoughts,
his humor, his stories begin to come from the
simple things at hand . . . his cattle and his horses,
and his companions? Would not these things become the larger part of his thinking, regardless of
his background?

He looked at himself in sudden surprise. Had he
not come to be pretty much like them himself? He
had not ridden back to camp sick and disgusted the
second time he made a trip to Judith Gap. And he
had gotten drunk, too. Just as drunk as the rest.
And hadn't he tried to shoot out as many street
lights as the others when they rode, in a roaring
spree, out of town?

If these were the actions of the crude and ignorant, then he must call himself crude and ignorant. If he tried to excuse himself and say it was
merely circumstance, then he had to remember the
circumstances were theirs, too. And then understanding the circumstances with which a man lived
on the cattle trail, out in the lonely country . . .
how could he question the actions or attitudes or
beliefs of another unless he questioned his own?
How could he assume that another's sparing use of
words, his silence, was a wall to hide bad things,
when he found himself less inclined to talk? That
tremendous sky and the endless land and the
fathomless stars of night that made them so insignificant . . it was not a place or time for endless
talking.

He thought back to Floyd Rogers, and how he
had not been able to stomach the idea that Floyd
was a wanted man. He thought of Cimarron, the
mysterious old Mexican whose actions and silence

and strange behavior seemed to speak of dark places and evil ... who even now, for some unexplained reason, borrowed a horse every day and rode off to unknown destinations and came back to sit against the wall, not sleeping but retiring to some point in his mind to wait.

Circumstance ... only yesterday, these things were just the opposite. But now ... he could not question as strongly the old man's behavior as to whether it was good or bad. He felt no suspicion. Only curiosity. And Floyd, sleeping back there in the river many miles away. He did not wonder at the man's guilt or the ugliness of his face, but how lonely the man must have been.

Circumstance ... necessity ... the way a people had to live with it and not against it.

Adam came in then, and even looking right at him, it took a moment to realize what was happening. Preble was the first to look at Adam's hat and then out the window.

"Goddamn! It's snowing!" he yelled.

"It's too early!" Rev joined him at the window.

"It happened fast," Adam said. "Almost as fast as a Texas norther, if it'd had a little wind behind it. I don't think it means anything. Just squaw winter."

Wood stood up and looked out at the first snow he had seen since the train trip that had taken him away from Boston.

"Maybe it means an early winter," he said.

"Well," Adam almost whispered, "with all those birds and animals we've seen moving south so early, you might be right. They were six weeks ahead of time, but it could be just that."

Wood turned to look at Adam as he said it, but

instead he saw Cimarron who sat with his back
against the wall. His eyes watched the window and
rolled in some untold anguish. He rocked back and
forth, and sound rattled unintelligibly from his
lips.

Wood woke that night to find Adam standing by
the window watching the snow. Wood lay awake,
unable to go back to sleep. He watched Adam step
out the door and walk for a way into the crisp
white silence to look at the sky for a moment and
then come back to stand shivering by the window
again.

"How does it look?" Wood dressed and joined
him.

"Still coming down. I don't like the look of it."

"I wonder how often this happens up here?"

"How long they last is the important thing.
Why?"

"No particular reason."

"Worried about how cold it's going to be on
night herd?"

Wood sensed a little irritation in Adam's voice.
He let it pass, attributing it to the fact the snow had
Adam worried.

"No. But it is something to think about."

"Why I should think that'd be one thing you'd
be used to, the way it snows around Boston!"

"In Boston," Wood found himself using pretty
much the same tone of voice, "we don't spend
more time in it than is necessary."

"You don't think night herding is necessary
when it's snowing?"

"It is, now that we're here."

"What do you mean by that?"

"I was thinking how smart the others were. The ones who shipped by rail and were out of here before we even were halfway."

It was a mean thing to say. Just as mean and pointless as the whole conversation, and Wood knew it. But it was the truth.

Adam stood there, shaking.

"Don't ever mention railroads in this camp again!"

"Why not? Since when can't a man say what's on his mind?"

Adam grabbed him by the front of his shirt and gave him a shove. Wood sprawled on the floor and saw the trail boss turn and walk into the snow. Several of the boys stirred and grunted in their sleep, but did not awaken.

He got up and followed, his boots crunching loudly in the new snow. He grabbed Adam by the shoulder and turned him around.

"You better go back inside, Wood!"

"No, not yet! I don't like getting shoved around for speaking my mind! I've got a feeling that what I said was too true for your liking. The truth bothers you. It's there to see. Railroads, fences, new towns. Maybe you think it'll all go away if nobody talks about it."

"Take your hands off me, Wood!"

"And I have an idea it goes deeper than that! Maybe back to that fence . . . pigheadedness has its rewards, Adam! Old Adam Childress comes to a fence and finds it personally inconvenient. So old Adam Childress says let's tear it down. Now he can't forget it because he knows the people who put the fence there had a right to shoot, and now poor Charlie is . . ."

Adam jerked away and swung and the blow glanced across Wood's cheek. Wood shook his head and walked in, burying his fist in Adam's stomach. The old man grunted and doubled over. Wood brought one up from the snow, but Adam stepped around it and landed one that put Wood on his back.

"Get up," Adam grunted, his breath coming short.

He got to his feet and moved toward Adam slowly. The trail boss was crouching a little, waiting.

"Come on, Boston boy!"

Wood stood there without raising his arms.

"What's the matter, Wood? Had enough?"

"Suppose you find out?"

Adam bellowed and came in swinging. Wood ducked away from the blows. As Adam nearly ran past in the speed of his rush, Wood came down with a hard chop on the back of his neck. Adam stumbled and sprawled in the snow. He got up, slowly, and Wood hit him again, and the snow in Adam's hair flew in a diamond spray. The trail boss slumped and fell and was still.

Wood watched him for a moment, breathing hard. The falling snow felt good kissing his face.

He started to walk away, but the old man groaned and he thought better of it. Wood got his arms under Adam and lifted him and carried him back to the bunkhouse.

Red was stirring around and his head came up at the noise.

"What happened?"

"Fell off his horse," Wood told him. "He's all right."

"Oh," Red said and turned over.

XXX

They're feeding in the coulies,
They're watering in the draw,
Their tails are all matted,
Their backs are all a-raw.

—I'M A-LEADING OLD DAN

WHEN THE SNOW finally stopped, almost two full days later, it was deep enough to block the creek that had traced a welcome line around one side of the valley. Until it melted again, there was no water for the cattle. And it was ironic about the grass. Grazing had been good by comparison with any other they had seen. They had been lucky to find it, and for a while it looked like a reasonably happy ending to a drive that had been little more than one problem after another. But now they had to paw down through the snow to get it.

Adam rode around the herd, watching the clouds of steam that rose from their breathing and the warmth of their bodies. The longhorns were not so bad off. Their instincts and ability to survive came from their totally wild ancestors of a recent past. They attacked the snow with their long forelegs and got down to grass. The shorthorns

233

stood in small, pathetic groups. Some half-heart-edly made the attempt to get down to grass, and others fed where the longhorns had cleared a patch, but mostly they stood and bawled help-lessly.

The herd would manage. Longhorns had sur-vived worse times. But it was still not enough. The herd could do no more than hold their own. They could not gain the weight they needed.

He would have to hold here. Hold until the snow melted and wait some more in hopes that the herd could gain enough flesh.

But grass and water were not the only shortages. Even without this snow to remind them, it was ob-vious time was running out.

There had been a tendency to wonder at the strangely early migrations of bird and animal, and the presence of the arctic owl that far south. Man could look at a function of nature, and if its pulse did not match his own or seem logical, then he was inclined to look for other explanations . . . but it was simple enough to see now. Winter was coming, and it was coming early.

Adam turned back and headed for the shack.

Red Bellah was cooking the midday meal. He had pulled the wagon up against the shack when the snow had begun, and stretched a tarp out from the roof to provide a shelter and a place to work. The boys filled their plates and carried them inside, and Adam started to go in and talk to them about what must be done. But Wood stopped him at the door.

"What do you want, Wood?"

"I want to apologize, Adam. We've been avoid-ing each other, and there isn't any sense in it."

Adam brushed past and got the attention of the crew.

"I think we got a good spot here. There was water, and about the best grazing we could hope for. The question is how long can we hold here."

Adam put his plate down and rolled a cigarette.

"We'll all get our wages, so that doesn't enter into it at all. It's Jake Nance who comes out of this either in one piece or a broken back."

"We'll stick if you want," Ben said quietly. "You're boss."

"Yes, I'm the trail boss. But I'd be a damn fool if I didn't value the opinions of the men working for me."

"All right," Ben drawled. "What's your idea?"

"I say stick. I think the snow will melt and we'll be all right. Give them three more weeks here, sell, and head for home in the first week of November. I know you boys was hoping to start back sooner, and I ain't forgetting it means a cold trip all the way. But we might pull this thing out of the hat."

Ben nodded, and Adam waited for the others to agree or disagree.

"November it is, then," Adam said quietly.

The weather warmed gradually and the snow began to melt. It happened as Adam hoped it would. By the end of that week, it looked pretty good. The snow didn't leave the ground entirely, and perhaps it wouldn't before the real snows came. But there was enough grass exposed and the little creek ran free.

Spirits rose, and the boys found time to make the ride to Judith Gap to break the monotony.

Adam remained in camp with little doubt that he

had made the right decision, and what little worry remained he could not name. It seemed to come in the shadows of evening, just before the lamps were lighted and their soft glow filled the shack. For that was when Cimarron usually returned from his strange rides out to unknown places.

"One of these days," Preble said, "I'm going to follow him."

"Forget it," Adam advised. "We'll be going home soon."

But Cimarron still huddled in his place by the wall like a soul possessed. That was when the small, unnamed worry came like slow contagion.

XXXI

Then the blizzard howled, and I froze to my saddle,
And was up to my eyes in dying cattle.
                    —THE OLD CHISHOLM TRAIL

THE SNOW that had fallen in October had never really left the ground. Where the feeble sun touched, and where a warming wind could blow, it had melted and let grass come into sight again. But elsewhere, in the shade, in the deep and protected places, it held on like a promise. But the promise turned gray and crusted and insignificant because the days were good. Had it not been for a knowledge of time . . . had they slept for months and awakened to this, it might have seemed like early spring.

When the time came to move back to company ground, Adam looked at the sun and the cattle and decided to stay just a little longer.

"Go give Judith Gap a loud good-by," he told his men, "and when you come back we'll move them in and sell."

They talked of going home, like children, but time was gentle, and a few more days didn't matter. Jake Nance had been good to them, and fair. So for his and the Mexican Spur's sake, squeeze a little more out of that gentle time. It made no difference. Find the women once more and drink hard once more. It didn't matter whether they left tomorrow or had left weeks before. Winter would blow hard against their backs before they reached home.

So they went, and came back on the evening of November the third, and the timing seemed just right, for the men riding out to take the graveyard found clouds blanking out the sky and a stillness to the air that spoke of a coming change in the weather.

Before daylight had a chance to come, every man was in the saddle, fighting to keep the herd together and knowing they had stayed too long. They could only ride in astonishment and wonder how a blizzard could hit so quickly . . .

The winds screamed and grew. The snow came in heavy, scudding curtains that stung and blinded and took an instant foothold on the earth. Light never really came. The cattle bawled in abject terror, and putting it to their backs, began to drift.

There was no way to stop the drift. In the instincts of every frightened animal there was a wall somewhere, the gentle side of a mountain where the weather changed. It did not exist here, but perhaps they looked for it and nothing could turn them. But, if nothing else, they had to be held together for the warmth and protection of their own bodies. If they were allowed to break up, they would be scattered hopelessly, and some, if not many, would perish before the storm ended.

There was no time to eat. One at a time, when strength began to ebb, the men could ride in hard and gulp down the scalding, reviving coffee Red

kept going, change horses, and then ride back into
the wind that seemed to have lost all barriers from
pole to pole . . . the world, lost and dark, and bar-
ren, helpless against this thing that battered and
gripped it and howled almost alive.

Time was lost.

The day came and went and the darkness which
followed was little different. They rode like ghosts,
like dead men who had forgotten to be tired or cold
or frightened.

Perhaps for a time, Adam dreamed of the gentle
evenings at home, with the smell of beef turning
over an open fire, and the Mexican beans, and the
folks of neighboring ranches coming to call . . . and
how brother coyote would smell the goodness on
the wind and come to sing from not far away, and
how the Mexican hands would smile and shout
cantad, amigo! . . . and Preble dreamed of the
girl with the rose petals and the way the Texas night came warm through her window . . . and
Rev Marsh, still without a new coat but using a
blanket around his shoulders because he had decided òn it himself, remembered the puppies he had
once raised in a box in the warm place under the
wood stove at home, wishing he could go back and
somehow join that whimpering, dreaming, squirm-
ing warmth. Go back and forget the thinness of his
clothes that were a matter of pride and bigness and
equality as a man, and the whispering that kept
saying, *I'm as good as they are. I can take it if they
can. I can take more than they can* . . . and Charles
Wood thought of the easy snow on Boston falling
beyond a window, beyond the walls and warmth of
a fireplace, and perhaps, most of all, the strange,
sweet and compelling warmth of Katherine Nance

on that night that seemed so long ago.

But only for a time, for the night and cold and the forgotten time they had spent in the saddle overcame thinking and feeling and left only the shell.

When daylight came again, the storm had blown itself out, and the world held still under a deathly silence. The sky cleared and the sun came out, but it was like a sun that had too long been consumed by its own fire and now swung across the sky enfeebled and dim. The cattle stood as if stunned, hardly moving, their breath rising as clouds of steam in the frigid air. They had not drifted as far as had been imagined. The little valley was not far. The herd had moved in a long half-circle, never finding distance in their curving, blinded walk.

A guard was established, and the rest rode their horses back to the barn, took care of them, and then went to eat and sleep.

When the worst of fatigue fell away and life came back into their bones, Adam talked to them.

"I pushed our luck too far."

"We pushed our luck too far," Ben reminded him. "We all agreed to stay, remember?"

"Be that as it may, common sense would tell us to get out now. The weather has cleared, and it looks like it will hold."

"It ain't that simple," Sweet looked out the window.

"That's just it. That snow is deep, and those critters are worn out. But we got to get them out of here."

"That blizzard was a good six weeks early," Preble pointed out. "Maybe we'll have a long spell of good weather before it hits again. We could hold here and see what happens."

Adam shook his head.

"I don't want to count on it. It's too cold out
there. If we could get them back they could be sold
and shipped out of here."

Sweet poured a cup of coffee.

"Aint' no railroads running in this."

"No. But if we start now, and this weather holds,
they might be by the time we get there. I reckon we
can move five or six miles a day. We can be there
in a week or ten days."

"Well," Ben let his breath out slowly, "we ain't
doing no good sitting here."

Giles frowned and paced nervously.

"Awful lot of cattle on company ground."

"We can't even think about that. I think we've
found the only chance. We'll move out the first
thing in the morning."

Outside of the little valley, the snow was not
quite as deep. The open ground had not felt the
impeded winds where snow could pile against the
sloping hills and cling and grow deeper. But it was
still deep enough to make progress painfully slow.

Red Bellah followed in the wake of the herd with
his wagon, to take advantage of the trail broken
there. He rode with a blanket over his lap, with the
coal-oil lamp sitting on the floor boards beneath
his legs.

Adam rode ahead to point the way, trying to
judge by the lay of the land where the most shallow
snow existed. He led them to the southern edges of
timber stands, and away from the pockets he remembered. His horse plunged and struggled
awkwardly, as did the rest, except for Andy Giles's
back at drag. With the snow flattened and a trail

ready-made, it was the one time that the drag spot became the easiest job of all. The others glanced back in envy from their pitching saddles, and particularly when they dismounted every few minutes to lead their horses on foot.

Slowly, the place where they had first entered the valley fell behind. Gradually, the sun rose in the sky, but without warmth.

"I wonder how far?" someone muttered when the first halt came.

"I'd say offhand about three miles," Adam guessed. "If we can do three or four more today, we'll be doing as much as can be expected."

Wood stood up and looked at the herd thoughtfully.

"How about switching ends and giving the lead cattle a rest?" he suggested. It was intended for Childress.

Adam busied himself with cleaning snow off his boots and said nothing, but Ben nodded his approval.

"That's a good idea. How about it, boss?"

"All right. And let them find their own pace, and if need be, we'll keep going for a little while after dark."

The others were silent, looking at Wood.

"Now how come Arbuckle thought of that?" Skinner drawled.

Wood reddened and the others laughed a little.

The days and miles passed slowly. They began in the bitter cold of dawn and ended in the equally bitter cold when the sun sank behind the horizon and the stars came out. They would halt and eat and build the fire high and try to sleep while the

warmth could still reach them. Invariably, while
dawn was still faraway, the cold would reach them
again and sleep became a dream-laden, disturbed
thing. It was better to sit up and huddle by the em-
bers for the remainder of the night. While breakfast was being cooked, a few would be delegated to
ride out in search of fallen trees whose limbs, sticking up above the snow, could be snaked back to
camp to replenish the supply of fuel. Then they
would eat, and stand with trembling legs to drink
one more cup of coffee, and the day would begin
again.

On the third evening, they slumped around the
fire, shivering, waiting for its heat to dispel the
stiff, aching chill that had been in their bones since
the last fire of too many hours ago. The men stared
at it in hollow-eyed melancholy. There was not
enough cheer in the crackling blaze to erase the
miles of that day.

"Well, I reckon we've passed the halfway point.
Eighteen or twenty miles. I think it's going to be all
right. The weather's holding. Two more days ought
to get us there."

"Two days. Only two days," Skinner observed
caustically.

Adam didn't argue with Skinner's attitude. He
felt the same way about it. It didn't matter how
much of it was behind them or how much remained
ahead. The only thing a man could hold in his
mind was the fire he could see and feel that moment.

As the sun crept down with late afternoon on the
fifth day, they spotted the buildings of the
Musselshell Cattle Company, which, in the snow,
looked more bleak and unpromising than ever. For

themselves, the crew of the Mexican Spur could take cheer. In an hour or two, the brutal drive through the snow would be over. They would find warmth and rest for a day or two and then head for home.

But for the herd, they could feel only despair. The race with the weather had not really been won. They had watched it building all day. There had been that stillness again, and an oppressive closeness that touched the nerves of every man, and a yellow haze lay along the northern horizon. The dark, boiling clouds followed.

After the boys had secured a company bunkhouse that evening, Adam rode over to Barnaby Hall's cabin. When he reached the front door and knocked, the wind was rising and drove before it the first new fall of snow.

"Well, good evening, Childress."

Adam sat down in a chair, heavily, letting the warmth of the room sink in.

"I've come to sell. They're as fat as they'll ever be."

"Yes, that blizzard was a most unfortunate occurrence."

Hall lurched a little as he walked to a cabinet and pulled out a fresh box of cigars. Adam realized for the first time that Hall had had a little too much to drink.

"Is it still eight to ten dollars a head?"

"That's the current going rate."

"Well, I'll take it."

"Looks like another blizzard blowing up."

"That's why I want to sell and get out. Me and the boys want to leave before we get pinned down for the whole winter."

Hall turned around and faced him unsteadily.

"I can't buy your cattle, Childress."

Adam looked at him, unable to believe what he had heard.

"Can't buy them! What do you mean?"

"Exactly what I said. I can't buy them."

"Now listen here. . . ."

"There's another blizzard blowing up, Mister Childress. It looks like another bad winter. A lot of cattle died out there last winter. A lot of companies went broke because of it."

"Last year doesn't concern me, Hall," Adam spoke angrily. "This one does. I've got nearly three thousand head out there and a contract with you that says you have to buy them."

"That contract doesn't mean a thing."

"That's one opinion a court of law wouldn't go along with!"

"It's just paper."

"Goddamn you, where I come from you can depend on a spoken agreement and you're telling me it ain't even worth anything written down!"

Hall backed off and began to whine.

"It isn't my fault! It rained so much last fall . . .no strength in the grass and the cattle weren't fat enough when the blizzards hit. And you remember what President Cleveland did . . . ordering two hundred thousand head removed from the Cheyenne-Arapaho reservation . . . a good part of them came here. You know that! They overstocked the ranges, and then you boys from Texas kept coming in with more . . . and the water was low and . . . you know what that does to the market. And now winter's going to hit hard and the bottom will fall out of the market again. . . . how could it be my fault?"

"By ignoring all that and keeping on contracting

for beef. More than you could handle! All the companies!"

Hall sat down and avoided Adam's eyes.

"Maybe so."

"You know damn well it's so. You saw all them critters coming up and got grabby, just like anyone else. You were going to get a wagonload of money. Only in the doing you knocked the wheels off that wagon before it ever got here. A little common sense would have told you to start turning them boys back when space ran out."

"All right . . . now you're recommending I bust contracts. Seems like you can't agree with your own advice, Childress!"

"Certainly, I agree with it!"

"Then why are you getting sore because I'm busting yours?"

Adam walked closer to Hall, anger growing hard and icy.

"My contract was made two years ago! You're obliged to take care of the old contracts first!"

"That'd be simple if the herds arrived in that order. But they don't. A fact I'm sure you're well aware of, Childress."

"That's right, but when the range begins to run out, common decency would tell you to reserve a place, and take the old contracts into account. I ain't holding it against them boys who signed up their herds after me and sold out before I did. I can't tell them to stop and go back. But I resent being first and not getting in the door before it closes!"

"What do you want me to do? The situation is out of my hands!"

"I'm holding you to that contract, Hall."

Hall looked at him and suddenly shifted his defense.

"Very well, and I shall honor the contract too," he said with a strange little smile. "Sometimes I think you're a child when it comes to business, or maybe you're too accustomed to those verbal contracts you talk about."

"That might be, but I also know I can hold you to what you've written on paper!"

"Certainly, only you will find, if you read the contract with care, that it doesn't require me to buy your cattle at any specific date, or any cattle that are in substandard condition. It's obvious your cattle are too thin, and I'd rather not purchase them at this particular time."

"I know about that part of it," Adam roared helplessly. "But I never thought I'd see a man who would stick to something like that when cattle faced death by the thousands! In a short while, they'll all be dead or scattered from here to Mexico!"

"That," Hall said quietly, "is not my concern."

Adam's hand touched the pistol on his belt and anger was busting loose inside. He turned and left quickly before he lost control of it.

He found his horse and rode away, numb with the thing that had happened. Hall had him pinned down. They had driven three thousand head of cattle from Texas to Montana for nothing.

"That's what he said, boys, and it's the same as saying he won't buy them at all."

"What can we do now?" asked Giles.

"Ride her out. That's all. Maybe in a week or two we can take them south, maybe find lower ground where they have a decent chance of lasting the winter. It depends on how wide this storm is spreading. There isn't time to figure it out now, though. Get what rest you can. This storm is building fast. It might be a good idea to plan to come in two or three at a time every hour for fifteen minutes to rest and get coffee. But no more than that. Ben and Rev and Andy can come in after the first hour. And then Wood, Skinner, and Preble on the second."

"How about you, boss?" Ben looked up.

"I'll get in there somewhere. Somebody be sure to tell Rev and Andy when we get out there."

The wind swiftly picked up in force and changed the falling flakes into hard pellets of ice. Darkness was merely an absence of light, but the wind filled it and made it alive and solid and moving. It pounded the strings of the earth and grew in voice, but it was not the often described wailing of lost souls. There was nothing in this sound that could, in illusion, seem to be human or what once was human. It was the sound of pure and ultimate fury, the struggle between earth and sky, in which anything living or dead became only incidental and unfortunate dust.

At close to one in the morning, the second bunch was coming in to sit exhausted and frozen in front of the stove. It was these riders who discovered that Cimarron was missing.

"Anybody see him?" Preble poured coffee with shaking hands.

"He wasn't here last time we came in. Before that, I couldn't say. Forget it," Skinner advised. "He's around somewhere. We ain't got much time before we got to get back out there."

"I ain't got any more use for him than you, but you can't let an old man wander around on a night like this. It ain't right!"

Preble finished his coffee quickly and went to the door. Wood and Andy Giles followed. Ducking against the sudden blast as the door opened, they stepped out into it and began the search. They had not gone more than a hundred feet when Wood let out a yell.

"Here he is! If I hadn't stumbled over him, I'd never have known he was there!"

"He must've gotten lost," Preble yelled against the storm. "Damn snow! You can't even see the bunkhouse from here!"

They got him inside and laid him out on one of the rolls. He was still alive.

Peewee came in from the shed in back where the remuda was sheltered. He shivered, rubbing his hands.

"What's going on?"

"The old Mex was lying out in the snow."

"You mean he's been outside all this time?"

"What do you mean, boy?" Preble looked over his shoulder.

"I saw him when he went out. Must've been four or five hours ago. He was acting funny. Sat up like he heard something. All I could hear was the blizzard, but he sat up like someone had called him, and he went out. I thought he was back long ago."

Cimarron slowly opened his eyes and looked up at them.

"I think he's dying," Preble whispered.

"Quiet," Wood raised a hand.

Cimarron rested for a minute more, like a man trying to gather breath, and then he spoke for the first time.

"He is out there, somewhere. This I know, my friends. I heard him speak. He is here, somewhere. This is a bad place. A very bad place . . . Juanito . . . Juan . . ."

"Who is out there?" Wood asked. "Try to tell us."

"He's gone. He don't hear you." Preble stood up.

They wrapped Cimarron in his blanket and put him outside in the snow to await daylight when they could see to bury him.

"He was always looking for something or someone," Wood murmured.

"He just acted crazy, as far as I'm concerned," Skinner discounted the idea. "If he was looking for something up here, why should he act spooky all the way up the trail?"

Wood didn't know.

"What was that name he mentioned just before he died?" Red Bellah asked. He had been out in the barn seeing to his mules when all of this had happened.

"Juanito," Prebble told him.

"Mean anything to you?" Wood wondered.

"It's a common name."

It was time to go back out to the herd then. Back into the dark, screaming world. The storm swept Cimarron from Wood's thought. Even from a distance of a few feet, the bunkhouse could not be seen and therefore became remote.

He found a longhorn standing apart from the

herd and tried to move him back in, but he stumbled and fell and died before his eyes. Sharply, he came awake, throwing off for a moment the stupor of exhaustion and cold and realized fully for the first time the full impact of this thing that howled down out of the darkness.

XXXII

I may not see a hundred
Before I see the Styx,
But, coal, or ember, I'll remember
Eighteen-eighty six.

—Prose and Poetry
of Livestock Industry
of the United States

For less sober men, it might have appeared to be the ending of the world. For those who had not seen it before, life might have been plunged into irrevocable darkness to wait and make the pitiful attempt to survive while earth and dark wind made the final struggle.

The pattern did not fit nature's normalcy, its usual and precise scheme. It seemed to come from beyond. A man could listen to thunder and the pelting rain and see the flashes that light up the wilderness. He could huddle in a cave, or shield himself with canvas or shut a door against it, and he could understand and accept it because the pattern had been there for as long as he could remember.

But the migration of birds and animals, the race for southerly climates had not been just early, but weird. The pattern was gone. There was a wild cry there, a frightening undercurrent that could not be heard but sensed; an ancient tremor that could not be felt, but somehow remembered. Man had sensed it in the dark avalanche of a buffalo stampede, and remembered it somehow in the eyes of cattle as they rose in terror against something unseen. He had seen buffalo and cattle do this before, and he knew it was normal, but the sense and memory were there and they were older than he.

So it was with that first snow of squaw winter, and the first blizzard, and the second blizzard which followed a few days later. But it had stopped and the sun had come out, and ancient fear faded. The inconvenience was all that remained.

And yet, even with calm and sunlight, the second blizzard never really ended. The kind space could not be remembered under the onslaught of the thing that followed.

One blizzard after another swept down on them. The undercurrent returned and became a roaring and a fear, and still there was no understanding. The pattern was gone.

Time was blown aside. Men rode until they knew little else. They fought and were not equal. Some died and their cattle wandered like lost souls, their tails to the blast. They froze to death standing up, to become grim monuments of the glorious trail. They wandered blindly against drift fences and died in great piles. They were seen at cabin windows, driven by some instinct that told them man might help them . . . man who had taken them to this place of hell from a gentler range.

Adam Childress, in spite of his deep weariness, slept poorly when the chances to sleep came. He

had lost ten per cent of his herd, and while it was
not a bad loss when the circumstances were con-
sidered, he could not forget the sight of them, nor
the sight of the others suffering endlessly. He could
not forgive himself for not selling them the first day
they came.

His dreams were filled with the trail, all the hard
things of going north, fences and hatred and dying
men and constant bad weather. He defeated these
things in his dreams and readied himself to stand
triumphant at the gates of the Musselshell. But
each time, Barnaby Hall stood at the end of the
trail, laughing and sneering. He killed Hall in a
thousand brutal and gratifying ways. But Hall was
always there the next time he slept, with the sound
of dying cattle unable to drown out his whining
voice.

Once he had thought they would be back cross-
ing the Red by November. The Red River, and
Texas, and home again . . . now it was January.
The last of January, and they were still here . . .

"Boss . . ." a hand shook him awake. "Wake
up."

He rose on his elbows and saw Skinner, and
heard the silence. The silence that had begun only
recently was still there, outside. He found little
comfort in it. It could end just as quickly.

"What's the matter?"

"It's almost dawn. I got to get back out to the
herd, but I thought you'd like to know. There's a
warm wind coming up. It looks like a chinook."

XXXIII

When I dream of Texas, I want to go home,
Take me back there once, and I never will roam.
                              —THE OLD CHISHOLM TRAIL

THE WARM WIND grew, feeling wet and clammy as the beginning of sweat. It came from the south, and faltered and for a while seemed lost and defeated by the great white places which rose before it. But it grew again and became steady, and the air became more bearable.

It was there that first day, and the next night, and then the second day, and it kept on until it was an accepted thing. The snow began to melt. Its surface became covered with water, and here and there, there was a hint that grass might show itself again. If it could come to that, the longhorns might survive.

Charles Wood watched the herd slowly come to life again in the warmer air. He had come to know the Mexican Spur cattle as the other men knew them. He found pride in their durability, the way they could, given half a chance, survive on air and scenery and little else. He looked upon them as one would look at a pet, a friend. He was saddened by anything that hurt them, and grateful when they

lifted their heads and began to look a little like the
proud animals that had taken the trail from Texas.

There was a feeling that winter had done its
worst. Normality had to come sometime. Snow
would fall again. They held no illusion that it
wouldn't, but it had to taper off. It had to be rea-
sonable and almost gentle, because no winter could
hold more than it had held already.

There was talk of home once more, although no
one had any idea under what circumstances it
would come about. They would not desert the
herd. In the spring, perhaps the market would recover and they could sell and get out. The market
failing, it might be possible to trail them to Fort
Benton, farther north, and sell them to the army
for Indian beef, or on into Canada where fewer
herds were trailed. If nothing else, they could be
taken home again to fatten in Texas and wait for
another drive at a later time.

Wood closed the book of Shakespeare and
moved restlessly to the window. The chinook was
still holding its warming grip on the land, and to
Wood there was more in it to think about than the
survival of the cattle.

He could not look back to the months on the
trail and say it had been totally unpleasant, or that
there had been no beauty in it, no good times or
happiness. He looked for a life with purpose in it,
and there was purpose there. On the broad scale, to
provide beef for the nation. For now, to keep them
alive . . . not because they were worth money. They
were, of course, but the economics of it had become a secondary reason during the blizzards. The
purpose during those weeks was to help them be-

cause they were living things, suffering through no fault of their own.

Yes, he had discovered purpose. And he had looked for honesty and a clean, open way of living. People who were honest and open in their thinking . . . who judged and accepted another not on his social or financial background, but for what he was for himself alone. As Adam would put it, it didn't matter what kind of boots a man wore. It was the way he wore them.

It had taken time for the realization to come, but the men around him had always had these qualities. It had taken even longer to realize that, in his preoccupation with Floyd and Cimarron, it was Charles Wood who had been dishonest. He had looked for these qualities and had been unable to find them because they were lacking in himself.

It was strange. There was no geography to this thing. Boston had never had anything to do with it, nor did the people there. They could not be condemned for living a life that suited them. It became wrong only when an individual discovered he did not fit and then did not leave. This was the key . . . no one had held him down. The things he had looked for after months of wandering had unwittingly been found the precise instant of his rebellion and departure from Boston. And because he had not seen it, it was as if he had never left Boston at all, until now.

Wood looked out at the dreary snow and shivered.

It was all understood now, and past.

He was not a cowboy. He could not entertain the illusion that he had really earned his keep. He could not visualize a continuance of this kind of life. He was not made of hard bone and rawhide like the others.

The circle had come part way. He had left Boston and the life he could not stand. He had learned about heat and dust and thirst and cold and the lack of sleep. He had hardened to it and he felt cleaner inside than he could ever remember. But he could not harden all the way, not like the others. And the others had come to accept him, and he accepted them in return, but it would never be complete. To them he would always be that Boston feller, and to him they would be Texas cowboys. He could laugh and cry with them, eat and ride and get drunk with them, and never think about it as being strange. But the thought inevitably came. *What are you doing here? A city man riding herd on Texas cattle, getting drunk in frontier dance halls, chasing an Indian in the middle of nowhere on a dark night . . . clinging to a staggering horse, half-blind, frozen, and nearly dead in a howling blizzard. . . .*

He turned away from the window and went to stand by the stove. Adam Childress had been short-handed and charitable, too. That's how he had gotten the job. Not because of any other qualification. If for no other reason, he could not hang on and impose on them. *You could never be the equal of the others,* he thought, and wistfully, he thought of Katherine Nance. She was a Texan and a part of the cattle and big country. He could never be the kind of man she would want.

Adam came in and joined him by the stove. Nothing was said for a moment, and the silence was awkward.

"You'd like to be on your way, wouldn't you?"
Adam asked, finally.

Wood looked at him for a moment and then
nodded.

"You're right. I do feel like I ought to move on.
I'm not a cowboy, and never could be."

"When do you want to go?"

"I didn't plan to run out on you before you were
finished."

"No use in worrying about that. There isn't
much to do now."

"Winter isn't over yet."

"No, but the worst of it is, and there ain't no
sense in you hanging around if you feel like you got
to get moving on."

"Well . . ." Wood let out his breath. "If you say
so."

"When do you want to go?"

"Tomorrow is soon enough, I guess. Tomorrow
morning."

He had gone to bed that night, feeling strange
about not having any more graveyards to ride, and
knowing that coosie's call to breakfast in the morning would be the last he heard. He was anxious to
move on and feel the touch of good clothes and hot
baths again. He had no desire to return to Boston
and take up things as they were, but there were
some things, certain habits of that life that he could
not shed. There had been good things. Music, liter-
ature, the arts, certain comforts. It would be good
to be in touch with some of that once more, to have
it within reach when his mind hungered for it.
There had to be a permanence somewhere in

himself. A place to go when his day was over. A home and family, a place to belong to . . . it was as simple as that.

But just as simply, there were regrets in leaving the Mexican Spur behind, this life on the trail. He had felt close to the earth and close to the stars, and there was something in both that a man learned and never would forget for the rest of his life. The real truths, the real beauty, an acquaintance with eternity. Yes, there were regrets, and because of them he slept only fitfully, waking often to stare against the darkness.

Something else crept into the room. It was hard to tell exactly where it began and where after that he realized what it was. But the men began to stir in their sleep, and after a while Adam got up and dressed and went outside. When the door opened for that brief moment and closed again, Wood came out of his half-asleep state and sat up. The temperature was dropping fast.

He went to the window to look up at the sky. The heavens were sharper and clearer, with the frost-fire of the Milky Way flaming white and cold, than he could remember. The night was utterly still and peaceful, and alarm died away. He turned and built up the fire in the stove and returned to his bedroll.

The chinook had ended, that was all. There was no reason to worry, but he could not sleep anymore that night, and Adam Childress didn't show up again until Red Bellah built his fire.

Wood washed and shaved and got his belongings together and then went out to the chuck-wagon fire to get his breakfast.

Adam's mouth was tight, and his eyes were hard with worry.

"What's the matter?"

"You can feel it, can't you?" Adam snapped and went inside.

Wood watched him go and then turned to Red.

"The temperature dropped hard last night, kid. It froze the water sitting on top of the snow. Got a thick, hard sheet of blue ice over everything. Cattle can't dig down to grass."

Wood, disturbed by the meaning in Red's words, took his plate inside and sat down to eat.

Adam stood by the window, silently, and Wood wished he could say something. But even if they had been on good terms, it was not a time for talking. He wondered ... *don't count on it* ... the weather ... perhaps it was only the pessimism that comes to a man as an aftermath to disaster, in which everything is judged from its gloomiest aspect. Or, maybe men like Adam and Red did see things in the weather that he could not see.

Wood finished eating, and Adam strapped on his gun and put on his coat, and went back out. Wood saddled a horse and strapped his belongings in back of the saddle. When he mounted up, he paused for a moment, looking around. He didn't want to say good-by. What once would have been easy was now a tight-throated and uncomfortable thing. He gave a little wave of his hand to them all, and they returned it. Suddenly, nothing more was needed.

He turned his horse and rode out of camp, thinking about Adam. Adam, and the way he was acting a few minutes ago. The more he thought about it, the faster he urged his horse. He knew where the trail boss had gone . . . with that worry in his face . . . the worry more like a final anger, the last yielding to a burden, strapping on his gun and walking out of there with that look in his eyes. The company buildings. . . .

Wood spurred his horse on and grew impatient with the snow that slowed them.

When he got there at last, he found Adam's horse tied out in front. He jumped down and ran inside where a boy was lazily pushing a broom down the worn boards of the floor.

"Where's Hall's office?"

The kid pointed up the stairs.

Wood ran up to a hallway with a door at the end. There were loud voices coming from behind it. He threw it open, and kept on running. He caught a quick glimpse of Hall's sickened face as he grabbed Adam's pistol and pushed it toward the ceiling. The pistol went off, and bits of splintered wood showered down on them

"What are you trying to do, Adam?"

Adam broke away and stood there shaking.

"Who asked you to interfere, goddamn it!"

"But you were going to shoot him!"

"Why not? This man is responsible for the death of three hundred head of our cattle. And more are going to die because of him. You think he ought to get away with it?"

"You think shooting him will change the weather?"

"What do you know about it?"

"That's right, I don't know much about the way people do things out here."

"Then go back to Boston! Get the hell out of

here and mind your own goddamned business! I've
had enough of your preaching!"

Adam leveled the Colt .45 again, but Wood
stepped between him and Hall.

"Get out of the way, Wood!"

"You can't shoot him."

"You know a better way?"

"Look . . . you've got a right to be angry. While
I'm yelling at you not to shoot, I have a little voice
inside that says go ahead. Hall deserves it. But
where is there any satisfaction in it? It's over too
quick. And then when they hang you for murder,
it's like him having the last word. Seems to me
there'd be real satisfaction in going after him with
your fists."

Adam stood there a long time, looking at Hall.
There wasn't a sound except the sound of their
breathing and the ring on one of Hall's trembling
fingers chattering against the top of his desk.

Adam lowered his pistol.

"You might be right, Wood. Take it. And if anybody comes in here and tries to stop us, you hold
them off."

Wood took the pistol and stepped back.

Adam took a deep breath, and with a fierce, glad
thing in his eyes, walked slowly toward Hall, tight
and awkward with anger.

Hall stuttered like a frightened child and kept
backing away.

"I . . . I won't fight you . . . I won't . . ."

Adam drove his fist into his stomach and
doubled him over. He brought his other fist hard
into Hall's face, and Hall slumped against the wall
and slid down. He pulled Hall to his feet and the
man tried to run for the door, but Adam grabbed

him by his coat and spun him around and hit him again. The force of it sent Hall backwards to sprawl and not move again on the top of his desk.

"How can you get satisfaction out of a man like that!" Adam said, breathing hard. "He gives out too quick!"

They got their horses and started back, listening to the ice beneath the hooves of their horses.

"I guess I'd better be on my way, Adam."

Adam pointed to the horizon.

"I don't like the look of that."

The wind was slowly rising and clouds were piling up on the horizon.

"Looks bad. I'd better stay."

"It ain't a matter of needing you. It's up to you. But if it were me, I wouldn't want to get caught in that if it builds up to something."

Wood watched the clouds. They did not appear to be moving and there were not as much, nor did they seem as dark as before. But there was something about them and the way Adam talked. He decided to stay.

They rode back to the bunkhouse, and in a way, Wood was glad. It would not be easy to say goodby to Adam Childress, no matter what their differences were, and regardless of the weather, it was a relief to delay, to put off the time when he had to do it.

XXXIV

THE WEATHER steadily worsened. Clouds gathered in awesome council and the sun was lost. The wind lost its mournful cry and became despair itself. The cattle saw the devil, and hell whispered across the flat and echoed in the hills. Time was coming to an end again, and there was nothing to be done. The herd could only stand and wait. And the men who guarded it could only watch in hopeless anger, or sleep if they could and gather strength for the ordeal which was to come.

Rev Marsh rested on his bedroll and thought of home. Home with the nights that were like perfume, warm and slow. Even the stars seemed warm there. And the rains. Warm and heavy, and wet, striking the dust of the earth and bringing up that sharp, clean smell. A man could get out in it and stay all day and be wet clear through and never mind. Sometimes the rains didn't come, and the land dried up and tried to blow away. Cattle and men alike went thirsty and hungry. But the severity of it never seemed to be like this. Water could be found somewhere. Maybe a man had to ride far to find it, but it could be found. The bigger rivers, the eternal springs, and nowadays, deep from the ground, sucked from the earth by the groaning, squealing windmills. For a while, a man could put his mouth to the end of the pipe and drink it as fast as it was pumped. But the water kept coming, and it would fill a mud tank in time. Yes, even in the driest of times, a man could find water if he went far enough or deep enough. And besides, that country back there at the beginning of the trail had another quality. It had the quality of being home.

Here, it was nothing but strangeness. Perhaps beautiful in the golden summers, perhaps in a good year the best grazing country to be found. Longhorns could thrive in the sparse rangelands of Texas. Here, they could grow sleek and fat. But when the snow came, when the blizzards struck ... where was the quality of home? Where could you go to escape? There was warmth in a fire during the howling hours, but no comfort. No feeling of strength and familiarity, but a sense of being lost and exposed.

You could only wait, and let it happen.

Always, it was the waiting. . . .

He crawled in and tried to find sleep. Waiting. . . .

"All right boys, it's here!" Adam's voice shattered sleep. "Crawl out! Come on! Coffee's hot and the horses are waiting."

Marsh swung out, first as he always was. That

was the part of pride, pulling on his boots and standing up. He pulled on his thin canvas coat, jammed his hat down on his head and went to the coffee pot Red had set on top of the stove.

"Bad as before?" a sleepy voice asked.

"Worse," Adam said quietly.

Marsh went to the window and could see nothing. It was around dawn, but there was no light. He could see only the bulletlike chunks of snow being driven by the window, flashing in the light that came from inside. But he could hear it, the high and far reaching roar of it, the shack groaning and shaking in it.

Skinner finished his coffee quickly and stepped to the door. He opened it and hesitated. Everyone could see and sense it. The Abyss, the Maelstrom, Hell . . . right there at the door.

Skinner turned and his face was white.

"There ain't no sense in it! We can't do anything for them."

Adam buttoned his coat and tied his hat down.

"You're probably right. We'd more'n likely do just as well closing that door and sitting it out. But as long as a single longhorn out there can put one foot in front of the other, we've got to try and help."

"Come on," Marsh grinned at them, and wrapped a blanket around his shoulders and tied it there. "Wood and Sweet cain't hold 'em forever!"

One by one they pushed through the door and headed for the shed that sheltered the remuda. With already stiffened fingers they saddled what horses Peewee had not prepared already. They rode out into it, bent over the saddle horn, trying to see in a darkness that was deeper than night.

By guesswork and luck, more than by knowledge of where they were going, they found the herd and began the battle of trying to keep them together while they drifted, tail to the blast. They had to be kept from the gullies and the deep drifts, and the fences where they would die in great pile-ups.

Rev Marsh sat stunned in the saddle. It was not mere cold that slashed through his thin and worn clothes. It was a thousand sharp and hard driven pains. The cold seared like fire. It ripped and tore and slammed, and it numbed the mind.

He thought of turning back to the bunkhouse, but the bunkhouse was lost forever. He thought of home, but it too was lost. It was a void that held them, a raw, bleeding fragment of earth thrown free to spin and disintegrate in emptiness. Nothing lived or died here. There was no boundary, no end, no escape.

Rev wrapped his reins around the horn and slapped at his body as if he were attacked by a swarm of insects whose stings were like fire. He swung his arms and tried to breathe against the blast that sucked the wind from his lungs.

His horse brushed up against another in the struggle and Adam caught his arm.

"Better head for the bunkhouse, Rev! It's hitting forty or fifty below, and you ain't dressed for it!"

"I'm all right, boss! I got me a blanket!"

"I kept telling you you ought to get a warmer coat! Don't be such a stubborn, thickheaded . . . mule!"

"I'm all right! Honest, I am!"

Marsh pulled his horse away and crowded a longhorn back into the tightness of the herd and Adam was lost to him. He thought of the trail boss almost angrily. A mule? That wasn't what Adam had started to say! And hovering over him like a mother does a child. Always talking about a warmer coat! When they got the idea he could make his own decisions, he'd get one.

He shoved the anger from his mind. Old Adam Childress was all right. He didn't mean anything by it. Adam and the others . . . they didn't mean anything by it. They knew he was as good as they were. He was a good cowhand. He could take it or hand it out as well and better. They knew . . . but why didn't they act like it!

"Big dumb nigger," Floyd had kidded him once, "don't know any better!"

Go back to the bunkhouse? Not as long as anyone else was out here. He was all right. He was all right for sure.

A mighty blast of wind caught at the blanket and tore it away. He reached for it desperately, but it was gone. He sat rigid in the saddle, and then discovered it didn't really matter. He unwound his reins and fought the drifting cattle. Forty or fifty below? It couldn't be. Maybe a little while ago, but not now. Just a big wind, was all. Why it was getting warmer, and warmer . . .

They kept the herd together as best they could, but what was unbelievable became worse, until it was impossible to keep them together any longer, or for that matter, to even see them.

In twos and threes, and in larger bunches, the herd dwindled and became lost to them.

The time had come when a man must stop trying, when he can no longer remain where he is and survive. There is no decision to quit and run,

nor is there a question of an alternative. There is
merely a wall that is too high to climb and for
which there is no going around. It is not failure or
defeat, because there was perhaps no chance from
the beginning. There is no emotion. Emotion can
only come later.

Adam gathered his men and they went back. The
time had come perhaps an hour before, but they
had gone on as if in a terrible dream of dying cattle.
They had gone on, because it was the only thing to
do. But for all of that hour, the wall had been
there.

One by one, and silently, they rode into the shed
and tended to their horses. And one by one, they
fought their way to the bunkhouse and collapsed in
its warmth. They held cups of coffee in shaking
hands and stared at the walls, more dead than
alive.

Adam watched the window, not seeing it but just
staring in that direction until an image appeared
there. The wild eyes, the great horns, its voice
bellowing and lost in the holocaust.

Adam stood up and went outside. He stumbled
up against the beast and placed his pistol to its
head and pulled the trigger. The longhorn fell and
kicked and then lay still and Adam looked at it for
a moment. Slowly, he went inside and sat down,
and cried.

"Goddamn it! *Goddamn it* . . . they're *in* hell
before they die!"

Andy Giles put his cup down and stood up.

"Where's Rev?"

Adam looked around.

"Was he out in the shed? Did he come in there
with us?"

Preble's eyes opened wide.

"By God, he wasn't!"

Adam watched the door and had it opened before he realized what had happened. The only thing that could have happened . . .

XXXV

When I bend my head low and listen at the ground,
I can hear vague voices that I used to know,
Stirring in dim places, faint and restless sound,
I remember how it was when the grass began to grow.

—A. H. BRANCH

IT WAS INEVITABLE that winter would end. There
were times when the pattern was in doubt, when
men huddled around their fires in despair and wondered if the winter on the land would ever end. But
the pattern was still there, and the sun did come
out and the snow did diminish. The scars would
not last long. Time and season had their way of
healing. It was the winter in man himself which
would not lift and let him live again as he remembered.

A man could ride out into the melting snow and
count what was left of his cattle, if indeed he found
any still alive, and blame the great blizzards, or he
could think of the years of mismanagement, the
wild financing, the overstocking of ranges which
accompanied the weather. It would have been hard
to say which made up the greater part of the disaster. But it did not make any difference now.

The great herds were gone. An industry, the like of which the country had never seen before and would never see again, was dead. A few of the cattle companies, the ones that had exercised prudence during the booming years, survived. But most left their doors swinging in the spring winds, carting away openly what few possessions were left. Some were gone overnight, departing in stealth to escape the anger of the cowman.

It was as if a sudden quiet had descended over the region, and it would be a long time before a man rode the plains and gentle hills and did not see the bones and horns mouldering under the seasons to remind him of what had happened here.

One by one, the trail crews limped away, and the skinners took their place to reap a grisly profit. Remnants of herds were sold for as little as what one cowhand made in a year, or allowed to scatter because they would never have made it home.

March, 1887, and nothing was left.

Adam Childress cinched up his saddle on the bayo coyote, and leaned on it for a long time, looking out over the country.

For a man who despised change and could now only hunker down and build the customary fire and talk earnestly about the old ways, this was a time of dying, perhaps. The hell that every man fears. But changed it had. The change had not begun with that winter nor with any specific date. Change had always been there, slow and inevitable. It only took a time like that winter and the thing that happened to the market to hasten it and bring it out sharply in hard contrast.

Adam had counted up a ninety per cent loss of Mexican Spur cattle, and sold what he could find of the rest to a man who was trying to put a herd together to sell in Canada. Ninety per cent, he found, when talking to others, to be common. But it was not just the loss of the herd that saddened him. Charles Wood had been right in the things he had said. His own fears had been justified, except that he had never allowed himself to believe they could ever happen in his time. But nothing remained but to head for Texas now. The days of cattle, as he had known the time, were gone.

There might be a few more drives north for some, but in a sense, they would be ghosts, no more than shadows of another time. Of the great herds that swung north, nothing remained but the deep-cut trails of their passing. The longhorn, with the increased use of railroads and the growing popularity of new breeds, would vanish. Of the rawhide, rollicking, valiant men who trailed them, only an echo would be left. The fences would crowd too closely now, and the plow would scar the land in a way the hoof never did. The big country, like the buffalo and cattle that walked it, would be only something to remember.

Red Bellah and Ben Sweet, too saddened to do anything else, had shaken hands all around, and with wagon and remuda had taken their own trail home. Andy Giles had left early for Brownsville and the family he had left behind. Preble and Bob Skinner, losing heart and stomach for the only kind of life they had ever really cared for, had gone elsewhere to find a new kind of life. And Peewee, somehow older now and ready to go on his own, had joined them. It was hard to picture them working at anything that did not have to do with cattle. Maybe they would show up again, someday.

What had been accomplished? What was the worth of it all? Floyd Rogers had found the only peace time could hold for him. Rev Marsh had died commanding the respect of all who knew him, and how many men, white or black, could hope for the same? The tragedy was that Rev never fully realized it. And Charlie Baggett? And Cimarron? Cimarron had been an old man and maybe it didn't matter so much. Charlie had died with a good drunk on, and maybe that was a happy way to go. But where was the real worth of it? Where was the thing that kept it from being a waste?

"Mind if I ride with you a way?" Wood reined to a halt.

Adam came out of his reveries and swung into the saddle. He looked at Wood and nodded. The stiffness and embarrassment were gone. The reason for anger, if there ever had been one, was gone. What was the use? Where had there ever been any use? Wood had not caused history, but merely predicted it.

"I was going to ask you to," he smiled.

They rode several miles without a word, each caught in a sadness that made talking difficult.

"What are you going to do, Wood?"

"I haven't given it much thought. Too much has happened here. You?"

Adam shrugged.

"The Mexican Spur will go broke. It was in a bad way as it was without this happening. I'll go down and say good-by to Jake Nance, and see if there's anything I can do for him. Then I guess I'll head for La Vaca County. Back to the old house and spread the folks had. I reckon I'll sell it and maybe get enough to live for a while."

"It's too bad, the way things have turned out."

Adam found no way to reply. The thing touched too deep.

"You know, Adam. I was really beginning to like it. Maybe at the time I didn't realize it, but before those blizzards hit I didn't need to leave and look for something else. Now it's gone."

"You're just a yearling yet. You'll find something."

"I suppose, but . . . it makes me wonder what it does to a man who had never known anything else."

The kid was asking in his own way what would happen inside old Adam Childress, and he replied silently in his thoughts. I don't know. I don't know. . . .

They rode for a long time together, saying little, neither having the courage to say good-by. It was only for two days, but it seemed like forever and as empty of life as the land and its thin blanket of melting snow.

They came to a low rise and climbed it and stopped to look at the country before them.

"Looks like a bare place over there. We can build a fire and fix some grub," Adam decided.

They rode to the place and dismounted and found some wood and gathered it in a pile. Adam bent down to start the fire, and saw the new green growing there . . . the tiny beginnings of new life. He felt a strange catch in his throat.

"Look!"

Wood squatted down and ran his fingers over it.

"New grass," Wood whispered. "The ground lies frozen for months on end. Man and beast walk-

"ing across it can die, as big as they are, but this tiny thing waits and waits, and exists, and one day reaches for warmth and light. It's a wonderful thing . . ."

The first new grass . . . the re-occuring miracle of grass. Adam stood up and wanted to cry. The strangeness in his throat was growing, but he could not speak.

Wood saw his face and seemed to understand, turning away to start the fire and fix coffee and bacon, and saying nothing.

They ate silently and sat quietly until the fire burned itself out and only the smoke remained.

"You're an old fool," Wood said quietly.

Adam looked up, wondering.

"You're the one who told me," Wood went on, "as long as grass comes up each spring, there will be cattle to graze on it. You told me that once. Have you forgotten?"

"It's no use, Wood."

"Oh, I know. What I said before still holds true. Progress, I called it. Fences, cultivation of land, new towns, railroads, people coming in by the thousands . . . by the hundreds of thousands, the end of the trail drives, the end of the longhorn. That's happening right now. It's been happening, it's happening, and it will continue to happen. But still . . . as long as there is grass, Adam, there will be cattle, and there will be a market for them."

"Yes. You're right. And I was an old fool to think it couldn't happen in my life. It began during my life. How could it end in one man's lifetime? Yes, you were right. But I'd be a bigger fool to think I could change."

"Well, whether you like it or not, you *are* chang-

ing. You won't be taking longhorns north anymore. All that vanished back there," Wood
pointed north. "The question is, how far are you
going to let it change you? I saw you turn into a
bitter old man inside of a week because of a fence
and a man dying. I saw you get a little more tired
each day because of drought and stampede and . . .
everything hard that happened. There's no point in
dragging it all up again. But I saw you get pushed
down, and then wiped out. Is that the way you're
going to leave it? Are you going to sit on a porch
and read papers and die with nothing more than
memories on your mind? Or are you going to take
that land your folks had and put some cattle on it
. . . yes, Herefords . . . and put them on the railroads! That's something, isn't it? It's certainly better than sitting around mourning something that
can never be brought back!"

Adam looked at the new grass, wistfully, hungri-
ly.

"Listen, you've told me. Texans took what they
had . . . longhorns . . . and made a life of it. They
branded the wild cattle, and it didn't matter how
far the market was . . . *they took them there!* All
right, do you think they're going to quit now? No!
They'll take what they have this time and make a
life of it again. It can't help but be different! But in
its own way, it will be just as good."

Adam touched the new grass, gingerly and
carefully.

"How tall will it be when you get home, Adam?"

Adam raised his hand to show him and stopped.
He stood up quickly, the strange feeling suddenly
giving away.

"Tall enough!" he shouted.

He swung into the saddle and Wood jumped to catch up and they rode a long way at a gallop before Adam reined back and they rode quietly, laughing.

Home ... he could remember it not being enough ... well, maybe a man did have to wander before he knew what he wanted. Like Wood wandered now. But home ... he was ready for it now. A place to belong to. ...

It should have come sooner. It would have been good to have a family. The land a man sets aside is, in time, indistinguishable from the land that surrounds it. The adobe he erects soon crumbles in the rain and in the wind until it is no more than the dust that blew across the trail. A family would have carried his name, and it would have been a small share of immortality. A man ought to leave a mark of some kind, to let others know he had been there. But at least there was peace now, a warmth. He had changed. Not all the way. Not ever ... but it was enough and it was all right.

"Be the first hand I hire," he said.

"Me? I'm not a cowboy, Adam. At least not a good one."

"I don't know. When was the last time you were called Arbuckle?"

"I don't know," Wood said with some surprise. "I can't remember!"

"It doesn't matter. What you don't know, I can teach you. Besides ... call me a damn fool if you like, but ..." Adam lapsed into an embarrassed silence, and Wood filled it quickly.

"I like the idea. Don't think I don't. You know, my father was a good man. He gave me a good education, appreciation for many fine things. I'll always thank him for that. But he provided too well. You know how that is. So I ran away from it, and it seemed at first like I had taken on too much. It was like stepping from one life into a completely new one. The things I learned at home never prepared me for this. If it hadn't been for you . . . well, if I didn't think you'd knock me out of my saddle, I'd say you've been sort of a second father. I'd never have made it on my own."

Adam looked away, not knowing what to say. What he hadn't been able to put into words, Wood was saying. He wanted to run from it. It seemed ridiculous that two grown men should act this way. Sentimental and full of affection . . . but he couldn't stop it. It was what he wanted, like between a real father and his son, and he could only sit there on the embarrassed edge of it and remain silent. Angry with himself and the moment, he adjusted his stetson and occupied himself with the horizon.

"I don't know, Adam. Maybe it would have been the same anywhere I went. I keep saying I'm not really a cowboy. With all the preparation I had at home I would've found myself saying I'm not really a banker, not really a lawyer . . . doctor, shoe clerk . . . no matter what I chose as a profession, I would have had to say that. Each would have been just as hard in its own way."

"Then why leave?" Adam said awkwardly. "Stick with me."

"I'd like to. I'd really like to. And I'd like to see Katherine again, and maybe . . . but what the hell, Adam!"

Adam Childress saw the uncertainty, the wondering at himself in Wood's face. Wood, who could never be called Arbuckle again.

"You'd do to ride the river with."

They continued on, and Adam settled back and watched the country, content now. Some things are forever, particularly in the heart of a man. It would only change on the surface. The trails would vanish, but the deep imprint of hooves would not.

The *ladino* walked south slowly, the sun glinting on his great horns. He grazed as he went, terribly thin, and the wildness growing in him again. He raised his head and looked at the two men approaching on horses, and for a moment thought of doing battle, of running . . . but then it did not seem to matter. The sun was warmer and the new grass was coming. The moment passed and he lowered his head to graze again. They joined him and he started the slow walking again, south.

Sharp Shooting
and
Rugged Adventure
from
America's Favorite
Western Writers

44464	**Kinch** Matt Braun	$1.75
83236	**Twenty Notches** Max Brand	$1.75
56025	**The Nameless Breed** Will C. Brown	$1.50
82403	**Trigger Trio** Ernest Haycox	$1.50
51860	**The Man On The Blood Bay** Kyle Hollingshead $1.50	
04739	**Bandido** Nelson Nye	$1.50
62340	**Omaha Crossing** Ray Hogan	$1.50
81132	**A Time For Vengeance** Giles Lutz	$1.50
87640	**Wear A Fast Gun** John Jakes	$1.50
30675	**Gun Country** Wayne C. Lee	$1.50

Available wherever paperbacks are sold or use this coupon.

Winners of the SPUR and WESTERN HERITAGE AWARD

08383	**The Buffalo Runners** Fred Grove	$1.75
13905	**The Day The Cowboys Quit** Elmer Kelton	$1.25
29741	**Gold In California** Todhunter Ballard	$1.25
34270	**The Honyocker** Giles Lutz	$1.50
47082	**The Last Days of Wolf Garnett** Clifton Adams $1.75	
47491	**Law Man** Lee Leighton	$1.50
55123	**My Brother John** Herbert Purdum	$1.75
56025	**The Nameless Breed** Will C. Brown	$1.50
71153	**The Red Sabbath** Lewis B. Patten	$1.75
10230	**Sam Chance** Benjamin Capps	$1.25
82091	**Tragg's Choice** Clifton Adams	$1.75
82135	**The Trail To Ogallala** Benjamin Capps	$1.25
85903	**The Valdez Horses** Lee Hoffman	$1.75

Available wherever paperbacks are sold or use this coupon.